LOOKING FOR LOVE

MISSING LINK 4

LYNN BURKE

LOOKING FOR LOVE

With more curves than a country road, Madeline Young makes me want to take a slow ride around every bend and dip of her body. And her husband Hudson has that sexy silver fox thing going on that clicks all my needy buttons his wife can't reach.

They share a marriage found only in fairytales and make me want the same. When I find out the Youngs are on Missing Link, I think my dreams have come true.

The problem?

They just want to play...and I'm looking for love.

The masochist in me agrees to one last hookup before searching out my forever couple, and while wounds from their past keep their hearts locked up tight, I fall in deep.

But there's a ticking bomb manipulating behind the scenes, one that makes emotions run high and bares vulnerability.

Will Madeline and Hudson allow me the opportunity to help them rebuild what they lost, or will the explosion of truth lay waste to my heart?

1

COLTON

Madeline Young was fine as fuck.

With more curves than a country road, she made me want to take a nice, slow ride around every bend and dip of her body while wrapping her long, golden brown hair up in my fist.

Leaning against the railing of the deck I'd built for her and her husband, I stared after her gorgeous, swaying ass hidden by black yoga pants as she walked away from me.

She went back inside the house, leaving the slider open to catch the early summer breeze through the screen.

"Goddamn," I groaned quietly, fixing my dick strangling in my work pants.

With a long pull on the lemonade she'd gifted me, I enjoyed the coolness sliding clear to my stomach. The drink didn't do shit to chill my blood as I watched her move around the kitchen directly in my line of sight.

The soft swish of the fridge door reached my ears, and she bent slightly, giving me an eyeful of her lush backside.

I stifled another curse she would easily hear through the

screen and settled in to eat my lunch beneath the rolled-out awning over their almost-completed back deck.

If fraternizing with clients wasn't a big no-no, I'd have asked if she and her older husband were interested to a third—because her other half had that sexy silver fox thing going on and clicked all my needy-as-shit buttons Madeline couldn't reach as a woman.

What I wouldn't have given to be a piece of meat in a Young sammie. God knew I'd been fantasizing about that very thing since arriving at their house.

The Youngs had hired Harper's Construction to tear off their old wooden porch and build a new one. Lucky me, I'd moved into town about a mile from their place and got assigned to the job that had fueled my spank bank for the previous two weeks.

But the work drew to a close with only AZEK trim left to hang, something I would finish up by the end of the day.

I would miss break time and the chats she and I had. I would miss her husband hovering in the mornings before he went to work and when he came back for lunch and bull-shitted with me about sports. And I would definitely miss devouring the eye candy every second I could for those long nights spent fantasizing alone in my bed.

Shoulders sagged, I opened my lunch box and pulled out the first of the two PB&J sandwiches I'd made that morning while Madeline kept herself busy a few feet away from me.

She and her husband Hudson owned Young's Tree Service. They didn't have any children, but she mothered the hell out of him and me—coffee and fresh muffins or homemade cinnamon rolls every morning. Freshly squeezed lemonade or sweet tea for break. Cupcakes and cookies always ended up in my hands at the end of the day too.

That nurturing way about her did funny shit to my insides.

Made me want more. Stability. A real relationship like they shared and I envied like a motherfucker.

A flash of movement in my periphery from inside the house drew my focus off Madeline. Hudson had entered the kitchen, and he went right up behind her, gently wrapping those strong arms around her middle.

"Hey, love," he murmured, loud enough that his low tone moved over me like a caress.

A shiver slid straight to my balls, and I tipped my head back against the railing, taking a long look at the tall drink of water.

He had probably fifteen years on both me and his wife, but the sexy man was as fit as a guy half his age.

Steel-toed boots, worn jeans hugging his ass in all the right ways, T-shirt on the tighter side stretched over his muscular back...fuck, what a sight he was. Toss in a bit of sawdust sprinkled in his salt and pepper hair and atop his shoulders, and my mouth took to drooling for a taste of the sweat on his skin.

"Hi." Madeline leaned back against him, offering her neck like she always did when he wrapped her up like that. He kissed beneath her ear, but I forced my attention on my lunch before my mind got too carried away over planting myself between the two of them for yet another daydream full of roaming hands and tongues. Hard dicks, hungry mouths, and tight holes.

Jesus Christ.

I swallowed audibly, refusing to watch what would

tighten me up to the point of exploding then leave me a puddle of goo.

They had one hell of a marriage from what I'd seen. She took care of him, and he adored the fuck out of her if his constant affection whenever he was around was any indication. What I wouldn't do for a little bit of both since I hadn't experienced either in my rough past.

"Chicken salad today," Madeline told him while I tore into my PB&J sandwich, my dick half-hard and brows furrowed.

"With purple grapes?" Hudson asked.

"Of course," she answered.

His groan licked over my groin, making me bite on my tongue to keep my answering one inside. "You spoil me, woman."

More fucking kissy noises. He probably loved on her neck like he'd done the day before when I hadn't been able to look away.

I closed my eyes rather than fighting off the need to gaze at affection and popping another full-on boner. My thoughts traveling the road of commitment and relationships wouldn't do me any favors, but I couldn't help myself.

I wanted a sandwich prepared in love, goddamnit, and grapes tossed in because my significant other knew I liked a little sweet crunch with the savory mayo mixed with chicken chunks.

While I'd always sworn off monogamy and settling down, since meeting the Youngs, I'd found myself yearning for someone—preferably *two* someones—to share my space. I dreamed about arms and mouths welcoming me home at the end of the day too. Soft breasts to nuzzle and warm curves to wrap myself around...rougher male hands that would wreck me in the best way possible so both of them could put me back together again.

The thought of giving that sort of trust though hit all my *hell no* alarms. Growing up in foster care made me well aware long-term didn't happen for someone like me.

But fuck, did I want it.

Maybe I should test the waters though...give up the playboy days for something worth a damn. Besides, thirty-six lay not too far in my future. Wasn't it time I attempted more with my life?

My sense of self-preservation screamed *NO!*, but my damned heart craved that sort of satisfaction to the point my chest ached.

I shoved the last bite of my first sandwich between my lips and pulled my cell from my back pocket. Time to shoot off a text to one of my friends who would be able to help me figure out how the fuck I went about finding what I longed for—if I was even sure I truly did.

I need to vent, and since you'll give shit to me straight, I want your ear. Call me so I can annoy you.

Within seconds, my phone rang, Rhett's name showing on the screen.

"You know me too well," he said when I answered.

I glanced back through the screen door, but both Madeline and Hudson had disappeared from the kitchen. Probably off for a little afternoon delight.

A pang of jealousy ripped through me.

"Yeah," I muttered with a deeper frown, "which is why I trust you to figure out a plan and tell me what the fuck to do." I put Rhett on speaker so I could finish my lunch and chat at the same time.

"What's going on?" he asked, and I leaned back against

the deck's railing and eyed my second sandwich. Boring fucking thing...

"Remember that variety I used to enjoy?" I asked. "Well, my dick has decided it's tired of being a playboy."

And I wanted Hudson's lunch, the lucky fucker.

Rhett barked out a laugh at my whiny tone while I took a bite of my sandwich and chewed.

"I'm serious!" I scowled. "All of my buddies had the same pussy-hungry attitude I used to—hell, a few work for Elite Escorts, so they're getting plenty, but I'm *bored*, man." I swallowed, the peanut butter that I'd slathered on the bread earlier that morning a little too thick. "Seriously. The only thing that interests me is something real, you know? Like you and Ash have. Guy, girl, I don't really care either way." I took a sip of lemonade to wash the sandwich down.

"Elite Escorts?" Rhett asked.

"You know..." I took another massive bite and spoke around my food, "*escorts*."

"Prostitution?" His tone didn't suggest judgey douche but more looking for clarity.

"Lots of them get paid to use their dicks, but sometimes it's just to be eye candy for events and that sort of shit. Why? Do you think it's wrong?" I asked anyway while grabbing a couple of chips from the plastic baggie on the deck beside me.

"As long as someone works hard to pay their bills, what do I care?"

"Hard." I couldn't help but focus on the word and chuckle before shoving some chips into my mouth. I could imagine Rhett rolled his eyes at my juvenile behavior. I spent most of my days with a bunch of construction guys. Our discussions tended to revolve around dicks, pussy, and getting off, not software and investment shit like Rhett probably did with his suit-and-tie friends.

"You're adventurous," Rhett stated the obvious to anyone who knew me. "Why don't you switch over to looking for relationships instead of hookups on Missing Link? See what you can find. There are thousands of profiles of people hoping for something real."

I rubbed the back of my neck, suddenly too antsy to discuss my wants versus fears.

I asked how his and Ashton's search was going before tossing the rest of my sandwich between my lips.

Rhett took so damn long in answering that I figured we'd lost connection.

It turned out some woman named Skylar had flipped his world upside down, and he went on a bitching fest about how perfect Ashton thought she was while I bit back a grin over his petulant tone.

"What's she look like?" I asked, stretching my legs out and eyeing the four melting ice cubes watering down the final couple of inches of my sweet lemonade.

"Gorgeous. Pale skin, auburn hair, and she has these big green eyes that are so damn expressive..."

I couldn't help my chuckle. "Someone has it *bad*."

"I do not." The dude totally lied.

"She makes you feel *alllll* the damn feels, am I right? *That's* what you can't stand. Go ahead and deny it, Rhett Stirling, Mr. I-Hate-Vulnerability Asshole." God, my tone stated *jealous jerk*.

"This doesn't sound like you venting," he grumbled while I finished my drink.

"Your life is more interesting," I said, laughing again and setting aside my empty glass. Madeline would eventually come back out for it—and I couldn't wait to thank her and steal a bit more of her time with idle chitchat. I wondered if she'd caught onto my neediness, how I asked questions to keep her talking.

"So. Missing Link." Rhett redirected the fucking subject after a throat clearing. "Change your profile to show you're looking for a relationship. Trust her to bring what you need."

"Like she did for you?" I couldn't help but toss out there, knowing it would rile him up.

"Fuck off."

I did a few minutes later with a plan.

Missing Link led my ass over a rainbow into a pot of gold every goddamn time I went searching to get laid. Couples of all pairings—I didn't discriminate and enjoyed the fuck out them depending on my mood.

But lately, I'd been seeking MF because my damn heart had started dreaming about both.

And not for my usual one-and-done.

The fantasies I'd had going through my mind the previous two weeks since meeting the Youngs flitted through my brain like a pornographic movie on fast-forward.

Sucking. Fucking. Cuddling.

Even drinking coffee together in the early morning hours on a deck like the one I'd been sweating over for two weeks. Assurances of permanence in their affectionate touches and edifying words.

No such fucking thing.

Lips pressed tight, I cleaned up my lunch shit, got off my ass, and strapped my tool belt back on.

Those goddamn longings inside my chest for something

more needed to take a back seat because forever didn't exist no matter what promises were made. I'd heard them one too many times as a kid, only to have my heart ripped in half.

I had a job to finish before the end of the day.

It was best to focus on reality.

2

HUDSON

I couldn't see Colton from where I'd leaned against the far kitchen counter to eat my lunch, but I could hear every word he spoke.

Mads had gone upstairs, and I'd stayed in the kitchen so I wouldn't track sawdust through the dining room where I usually sat to eat lunch.

Only a screen door and a few feet separated me from the hot young guy Blake Harper had sent over to build our deck. Colton and I had connected from day one, getting caught up in bullshitting about the Red Sox and Pats. Like any true New Englander, we both loathed the Yankees and believed Tom Brady was the GOAT.

The day before, we'd talked stats over our lunch break, and our easy conversation swept us well past the half hour I'd allotted myself.

Something sparked inside me whenever I hung out with the younger man. He drew me in to the point that had I been in a different frame of mind, I'd have let my imagination run wild with inviting him over one weekend for a little bit of fun.

As it was, Mads and I had hit a goddamn wall a few months earlier, and all thoughts of sharing our bed had gotten shoved onto the back burner in our minds—same as our own sex life.

Neither of us had fully gotten over the grief of losing our baby along with her ability to conceive. I doubted we ever truly would, but it was bitterness toward the catalyst of our sorrow that kept me up late at night when my wife finally slept.

She went to weekly meetings that hadn't done much to help her depression or the hesitation to move on from our loss. The unused nursery upstairs looked the same as it had six months earlier, and the third bureau in the master bedroom still sat empty without the possibility of it ever being filled with another's clothing.

Our passion had dried up although her tears continued to fall. She didn't avoid my advances to be intimate but didn't initiate or show any desire for me, which messed with my head and affected my ability to get hard.

I was tired of wading in stagnated waters, going through the motions—without *living*.

And Colton had zapped something awake inside of me, the desire for more, but the idea of opening myself up again, allowing another man access to my heart and body...

My stomach churned at the mere thought of giving someone that kind of power over me again.

"Why don't you switch over to looking for relationships instead of hookups on Missing Link?"

The muffled question coming from Colton's cell on speakerphone brought me back to the kitchen and the fact I still held my favorite sandwich in hand that I hadn't yet taken a bite of.

Missing Link.

I'd heard about that app when it had first popped up in cyberspace a few years earlier, but by that time, Mads and I were already in a committed triad.

But his poor choices got him tossed from our home.

And we still suffered.

Although I fantasized about another man between me and my wife, I had no wish to be vulnerable.

But maybe that was what Mads needed.

Setting aside my sandwich, my appetite gone, I listened in on the rest of Colton's conversation, taking note of the emotions he couldn't hide from his tone. He made fun of his buddy for falling for a woman, but clear longing lay in every word he spoke.

His friend brushed aside his banter by bringing back up the poly dating app and suggesting Colton try for something more.

It sounded like Colton's interest and heart's desire lay in the happily-ever-after side of a triad, something I had zero interest in attempting again.

But Missing Link offered hookup profiles too.

I rubbed a palm over my whiskered jawline, considering the idea of bringing a spark back to our bed to rekindle the flame Mads and I had lost.

The saw turned on outside, and I shifted to the window above the sink to watch Colton work. Something about the kid attracted my eyes like a magnet, and I couldn't help but check him out same as I did every chance I got.

He faced away from me, cutting a piece of white trim material. His wide shoulders filled out the navy blue shirt with Harper's Construction logo on his back, dark, short hair peeking beneath the bottom of his old ball cap stained by sweat. He stood a good inch or two taller than me, something that usually turned me off toward men, but he'd held my full focus since starting on our deck.

There were no shifty gazes, no immaturity outside banter when we shot the shit. He seemed...real. Genuine. Definitely a hard worker—and had the body to show for it. Twice, I'd caught him without a shirt on, and the one time he'd lifted the hem to wipe sweat off his brow while I stood beside him, I almost got caught ogling his eight-pack.

Colton pulled down the miter saw's lever, the whirl of the blade louder for a few seconds as it sliced through the material he held. One small piece of AZEK fell to the ground, and he flicked off the power switch before lowering the headphones he always clamped around his ears when cutting.

I leaned on the sink and watched him use the finish nail gun to hang the piece of trim before measuring for the next.

He would complete the job before the end of the day, and I was bummed to lose my favorite part of lunch break the previous two weeks.

I quickly ate half my sandwich, my mind preoccupied with the backyard and Colton's ass in his tan Carhart pants. How snugly they fit his backside, how they tempted me to yank them to his knees before bending him over the deck's edge.

It had been too damn long since I'd allowed myself to let loose with a man, and my dick woke up in total agreement as the scene played out in my head.

Colton emanated pure masculinity, but I got a sense he would take every inch of my cock like a greedy little cock slut and beg me to fill his hole. I would pump him full of cum and watch gobs of white dribble from his asshole as it winked at me.

"Fuck." I scrubbed a hand down over my face, my entire body vibrating with need.

The saw whirred again, and I studied the ripple of muscle over Colton's back through the sweaty shirt clinging to him. I wanted to slide my palms over his skin, knead the knots from his body, and soak in the groans of pleasure as he relaxed beneath my oiled hands.

I'd told myself I wouldn't bother him on his final afternoon finishing up our deck, but I found myself striding out the slider before thinking it through.

He glanced up from where he tacked up the AZEK along the deck's base. Heat flared in his eyes for the briefest of seconds before he shut it down just like every other time I made my way outside with the intention of hanging out with him for a little while.

Without doubt, Colton would have gladly jumped into our bed if given the chance.

Too bad he wanted more than one night.

"Hey, Hudson," he said, his smile making my stomach feel like I rode a roller coaster.

I nodded, taking the stairs along the side. "Catch the game last night?" I asked, rounding the deck to get closer to him to soak in that feeling of...exuberance. Every inch of my body urged me to keep going—crowd the fuck out of him until he dropped the finish gun and gave me what I craved.

He snorted, but his quick once-over didn't go unnoticed by my eyes or my dick. At least his gaze didn't linger long enough to see my bulge buck. "That was a goddamn strike if I've ever seen one. Our boy deserved that shutout."

Instead, the pitcher had gotten *kicked* out in the final inning because he got up in the umpire's face. That had brought the manager from the dugout. Then half the team cleared the bench to back their boy.

"Reyes should have kept his ass clear," I said about the batter who got caught up in the middle and ended up with an elbow to his eye. Crossing my arms and leaning against the edge of the deck, I settled in to enjoy every second of being near Colton.

Both teams had ended up on the field, fists has flown, and the rumors on sports radio that morning promised lawsuits would fly too.

Colton and I went back and forth, sharing what we'd heard and who we thought might end up suspended for the rest of the season.

Same as every time I lingered and kept Colton from getting his job done, I didn't feel a bit of remorse. Over the two-week period, I'd probably used up almost a good six hours that he should have spent working.

But he'd given me something to look forward to every day, and I couldn't fucking leave him alone. He was like a damned patch of poison ivy you couldn't help but scratch until it took over your whole damn body.

"Still planning to finish up today?" I asked as he straightened from where he'd leaned alongside me.

"Yep. Gonna miss your wife's baking, that's for damned sure."

I'd seen him checking out Mads plenty of times—he would be missing more than her kitchen skills.

"You're welcome to place an order and stop by anytime." I might have added a hint of suggestion to my voice even though I knew he wanted more than a one-and-done fuck. I should have thought to offer before he decided to go looking for love like I'd overheard earlier.

"She ought to open her own shop," Colton said, not for the first time while turning to measure for the next piece of trim to be hung.

God, what a view he offered my hungry eyes.

I drooled over his round backside and had to swallow the rush of saliva. "It's a hobby, one she's not interested in building into a business," I reminded him, my gaze flitting away from his ass as he headed toward the saw once more.

"Damn shame. That woman makes my mouth water every morning and afternoon." His voice held the same hint mine had.

I kept my silence for a few minutes, simply watching him work and soaking in the show of youth and virility he exuded. To have that type of man in our bed, someone closer in age to Mads than me, would stir up a shit load of lust, I didn't doubt. Fuck knew being a few feet from him made me crave things I hadn't taken pleasure from in months.

No.

I only needed a flash of memory to knife my chest and lock my daydreams up. "Well, I guess I should get back to work too and leave you alone," I said as Colton set a piece of AZEK on the miter saw.

He turned, thrusting out his hand. "It's been great getting to know you, Hudson. Fingers crossed the Sox kick ass tonight, and I hope the two of you enjoy your new deck too."

I clasped his palm, heat and electrical pulses jetting straight to my hard cock, same as when I'd greeted him on day one of the job.

Neither of us squeezed to show dominance, nor did we pull away. We hadn't touched since he'd introduced himself a couple of weeks earlier, and that instant lust I'd felt had only grown stronger at having spent a little time with him.

"I appreciate the extra hours you worked to make up for all those I stole from you," I said, studying the slight swell of his pupils while wondering if he would put up a fight or submit to my leading in the bedroom.

His slow smirk revealed a dimple that would have gotten Mads's blood pulsing through her body months earlier. Fucking shame the boy wasn't looking to hook up anymore. He'd have given us both a night to remember.

"My pleasure," he murmured with a *definite* hint of interest.

Fuck.

"I've enjoyed hanging out and shooting the shit with you. You're a good man, Hudson."

I released his hand as the desire to yank him against me and claim his lips rolled over me. Clearing my throat and stepping back, I nodded. "Hope to see you around, Colton."

"You too," he said, and I forced myself to turn away before I said something stupid. Like invited him to stick around for a beer after work and maybe find out what my wife enjoyed in the bedroom.

My backside burned as though he stared at my ass, my balls tightening against my body. I needed release, and the thought of my hand didn't appeal. I wanted warmth and wetness wrapped around my length.

The saw sounded behind me as I bagged up the other half of my uneaten, semi-stale sandwich and considered my options. Quickie hand job or go upstairs to my wife who wouldn't enjoy my dick like she used to?

"You didn't eat your lunch," Mads said, coming into the kitchen and making the decision for me.

My body buzzed to the point my hands began to shake like a teenager faced with pussy for the first time. I tossed my sandwich into the fridge and turned toward my wife. She wore black stretch pants as usual—easy access to her fine ass.

She opened a cabinet and stood on her toes to reach an upper shelf. Her shirt rode high, gifting me a flash of her pale belly and the hint of stretch marks, the constant reminder of what we'd lost. She hated them, wouldn't allow me to touch the silvery lines on her skin I wanted to lavish with love.

I wrapped my arms around her like I'd done earlier when I'd arrived home, but this time, my hard dick pressed against the top of her crack. My lips found her neck, and she tilted her head, offering me access. While her body didn't tense, Mads didn't exactly melt into me like she used to either.

Reaching around her front, I slid my hand over her leggings, palming the heat of her core while nosing along her ear. "Can I have you, Mads?"

She shivered but didn't moan. "Yes," she whispered, and at least the haggard tone of her answer was laced with want for intimacy, assuring me of her love.

I dropped to my knees with thankfulness, pulling her pants and panties to the floor. "Fuck, I've missed this ass," I growled and grasped her cheeks, spreading them wide. A lick up through her crack shifted her hips back toward me, and I took another slow taste, groaning at her musky flavor on my tongue.

Dipping down, I lapped at her lower lips, not surprised to find a lack of dampness beyond her natural state. Still, she tasted sweet as honey, and I enjoyed the fuck out of eating her pussy and ass until my dick dripped with need.

She didn't writhe with want. Didn't pant or beg for my cock like she used to.

A whisper of guilt shot through my brain at the knowledge I would take pleasure in my wife even though she wouldn't enjoy it as deeply as I would, but I was too far gone in my lust—and she'd given me permission to find release in her body.

Goddamn selfless woman—I'd been blessed with the most awesome wife on God's green earth.

I worked open my jeans and palmed myself, a few slow tugs smearing pre-cum over my length since the extra lubrication would make Mads more comfortable.

Standing, I glanced out the slider's screen, then through the window above the sink, noting the lack of noise. No saw. No nail gun. No extending or releasing of a measuring tape.

Had he heard my groans while I'd tongued my wife's holes?

Was his dick hard and leaking like mine?

"Fuck," I crowed against Mads, burying my nose in the softness of her neck and rubbing the back of my pre-cum slickened dick between her cheeks. "This okay, love?" I murmured, swiveling my hips, needing to hear her consent one last time to erase that thread of guilt still weaving through my head.

"Yes," she whispered, arching her back deeper and widening her stance.

I bent my knees, which shifted my cock lower between her thighs. "You're such a good girl, Mads. Love you so fucking much," I whispered while sliding home into her tight pussy.

3

MADELINE

Hudson hadn't initiated sex in weeks.

But neither had I.

Our loss had left a gaping hole inside me, and nothing functioned as it used to. My lips rarely curled upward from welling happiness. My heart never thrummed with anticipation or excitement about anything. My body no longer warmed from my husband's gentle touch.

Even though his sensitivity to my lingering depression comforted me, arousal seemed beyond reach no matter how hard I tried to focus, to feel more than the connection between our souls that hadn't ever lacked, thank God.

He held still, buried inside me, his hot breath on my ear.

I squeezed my inner muscles around his thickness, and he groaned, stuffing himself a bit deeper. "Love you too," I promised through the tightness of my throat.

"I could stay here all day long." Hudson pulled out a fraction and burrowed back in, the heat of his thighs and groin pressing against my backside.

"What about work?" I asked, going for lighthearted, something I definitely didn't feel.

He chuckled. "I'd rather be here with my woman, enjoying the hell out of her curves and sweet pussy." Hudson palmed my breasts through my shirt and bra, but his words and touch that used to make me burn didn't ignite need through my core.

I swallowed hard and shifted back, creating space for me to prop my upper body onto the counter. Arms resting on the granite, I laid my cheek atop them and wiggled my ass.

Hudson groaned and slid his strong hands to my waist, grasping tight. "You feel so fucking good wrapped around my dick, love." He pulled out to his thick head and slid in to the root once more.

"Sorry I'm not wet," I whispered, and he leaned over my back, nipping my earlobe.

"You're fucking perfect. So hot and tight. The most unselfish woman, letting me love on you in the middle of the day even though you probably have a hundred things to do—I don't deserve you, Mads."

Warmth spread through me at his words, but the numbness toward anything sexual held strong over my body, keeping me from enjoying his slow, lazy thrusts, eased by his pre-cum.

I didn't deserve *him*. His patience, the daily assurance of his love, his empathy, and his intuition. He knew I needed to be treated with kid gloves without my having to say a word.

I should have gotten turned on by every display of his unconditional acceptance, but I remained a dried-out husk of the woman I used to be.

Hudson would apologize once he finished, same as he'd done the handful of times he'd made love to me in the previous couple of months, and that knowledge hurt me as much as my body's inability to appreciate his touch.

I was broken.

All because of that asshole...

I clenched my teeth to will away the memory of Peter's beautiful blue-green eyes and his soft smiles that used to tingle my insides.

It had been his betrayal that had shifted our world off its axis, and the resulting stress had taken a tight hold on my body.

The doctors claimed the loss of our baby had nothing to do with external circumstances, and they had also assured me I hadn't been at fault, but that didn't stop me from continuing to blame our ex. He'd torn out our hearts, and in my opinion, taken our baby's too.

"Mads." Hudson ran his hands up my back beneath my shirt, his warm touch pulling me into the present. "Are you okay?"

I nodded and relaxed again, not having realized I'd tensed up.

"Are you uncomfortable? Am I hurting you?"

"No," I whispered, overcome with love for my sensitive husband.

"I can stop if you want."

Tears stung my eyes, and I shook my head. "I want you to finish, Hud," I murmured through the thickness in my throat. "Want your cum dripping out of me so I'll never forget how much you love me."

"Jesus Christ, Mads." He backed out and thrust in deep, his hands once more grasping at my hips. "Your filthy mouth makes me hard as fuck."

Evidence of his claim stabbed into me with steady thrusts of his hips, and I arched, wishing I could draw him in farther, so his soul entwined with mine even more than it already was.

I should have been soaking wet, sloppy sounds of

fucking filling my ears. My body should have been burning with lust, my pulse throbbing and ears ringing as he whispered his desires, his appreciation of my body.

My heavy breasts swayed regardless of my suffocating bra, and the backs of my legs began to ache. Unlocking my knees helped a bit, and I focused on staying relaxed. Pliant. Soft and open to the love my husband showed me.

But I longed for more.

Once I'd lost my uterus along with the baby we'd been waiting years for, thoughts of sex and pleasure had dissolved like sugar in warm water.

Until two weeks earlier when a young man knocked on our door, his dark lashes framing bedroom eyes that should have soaked my panties the second they'd landed on my face.

A twinge had woken between my thighs that morning, a reminder I hadn't been buried alongside our baby, but it hadn't been enough of a flame to make me initiate sex again with my husband.

I doubted anyone's ability to fully rouse me if that young man from Harper's Construction hadn't been able to. He had the raw beauty, the sexual awareness that Hudson and I used to enjoy when playing with other men, but it seemed my body held little interest in intimacy outside that initial flicker.

Even the knowledge he worked a few feet away with nothing but a wall between us didn't turn me on.

I opened my eyes, catching a movement of shadow along the edge of the screened slider.

Did he watch?

That tingle, an awareness of sexual energy, once more flickered inside me, and I clung to the feeling.

Closing my eyes again, I imagined Colton studying how

I bent at the waist in offering to be used for my husband's satisfaction. Did Colton like to watch? Touch himself while imagining it was his body Hudson thrust into? My mind reversed our roles, and I stood outside on the deck. Hudson would let loose in ways he wouldn't allow himself with me. His thrusts would be harsher, his grip on Colton's body tighter—bruising.

I'm going to fill your ass with my cum. Gonna plug you up so I'm inside you all day while you're at work.

Arousal slid through my blood like warm molasses, and I sighed, sinking into the first hints of true pleasure in months as the fantasies continued to play in my mind.

Being squished in the middle, two dicks taking turns shunting in and out of me as Hudson and Colton chased their releases. Sprawled on the bottom, watching Hudson rail Colton as he writhed and whimpered between us.

Oh God, yes.

Riding Colton's face reverse cowgirl and clutching the backs of his drawn-up legs to offer my husband better access to his ass.

I'd seen Hudson checking out Colton as often as I'd done. Had we both been emotionally able, the young man definitely would have been invited into our bed.

But Peter—

The memory of his face once more flitted through my brain, stalling the need that had begun to rise inside my core.

A tear leaked between my clenched eyelids as the fantasies faded along with my desire.

Once more, I settled in to help Hudson finish.

If only I could find a way to fix what that man had broken so we could *live* again.

4

COLTON

They had to know I could hear them—that I could all but taste the scent of sex in the air wafting through the screen door.

Had their afternoon delight in the kitchen been intentional? Did Hudson hope to drive me fucking insane with lust as he railed his wife against their counter?

What had started as a hug from behind, same as when he'd gotten home, turned into a hell of a lot more.

I'd been standing on the ground near the corner of the deck, the angle offering me a nice side view through the screen of Hudson kissing her neck. Palming her pussy. Dropping to his knees and taking her pants to the floor with him.

My erection hadn't relented from the clasp of his hand when saying goodbye moments earlier, and the sight of him shoving his face in her gorgeous backside had jolted lust through my groin with enough force that my dick bucked. Hard.

Standing still, I'd held my breath, ears straining for

every word they spoke, my eyes drinking in the sight of him working pre-cum over his length.

He'd asked permission before angling his hips to push into her body.

"I could stay here all day long," he'd murmured, and Christ, did I agree.

Unable to help myself, I'd pressed against my aching dick as he poured out praise, my heart stinging with the need to hear similar sentiments. Love, not lust. Commitment, not a quickie to simply empty my balls.

Assurances and promises—things I'd heard as a child that hadn't panned out.

Could I really open myself up to the same devastating hurt I'd experienced as a kid? Did I have the guts to allow vulnerability that had the potential to tear my heart to pieces again?

Hudson paused, checking in with his wife, and she'd told him to finish so she could feel his cum dripping from her body.

His curse matched the one whispering off my lips at her filthy words. Could they be any more perfect? Pre-cum oozed from my slit, smearing the insides of my briefs.

Glancing around, I reassured myself of the privacy fence hiding my actions.

A quick pop of my button and downward drag of the zipper between my tool belt pouches, and I hissed in relief while pulling my aching dick through the gap in my pants.

Hudson's jeans clung to his thick thighs, and I zoned in on how the muscles of his ass flexed as he drove into Madeline with steady thrusts. Fuck, what I wouldn't give to be on the receiving end—or hell, on my knees in front of his wife, licking at them both as he filled her.

She would yank on my hair, clutch me close, and beg me to suck on her clit until she creamed all over his dick and my chin.

"Fuck." I gulped and squeezed the base of my cock, backing off the edge of spurting on the decking in front of me.

Madeline took him like a champ, a deep arch in her back, her ass high, the flesh jiggling with every slap of their skin meeting.

But she didn't whisper a sound. No moans. No begging for him to fuck her harder. No pleadings to come.

What—

Hudson turned his head, his gaze clashing with mine.

Goddamnit.

I swallowed hard, my heart racing, dick throbbing in my hand—but he didn't stop, didn't slow down.

His deep groan pebbled my skin.

The fucker enjoyed catching a Peeping Tom watching him fuck his wife.

"Ah, shit," I whispered harshly, my hand fucking my length in rhythm with his hips.

"You feel so good, Mads," he rumbled. "You're like silk wrapped around my dick."

"Christ," I muttered, my gaze dropping to said dick as he offered me a teasing peek before slamming back into her.

I'd gotten off to my fair share of porn, had sat and satisfied my voyeur kink countless times, but nothing compared to the sight of the committed couple beyond the screen door. If only I stood closer, had a better view—every fucking angle—

As though Hudson heard my thoughts, he shifted slightly and spread open his wife's ass cheeks like a camera zoomed in for a close-up of him stuffing his dick inside her pussy. A clear fucking shot of bare, pink lips wrapped around his glistening cock. The trimmed pubes around his base and drawn up balls.

A hiss escaped through my clenched teeth as pre-cum made a mess of my fingers gliding over my glans.

"Just like that," Hudson said, jerking my focus upward.

He wouldn't be able to see me below the waist from where I stood below the deck, but I realized my flexing forearm gave me away.

"Yes," he groaned as I didn't even break the rhythm of fucking my fist. "Jesus—fuck." He slammed into Madeline and held still, hips trying to buck him in deeper. A shudder ripped through him, and at the thought of his length spurting in pulsing waves, my own release shot upward.

I bit my tongue to keep quiet, grunts ripping from my lungs as ribbons of white fell to the ground at my feet. Gasping, I grabbed the deck rail with my free hand, eyes still glued to Hudson as he clasped his wife's waist in a possessive hold, drawing her up to stand. He gathered her hair in his hand, moving it to the side to access her neck.

As though I no longer existed, he whispered to her. Kissed and licked her throat. Nuzzled her skin.

Cursing, my insides a jumbled mess of longing, euphoria, and guilt, I stuffed my spent dick away, wiping my fingers clean on my boxer briefs. A few kicks of dirt from where I'd dug holes for new pilings covered the evidence of my perving.

My hands shook as I retrieved my tape measure from the side pouch of my tool belt and attempted to measure one last piece of AZEK to finish trimming out the Youngs' deck. I refused to look at them and yanked my headphones from around my neck and put them where they belonged. The built-in radio filled my ears, shutting out all noise from their house.

I focused on finishing the job I'd been hired to do rather than watching what sort of aftercare Hudson offered his wife.

Would he drop to his knees again and lick her clean? The thought made my mouth water.

Would he retrieve a wet towel and gently wipe his cum from between her thighs?

Would he offer to run a bath and pamper her like she deserved after being wrung out—

Madeline hadn't climaxed, I suddenly realized, remembering her lack of verbal involvement. Not one moan had left her lips.

My attention jerked toward the screen slider—but both Hudson and Madeline had disappeared. Thoughts of where they might have gone for Hudson to finish her off shot through my brain, but I shut that shit down before my dick went all happy again.

Lips pressed tight, I fit a piece of AZEK against the miter saw's guide, pulling down the still blade to line up the pencil line I'd drawn. A tiny shift, and I hit the button to bring the saw to screaming life. As with the silencing of voices, the radio blaring in my ears tuned out most of the blade's noise as it sliced through the trim material like a hot knife through butter.

A clean cut.

Exactly what I needed to do when leaving the job site that afternoon. Walking away with the knowledge I would never see the Youngs again or endure the heart-aching view of their love I expected would be easy.

But leaving the memories of them behind would prove impossible.

They'd stirred up longing. Fear. Curiosity.

Rhett's push to look for more had heightened those feelings, but my heart couldn't handle being broken again.

5

HUDSON

I didn't tell Mads that we had an audience. A year earlier, she'd have been thrilled like I was by that truth, but seeing as how she couldn't find enjoyment in my dick, I didn't have any wish to heighten her embarrassment. Colton had blatantly stared, and I'd offered him a better view, making my balls draw up tight in the process.

I'd finished first, but a harshly whispered curse had reached my ears from beyond the screen, enticing one last spurt up through my shaft at the thought of him getting off watching me come.

A second shudder rippled over me as I finished, and I pulled Mads against my chest. "Thank you," I whispered against her ear.

She clasped her hands atop mine on her belly where I rubbed over her shirt. "Mmm."

She hadn't come, but I honestly couldn't remember the last time she'd enjoyed release around my cock. My chest ached at the thought—I wanted so much more for us. Yes, our hearts remained connected, our souls bound with undeniable and unconditional love, but I missed the closeness of shared intimacy beyond physical touch.

"Okay?" I murmured while grazing my lips over her neck.

She squeezed her inner walls around my softening dick. "Yes. Promise."

I kissed her again and backed away.

Her hand appeared between her thighs, cupping her pussy to keep my cum from dripping to the floor.

"I'll clean you up," I murmured and caressed her hip before scuttling sideways to grab a paper towel from beside the sink. A quick glance out the window showed Colton with his headphones in place, measuring along the deck's outside joist.

A rush of longing swept through me, but I tore my attention from what I wouldn't allow myself to enjoy ever again.

I turned to find Mads had already left the kitchen.

I found her in the half-bath. She smiled at me through the door she'd left cracked open, but no happiness shone in her eyes.

"Headed back to work?" she asked while relieving herself, and I nodded, allowing her space to avoid the topic of her inability to climax that I'd attempted to discuss on more than one occasion.

Using the wet paper towel I'd gotten for her to clean myself up, I bit back the desire to push. She bumped the door wider with her foot and held out her hand for the used bit of paper I'd rumpled.

I gave it over for her to drop in the trash can beside the toilet and tucked myself away inside my jeans again. Leaning against the doorjamb, I waited for her to finish, flush, and right her stretch pants. "Do you have any baking to do this afternoon?" I asked, knowing she would appreciate a mundane topic.

"Cupcakes for Janie Callahan's eighth birthday party tomorrow."

"What kind?"

Mads turned on the water to wash. "Strawberry with buttercream frosting."

"Make an extra for me?"

"Don't I always?" She smiled again, that one hinting at the contentment she used to enjoy.

I grasped her chin, turning her face toward me even though she hadn't finished rinsing the suds from her hands. Pressing a firm kiss to her soft lips, I silently vowed to bring about a change—do something however drastic as needed to return us to the joy we'd lost along the way.

"I love you, Mads."

"Love you too, Hud," she whispered and pecked me again.

I turned for the front door, my stomach as empty as my heart. Should have finished my sandwich rather than teasing myself with a dose of Colton. Another amble to the backyard for one last glimpse of Colton and his tight ass wouldn't have made me any happier, so I left without doing so since he wouldn't be interested in what I had planned for my marriage anyway.

Regardless of how we definitely had chemistry, Colton wanted a forever couple, and my stance on never sharing myself emotionally again outside of Mads wouldn't be swayed.

My crew had already finished up lunch and had gotten back to clearing the trees we'd been hired to drop for an addition a few blocks away from my house.

They didn't need my help. I just enjoyed getting my hands dirty most days.

Once parked, I removed my cell from its dash holder, opened the App Store, and typed in Missing Link. A slow scroll allowed me to read a few testimonials and reviews of the polyamorous dating app.

Mads and I had been out of the swinger scene for so long and had left that part of us behind once Peter had moved into our lives. If she agreed, it wouldn't be with anyone we knew. God forbid lines crossed with someone we had a connection with and more shit got stirred and left us floundering a second time.

I downloaded the app but didn't sign up or begin creating a profile.

Consent had always been key for us, so I would leave the final decision to Mads even though my mind had already set on finding us someone to play with.

———

When I got home, the white truck with Harper's Construction painted on its doors no longer parked at the edge of our driveway.

For the best, I reminded myself, annoyed with the disappointment settling inside me as I brushed the sawdust off my hair and shoulders onto the front stoop.

No savory scents of dinner filled the air when I walked through the front door. No pleasant noises from Mads puttering around the kitchen like she used to do sounded from the back of the house. No plates and flatware sat atop the dining room table.

I was lucky to get a home-cooked meal once a week now when I'd been spoiled rotten six out of seven days before our loss. She still baked for the tiny business she ran out of our house, Mads Sweet Treats, which was a cash-only, word-of-mouth hobby that gave her a bit of spending money.

A hint of sweetness lingered in the air from the cupcakes she'd made that afternoon. Two dozen sat atop cooling racks on the counter I'd bent her over earlier in the day.

I shoved down memories of her tight heat and the dark eyes watching from outside as I'd found release in my wife's body. The last thing I needed was another damn hard-on I didn't want to deal with on my own.

Glancing out the locked slider, I took note of the completed deck and the lack of all construction tools and waste.

Colton was gone for good.

I exhaled heavily, wishing things had been different. Mads and I weren't always interested in the same men who drew our gazes and made conversation as though we'd known each other our whole lives. We'd only met one before, and that had ended in disaster.

After dinner, I'll bring up the idea of playing again, I told myself while turning away from the memory of Colton that left me feeling disappointed.

Rifling through the junk drawer, I found the menu I wanted, and a quick call ensured a hot meal would be delivered to our front door within forty minutes.

"Mads?" I called up the stairs, sure of her location since her car still sat in the driveway and she hadn't mentioned any plans about going out.

"Yeah?" Her voice didn't have the jolly tone it used to, the upbeat joy that had always made my insides smile.

I unlaced my work boots, left them by the door, and climbed the stairs on weary legs.

She sat in the nursery's rocking chair, staring at the

empty crib, her hands limp on her lap. I'd begged for weeks to return the room back to what it had been before she found out she'd been expecting, but she refused.

The scents of baby powder and lavender lotion filled my nose, and I slowly leaked a heavy exhale from my lungs.

"I ordered from that Italian place that just opened up," I told her, moving closer, hands shoved in my pockets.

"Okay." She continued to rock, not looking at me.

Lips pursed, I studied my wife.

She no longer wore makeup and rarely did anything other than air-dry her hair.

But she was still beautiful to me, achingly so.

My chest tight, I knelt in front of her and held her limp hands, deciding not to wait on what I wanted to discuss with her. "Hey."

She finally gave me her eyes. Blue as the sky but empty, they peered at me.

"I was thinking..."

Mads waited while I figured out how to bring up the subject of her fucking some random guy—Christ, we used to have zero filters, an ease when it came to conversations, but Peter had stolen that from us as well.

My jaw ticked as I glanced away.

"What?" Mads asked quietly, her soft palm cradling my cheek in a rare initiation of affection.

I leaned into her touch, my eyes closing. "We need to do something, Mads—"

"I'm not ready," she whispered, cutting me off as her hand once more dropped to her lap.

"Not about the nursery," I hastened to add before tears welled like they always did whenever I'd pushed her toward changing the nursery back into a guest room. "When we had sex earlier ...it isn't the same."

"I'm sorry," she whispered, and I cursed myself again.

"That's not—I'm not disappointed in you, love." I squeezed her hands. "I'm upset with myself for having allowed the passion to dissolve between us."

"We can have sex every day if you want. I don't mind." Her tone didn't suggest excitement or interest, which kept my dick in its flaccid state.

That wasn't what I'd meant either, but I wasn't sure how to explain what we lacked without causing her to feel even more broken than she already thought she was. We just needed to redirect our minds toward sex and intimacy.

"I overheard Colton talking about that Missing Link app today when he was on speaker phone with one of his buddies, and it got me thinking that maybe we could move on in that way."

"You want another man?" Mads asked, searching my face.

"No," I answered what my mind not my body desired while rubbing my thumbs over her knuckles. "But I would enjoy watching someone love on your gorgeous body. Make you smile, maybe give you pleasure again since I can't."

Mads studied our clasped hands, the sign of unity we'd had between us from the moment we'd met. "It's not your fault that I can't climax."

I held my breath, wanting to push for more—asking all the questions, making her dig deeper to explain why she couldn't come if it wasn't me.

"I've felt...numb. Emotionally. Physically." Her eventual admission escaped as a mere whisper, trickling relief through my mind and settling the unrest that had been a ball of turmoil in my guts for months on end.

We had been silent too long, hibernating in our own grief when we used to communicate so openly.

I tightened my hold on her hands, showing what support I could in her rare moment of honesty since that night with Peter. "Would you be interested in trying something different? Maybe a little kink would kickstart the beauty he made us lose."

She swallowed hard, and I cursed myself for even bringing up the memories.

"If that's what you want," she whispered.

I wanted a fuck ton more than that, but maybe Missing Link would help us take a step in the right direction.

6

MADELINE

I wasn't surprised Hudson had brought up the idea of inviting someone to our bed again, and I'd agreed—but only for him because I couldn't continue to let him suffer for my depression.

He was ready to move on, to go forward in finding happiness, and I'd done nothing but hold him back.

I didn't want to barrel into an unwanted future, but I would offer what I could. "I-I'm not sure I'll be able to enjoy playing again, but I'll try."

"That's all I ask, love." His smile fluttered my heart the slightest bit.

"I don't have the energy to find someone," I whispered. Just the thought of tracking down our old swinger group of friends gave me a headache.

"I'll do it." Hudson leaned up and pressed his lips to mine.

I longed to feel arousal at his soft touch, the scent of sweat and fresh sawdust clinging to his skin. Wanted to burn with desire like I used to whenever he put his mouth and hands on me, but I sat unmoved. Unaroused. Unable to feel beyond numbness.

My throat tightened up, eyes stinging, and I nodded when he pulled away.

"There's that new app for all things poly," he said, gently rubbing the tops of my thighs. "I'll take care of finding us someone to play with, someone to maybe ease us out of this funk, okay? Nothing serious, I promise."

"Yeah," I whispered and tried for a smile.

"That's my good girl." He kissed my forehead, his calloused, warm palm finding the back of my neck in a possessive hold that used to make my knees weak.

Warmth flushed through me but only with a sense of comfort and belonging. Far from the flames that used to flare between us.

"And while you're at it, maybe toss that third bureau in our bedroom out with the trash," I suggested, which earned me a deep, rumbling chuckle.

"Anything for you, Mads."

"I love you," I told him as a tear slid down my cheek.

He licked the trickle and pressed his lips to mine again.

I expected a flick of his tongue, a tentative request for more, but he backed away and smiled. "Let's go eat some dinner. I'll draw you a nice bath with Epsom salts, then rub you down with oil."

"Okay."

I didn't deserve his persistence in affection and edification when I'd given him nothing beyond my body a few times since Peter left and we'd lost our baby.

Goddamnit, I hated the emotional upheaval I'd been dealing with, more lows than highs, a tumble into depression that therapy and support groups hadn't helped me through.

But I felt powerless to change things. I didn't know how to move on from the heart-shattering grief that had robbed me of all my joy.

Depression hadn't taken away my appetite, unfortunately. I ate a pile of Italian food and had two pieces of garlic bread too many. Feeling like a bloated cow, I relaxed in the bath Hudson had drawn for me, a glass of wine in one hand while soaking.

The initial heat of the water had lessened by the time Hudson returned. He took up a washcloth, knelt beside the tub, and ordered me to sit upright.

We didn't speak, and I closed my eyes, enjoying as he sudsed the back of my neck and down my spine, brushing his fingertips along my skin in soothing circles. He shifted around to my front, taking his time on my breasts, the soft material of the cloth rubbing over my nipples and pebbling them slightly as a hint of arousal attempted to heat my core. The second he moved on, the feeling faded.

"Stand up, love."

I held his shoulders as he washed my pink skin, even propping each foot on the tub's edge one at a time for his devoted attention. He didn't linger between my thighs like he would've done before. Nor did he lean forward to kiss my pussy and demand I spread my legs for him to taste me there.

But with gentle, loving caresses, Hudson finished caring for me.

I sank back into the water, and he leaned forward to kiss me lightly on the lips. I sighed against his mouth.

"Okay?" he asked, and I hummed an affirmative, more relaxed than I'd been for days. "Want some more wine?"

"I'm good. Thanks." I tried for a smile, but goddamnit, it

seemed sorrow had my heart in a vise and refused to ease its hold regardless of his affection.

"Sit and relax as long as you want, then join me in the bed, and I'll rub you down."

I nodded, and he left me alone.

My throat went tight.

I'd been wallowing for too long. I knew I needed to accept our loss and make an attempt to find happiness again, but it was just so damn hard.

Sex had become a duty to perform, and my lack of excitement or initiation hurt Hudson. I could see it in his eyes when I caught him staring at me with desire in his gaze. Rather than approach me, he'd become complacent as well, and between the two of us and our sudden inability to communicate like we used to, we'd fallen into a rut. Unless he went too long without and asked me to ease his ache like I'd agreed to in the kitchen earlier in the day.

The fear of disappointing Hudson scared me more than not being able to open my mind and body to enjoy the thought of a third again. I needed to show Hudson that he was still the man I loved and that he held every part of me in his capable hands.

I could take those steps on my own.

I paused from climbing from the tub at the thought then continued drying off as my mind went down that road.

Sitting back and waiting for healing to come wouldn't benefit either of us. My lack of initiating physical contact the previous six months was evidence of that. So maybe it *was* time for a change—something easier for me to choose than cleaning out the baby's bedroom.

Shoving aside thoughts of what we'd lost, I slathered on Hudson's favorite honeysuckle-scented lotion, rubbing over my nipples in the same way he had done while washing me.

That hint of arousal blossomed, making my heart beat a little bit faster.

Clinging to that feeling, I walked naked into our bedroom, determined to restore what we'd allowed to fade into obscurity.

Hudson already lounged in our bed, propped up on a couple of pillows. He held a book but lifted his focus over the top of his reading glasses when I stepped through the door with my curves on full display. Heat flared to life in his eyes, and choosing love, I moved across the room and climbed onto the bed.

He set aside his book and glasses, watching me—but not reaching for me.

I slid down the blankets, revealing his bare groin and thighs. His dick lay soft against his thigh, and I gathered him into my hand.

"Mads," he whispered, cradling my face with his palms. "You don't have to."

"I want to," I told him, firm in my resolve and desire to rekindle the intimacy I missed terribly. I bent down and took him into my mouth.

"Christ." Hudson hissed as I sucked, his length thickening quickly on my tongue. "So good, Mads—so goddamn good. Love having your lips wrapped around my cock."

"Mmm," I hummed at his praise that fell down over me like warm rain. I rubbed his warm sack, playing with it and slobbering all over his dick until he grasped my hair and started thrusting gently. Excitement coiled slightly in my belly, that sense of power from commanding his body to arousal. I was no cock-sucking goddess, so I kept my hand wrapped around his base, jacking in time with my mouth.

Saliva and pre-cum leaked around my lips, and I rubbed the slickness down over his taint.

"Yes—fuck, yes." Hudson widened his legs, drawing his knees up, and I gave him what he wanted, smearing wetness over his hole. "Stick it in—fuck yeah." He groaned as I slid my finger up to the second knuckle. "More."

I popped off his dick and spat onto his asshole before giving him another finger, jacking his hard length with my other hand. Reaching deeper into his silken heat, I watched his eyes glaze over and lips part.

Rarely did he lower his walls to let someone take him there, but I knew he craved it as much as I used to.

"Feels so fucking good," he groaned as I rubbed over his prostate, and my pulse picked up, feeding that desire growing deep inside me.

"Want to come inside you," he rasped, fucking my fist while I fingered his ass. "Need you so fucking bad."

Not quite enough arousal slickened between my thighs for what he wanted, so I took him into my mouth again, soaking his length before pulling my fingers from his body.

"Mads," he groaned, and I climbed aboard, sinking down over his hard cock.

A swell of desire warmed my chest, my face, and I closed my eyes, willing the feeling to settle between my thighs where he stretched and filled me.

"My sweet girl," Hudson groaned, grabbing hold of my hips, his touch as sure and steady as it had been from the beginning.

I sank into the comfort of his acceptance. He'd been so damn patient with me, never pushing or showing aggravation at my reluctance to move on. Focusing on his love, the familiar way our bodies accepted one another, I settled on living in the emotions of *now* rather than our past hurts.

We rocked in perfect rhythm as always, our bodies finding that dance routine as though there'd never been any separation between our souls the previous couple of months. His tender touch, his low growls of encouragement...my chest ached with sweet pleasure. Intimacy drew us together, and my gaze hazed over when I lifted my eyelids to find him staring up at me with wonder and pure love.

One simple choice, one step of initiating toward my husband had cracked open the door inside my heart, reminding me of everything we shared, what we could be once more.

Hudson reached for my neck and drew me down, taking my mouth in a gentle kiss. Every slow swipe of his tongue along mine fueled the tiny flames in my core.

He filled his hands with my swaying breasts, fingers finding my soft nipples, rubbing and tugging until they firmed beneath his touch. Even more whispers of need swirled in my core, and I whimpered, wanting *more*, so damn desperate for it that tears slid down my cheeks.

Hudson used to strum my body like he owned it, telling me when and how to come, but he held back his demand same as he always did whenever we had sex since our loss.

But I wanted to give him my release. Ached for it.

Our mouths still fused, bodies still writhing, I reached between my thighs and teased over my clit with feathered touches.

A sweet ache swelled inside me, more dampness rising to coat my inner walls.

Yes...oh yes... I swallowed hard, my thighs tensing as I rode him faster, chasing after what I craved—what we needed to experience together again.

"You're so goddamn gorgeous, love," he murmured against my mouth. "Love your curves. Your sweet, hot pussy. The taste of you on my tongue."

I breathed against his lips in a non-kiss but needing the

contact, his exhales in my lungs. "Want to come," I whispered, my eyes clenched shut as I focused on the feel of his hard cock pushing up into my slickening pussy and withdrawing. Delicious friction paired with his hands on my breasts.

Hudson licked into my mouth in time with his gently thrusting hips, giving—always fucking giving. His hands moved around to my back, sliding over my ass cheeks. Feet planting on the bed, he thrust harder. Deeper. Angling for my G he never failed to locate when he set his mind to it.

I shifted away from his mouth, sitting— "Oh, shit," I gasped, my back arching as he stroked at just the right angle. "Yes, there—oh fuck." Clutching at his knees, I held still while he pounded up into me.

Hudson settled his thumb on my clit and flicked.

"Oh yes," I whimpered. "More—don't stop." Tingles rose inside my core, spreading down my thighs.

Finally—goddamnit, fucking finally.

Hudson grunted with every thrust, his curses letting me know he was close to finishing.

I palmed my own breast, scratching at my nipple with my thumb.

He pinched my clit, giving me exactly what I needed.

Euphoria welled up, and I cried out while tumbling over the peak into pure bliss.

"Yes, love—just like that—such a good girl coming all over my cock." Hudson thrust hard, ramming into my pulsing body over and over again, drawing out my climax as I shuddered and shook atop him. "Mads!" He slammed upward, his fingers digging into my waist to hold me tight against his groin.

Wet heat erupted inside me before I finished—so deeply

welcomed—his low groan rumbling the chest beneath my palms and pebbling every inch of my skin.

"Mads," he gasped my name again on one last shudder, and I burst into tears at the rush of emotional liberation just as strong as the release I'd allowed myself.

I hadn't realized how bottled up everything had become inside me, hidden beneath numbness I'd grasped with every bit of strength to ease my sorrow.

"Love you so much," I sobbed, my entire body tingling from aftershocks and release I'd needed desperately. "So sorry—"

"Shh. Come here," he murmured and pulled me down, kissing and licking the wetness from my cheeks.

I'd finally climaxed for the first time in over six months.

Six *fucking* months because I'd been burying my desire to feel anything.

Happiness rose to choking levels, and I couldn't stop crying.

Still lodged inside my core, Hudson rolled us, settling me onto my back while he planked onto his elbows, peppering my face with kisses. "Love you so damn much, Mads—there isn't anything I wouldn't do for you."

"Love you," I croaked out again, grasping at the muscles along his spine, holding him tight.

He smoothed my hair back, a soft smile crinkling the skin around his sated, sleepy hazel eyes.

"I thought I should take a step on my own first," I told him, unable to stop my tears. "I-I didn't want someone else to possibly give me pleasure before I found it with you again, you know?"

"I do, love. I do." He leaned down and kissed my forehead. "Should I still create a profile and find someone for us to play with?"

"Yes," I didn't hesitate to answer since I'd broken through the barriers of at least enjoying sex again.

I'd accomplished a baby step, but I wanted us to move forward together toward complete emotional healing.

If that meant giving Hudson the opportunity to watch another man love on me like he'd said he wanted, I would willingly offer my body to whoever he chose.

7

COLTON

Protecting my heart and staying single lasted a couple of weeks after my last day on the Youngs' job site. I stayed home every night at my fixer-upper and scrolled through my usual hookup suggestions on Missing Link.

Nothing clicked.

No profile image snagged my attention like Madeline's backside had done.

No poke roused my blood like when Hudson had offered me a better view of him thrusting into his wife's pussy.

No bio promised to quench the thirst for that desire for *more* inside my chest I'd been feeling since I'd gone all Peeping Tom on one of my boss's clients.

The idea of a dick up my ass or a warm pussy clenching around my cock offering mere release didn't satisfy the craving inside me that had begun thanks to vivid daydreams of a Madeline, Colton, and Hudson sandwich.

That metaphorical PB&J wasn't gonna cut it—I wanted the damn chicken salad: hearty meat with a hint of sweetness I woke up every morning still tasting on my tongue.

I didn't even bother trying to fill my hunger with

hookups that would prove unsatisfying. Emptying my balls by hand took off the edge, but the lack of sex when I'd been accustomed to a smorgasbord left me antsy as fuck and grumpy as shit.

Add in the fact I couldn't make a fucking decision about what I really wanted, and I behaved like a royal bitch.

Scowls dented my face rather than laugh lines during the work days, and the guys gave me a wide berth since I tended to get handsy in the wrong way if someone pissed me off.

My boss Blake had known me long enough to recognize the signs of trouble on the horizon. He pulled me away from the chop saw an hour into our day and ordered me into the makeshift trailer office on the condo job site.

An old air conditioner pumped coolness through the small space, offering respite from the day's heat as I followed him inside.

"Have a seat." Blake pointed at one of the two metal folding chairs facing the desk he rounded.

I released a slow exhale while doing as told.

Blake's office chair squeaked as he leaned back. Arms crossed over his chest, he leveled his dark blue eyes on me. "The fuck is your problem, Payne?"

I scrubbed a hand down over my face, the tension that had been riding me for a few weeks making me bounce my knee. The guys I worked with were aware of my sexual preferences. Hell, sex was all us playboys ever talked about while laboring beneath the sun, but none of them knew my background outside of my having grown up in the system.

"I haven't gotten laid in almost a month," I muttered the easiest part of my issue Blake would understand.

"The fuck?" he asked, his eyebrows shooting up.

"Right?" I tried to laugh it off, and the chuckle sounded forced to my ears.

"Everything okay?"

"Remember how I told you about the couple from the deck job a few weeks back? Gorgeous curves and silver fox?" I asked while brushing sawdust off my Carhart pants.

"Let me guess," Blake said, "the day you finished up, you weaseled your way into their bed, and now they're hounding you for more."

I snorted. No fucking way those two would even consider a third in their picture-perfect marriage. "Kinda the...opposite?"

"They offered, and you developed *feelings*?"

"Fuck off," I muttered. "I've kept my hookups to people I don't know outside apps for a reason."

"Less mess," Blake tossed out what I'd said dozens of times over the years of working with him. "So why the dry spell?"

I rubbed over my scruffy jawline, thoughts of Madeline's thick-as-honey thighs and Hudson's calloused hands in the forefront of my mind. Add in the fact I could talk sports with Hudson and baking with Madeline for hours, and the two of them were like a wet dream come true.

But dreams didn't *come* true.

"Do you ever think about...more?" I asked Blake.

He studied me until I shifted on my chair. "You're either bored, unsatisfied, or itching to settle down," he finally said, not bothering to answer my question.

I shrugged even though he'd hit the nail on the goddamn head. "All fucking three, but you know my background and can put two and two together."

Fifteen years of bouncing from house to house in the system didn't exactly cultivate firsthand knowledge of happily ever afters. Thank fuck I couldn't remember the first three years of my life. But I'd heard enough, learned where I'd originated. My single mom had been a piece of shit too, landing herself in jail for possession, and when she got out, she never came looking for me.

Blake nodded, understanding in his gaze. He might be a playboy bachelor, one of Boston's most sought after thanks to his family's money, but he *knew* shit without having to think too hard.

A quick rap on the metal door drew both our gazes over my shoulder.

Reid, Blake's best friend and foreman on the job, stuck his dark, sweaty head inside. "Making a run to Dunks. You guys want your usual?"

Blake and I both nodded.

"Here." Blake shifted to dig some cash out of his front pocket. "Break's on me today."

Reid hopped up the last stair and strode into the trailer, bringing a blast of heat along with him.

"Thanks, boss. So what crawled up your ass and died?" Reid asked me while pocketing the money.

"Nothing's been up my ass for weeks." I crossed my arms, my scowl back in full force.

"I'd help you out if I was into dick," Reid said with a shrug and clasped me on the shoulder.

"Get the fuck outta here," I grumbled, and he did just that with a chuckle.

Thankfully, Blake and Reid had known from back in high school that I identified as pan. For me, attraction had nothing to do with body parts, and they were cool enough guys to not give a shit about my sexual preferences.

"Maybe it's time to step out on a limb and look for something more." Blake's suggestion sounded a hell of a lot like Rhett's.

I glanced over at the window overlooking the framed condo building and the Merrimac River beyond rushing toward its destination in the Atlantic. The water's path had been set in stone, the promise of a peaceful existence until it evaporated into the air to start its cycle all over.

But sure things like that didn't happen for humans. Too many unknown obstacles lay in our path toward life's completion. And it was that sort of shit that rose in my mind like a ten-foot-tall stop sign.

"You really think I ought to get my hopes up only to have them come crashing down again?" I asked.

"If you don't take a chance on love, you don't get to complain when you're lying on your deathbed wishing you'd done shit differently."

I imagined myself as Blake had said, down to the loose skin and wrinkles covered by a white sheet. Oxygen in my nose, monitors hooked to my chest, and quiet beeping...slowing...

On my current path, I would end up in that hospital room alone. No one's hand to hold, no one to remember me once my heart quit beating.

What meaning would my existence have on the world once my soul got snuffed out by darkness? What the hell kind of legacy would remain after I'd gone?

"Fuck." I leaned forward, elbows on my thighs, rubbing my hands beneath my ball cap into the sweaty strands of hair beneath. Blowing out a heavy exhale, I righted my hat and clasped my hands between my knees.

Clumps of dirt tracked from outside scattered on the floor. Once they were swept up, nothing but a dusty residue would be left behind.

I'd often been made to feel like dirt under a shoe, but I wanted to find love and belong for once in my goddamn life.

"I'm gonna do it," I stated quietly to myself and lifted my head.

"What?" Blake asked.

"Put my fucking heart on the chopping block and switch my Missing Link profile over to relationships instead of hookups."

"That's the poly app, right? The one Rhett and Ashton built?"

"Yep—and it's supposedly worked for a shit ton of people." I sat back, slapping my thighs, mind and insides settling over finally having made a goddamn decision after two weeks of unnecessary aggravation. "What's the worst that could happen?"

A fucking broken heart, same as I'd gotten to wallow in as a kid when I'd been promised forever only to have it ripped away.

Fucking *twice*.

I knew better than to get my hopes up, but I couldn't help the thrill of excitement that leaked adrenaline into my bloodstream while I ate my boring-ass sandwich at lunch a few hours later and clicked through ML, changing up my preferences on what I looked for.

Love.

8

HUDSON

Wednesday night, Mads went to her support group, so I had the house to myself.

Rain poured down outside the house's windows, similar to the dreariness hanging over our lives for too fucking long, but I busied myself creating a profile on the poly app while sipping from a cold bottle of beer to keep my brain occupied.

I'd downed three before picking up my phone, and a nice buzz warmed my blood.

Skimming through the questions, I jotted the first thoughts that came to mind. I tended to trust my reactionary instincts when it came to Mads's and my bed, so there was no point in agonizing over answers.

A quick write-up finished our profile, the focus on my interests being all things wood—tree felling, I explained with a wink emoji—and Mads loving little sweets—baking, of course. Not that a hookup would need that kind of information, but it would hopefully draw people with more of a lighthearted vibe, not serious and intense as Peter had been.

I published our profile without double-checking or

second-guessing. Mads had given me the green light, so I was going to search for someone to help rouse our sex life beyond what we'd been able to find again.

But only for a night, maybe two. I'd go so far as to say three if that was how long it took to rekindle the uninhibited fire we used to enjoy with each other. Intimacy had continued at a slow pace over the previous couple of weeks, but we were still far from where we used to be.

We'd had sex a handful of times, Mads finding release in over half.

Positive steps. Slow, steady progression.

But I lusted for more, sooner rather than later.

Setting aside my cell, I pushed up off the couch, grimacing at the pop in my hip. Getting old fucking sucked. Aches and pains littered my body, typical for a person who'd worked hard their whole life.

Cutting down trees was no joke.

Back in the early days, my dad and I used to split all the logs by hand, a time-consuming task for selling firewood. But I'd been a teen then, filled out with muscle and brawn. While quite a bit of it remained due to our basement's small gym, I certainly looked older and felt it as well.

Mads swore by yoga, or at least she used to. But that passion had faded along with everything else.

I regretted not joining her all the times she'd begged and poked fun when I'd complain about my body hurting. It would have been another thing to share, something to enjoy together. Perhaps her seeing me lead by example would have drawn her back to that part of living again.

Standing in front of the open fridge, I guzzled another beer. Rarely did I drink more than three, but something about the storm outside and the excitement of finally making steps toward complete sexual healing had me craving that heavy buzz.

Four match notifications already hit before I sank back into the couch.

@CarpenterColt sat at the top, and my brain went straight to tan Carhart pants and broad shoulders before glancing at the tiny thumbnail of a profile picture.

Sipping my beer, I zoomed in—and choked at the unmistakable smirk and naked broad shoulders from the nose-down image.

"Fuck," I rasped, swiping my forearm over my mouth.

I thought the kid had grown bored of his playboy ways, but he hadn't updated his profile to make sure he got matched with the right couples wanting what he did.

He was looking for love...or at least that was what the conversation I'd overheard suggested.

Frowning, I went back into our account to double-check like I should have done before hitting publish.

"Ah, shit."

I'd somehow clicked on the wrong fucking reason for our signing up—the very first question to start the process when I'd been too hyped to get moving. I should have paid more attention to the wording on my cell's screen than that third cool beer sliding down my throat.

Missing Link was under the impression that Mads and I were searching for the same thing as Colton—relationships.

My finger hovered to update our answer to hookups... but I paused.

Chemistry with the young man wouldn't be an issue, seeing as how he'd jerked off while watching me fuck my wife. Perhaps he could be talked into one last romp between the sheets before he settled down.

Another long pull on my beer, and I clicked back over to

view @CarpenterColt's profile. It showed a green dot by his handle, which meant he was logged in.

I already knew he enjoyed working with wood as much as I did, but it was one of the first lines of his write-up that sealed the fucking deal.

He liked spending time in the kitchen, especially baking.

What were the fucking chances?

And had he already shared that information with Mads? I'd known she'd sat and chatted with him a few afternoons while he'd worked on our deck.

I ignored the rest of his hopes and dreams—cuddling, mornings sipping coffee together while watching the sunrise, finding his forever couple. That shit might have meant something to Mads and me once upon a time, but the memory of Peter reminded me of why I wasn't going there.

No way.

No how.

I would sit back and enjoy the show. Keep my hands to myself but point Colton in the right direction if he needed suggestions on how to please my wife. Getting off watching the two of them wouldn't be as satisfying as joining in the fun, but this choice wasn't about me.

Without another thought for the other possible matches listed below Colton, I clicked the poke button, fingers crossed he'd be in the mood for a final hookup before getting his heart involved elsewhere.

Within minutes of tense silence on my end, Colton poked back, which meant he was interested in our profile and had opened the lines of communication through the app's messaging system.

I blew out a heavy exhale and set my beer aside, but he sent a text before I even started typing on my screen.

@CarpenterColt: **Hudson?**

My forehead dented with a heavy line between my eyebrows. I hadn't listed our real names, and the image I'd uploaded was of me holding Mads from behind, my hands clasped atop her belly, hers atop mine. I'd cropped it from our necks down.

Colton sent another message before I could confirm what he'd assumed.

@CarpenterColt: **The red lotus on your right forearm is the same tattoo on a fine-as-fuck silver fox who's been haunting my dreams ever since I watched him bend his wife over their kitchen counter.**

Same, boy. Fucking same.

Hi, Colton, I texted back instead, needing to press down on my swelling dick.

@CarpenterColt: **How did you know it was me?**

The memory of his lopsided smile flashed in my mind. **Your smirk.**

@CarpenterColt: **Was the old man checking out my mouth and thinking about giving me something to suck on?**

Lust, hot and heady, shot through my system even as my hands itched to spank the sass out of him for calling me old. I'd imagined quite a bit more than his lips wrapped around my cock, but getting Colton into our bed wasn't about me or how much I would enjoy reddening his ass.

Me: **More along the lines of seeing that mouth all over my wife's body. Her neck. Her breasts. Between her thighs. Watching my wife come undone pleasures me more than any physical touch.**

A partial lie, but I wasn't putting myself on offer.

@CarpenterColt: **Fuuuuuuuck**

Oh, I'd dreamed that dream plenty of times. **She'd enjoy that too,** I let him know.

At least, I hoped the excitement of someone new, different from our mundane, would light Mads back up to full brilliance and make her open to enjoying physical touch again. I'd seen the way she'd looked at him with a definite longing for what used to be.

It took Colton a while to respond, but I sat patiently waiting, my beer growing warm in my tight clasp, my cock stubborn in his hardened state.

@CarpenterColt: **For clarification, your profile shows relationships, but you aren't looking for companionship for yourself, just Mads?**

Me: **That is correct.**

@CarpenterColt: **Is it that you don't like dick or...?**
Goddamnit.

I scrubbed a hand over my face. **I do,** I freely admitted since messaging with him came as easy as talking in person had.

@CarpenterColt: **Giving or taking?**

He included a smirk emoji, which I could clearly imagine on his mouth.

Me: **I've only given my ass to one man, and I regret it. Thoroughly.**

The fucker hadn't deserved it.

@CarpenterColt: **It was that bad?**

It hadn't been, but the vulnerability I'd shown those few times and the result of his betrayal...never again.

Me: **Let's just say it didn't end well.**

@CarpenterColt: **Shit, now I'm curious as fuck.**

Lips in a thin line, I messaged back, **Don't bother asking because it's buried in the past.**

@CarpenterColt: **Buried.**

Again with that damn smirk emoji.

I rolled my eyes, hearing his snort in my memory.

Typical of guys his age, he'd turned everything into a sexual joke whenever we hadn't been talking sports. Colton had a lot of things going for him when it came to Mads and my likes, but I loved his lighthearted attitude about shit too.

Me: **Not gonna happen.**

@CarpenterColt: **So there wouldn't be any physical interaction between you and I at all? Have to ask, because we have chemistry. Don't deny checking out my ass every chance you got.**

Little shit.

The thought of touching—owning—every orifice of that man made my dick throb, but no.

Me: **I'm only interested in watching, so don't bother hoping for more.**

@CarpenterColt: **I can be very persuasive.**

I imagined he could be. His body and gorgeous face were tempting enough, but I'd been hurt to the point where resisting wouldn't be an issue.

I inhaled a deep breath and typed out what should be said, what might turn him off from wanting Mads, but as with any poly relationship, honesty needed to be front and center. We knew from firsthand knowledge that going against that line created unrepairable fissures in supposed rock-solid foundations.

Me: **I clicked on the wrong box when creating our profile. Mads and I don't want something serious. We carry baggage that won't allow for more, but there's pain that bringing someone into our bed again might help heal. I realized my fuck up in creating our profile before poking you back but did so anyway since Mads couldn't keep her eyes off you—and I know the feeling is mutual. We're not looking for love, simply someone to bring** chemistry back to a marriage in desperate need of life after loss.

I breathed in shallow sips of air, waiting.

Hoping.

One and done? He finally responded as I went light-headed from the lack of oxygen.

Me: **Could be more. Whatever it takes to make our hearts beat in time again.**

@CarpenterColt: **And what if mine falls into rhythm with both of yours too?**

He needed to know I wasn't on the menu, same as that *more* he had told his friend he wanted. **Don't let it.**

@CarpenterColt: **You know why I'm on here.**

Me: **You're looking for love—but that's not going to happen with us.**

It took a while for Colton to reply, and I sucked down another beer while waiting.

@CarpenterColt: **I decided to try for more than my usual hookups because I've never had anyone I could call my own. I grew up in foster care. Missed out on getting adopted twice because I did stupid shit. I've never had a dad or mom, but that's not what I want from this app. It's not my kink. I long for a soft woman and a man with calloused hands, two souls that can take me to the moon and back. I'm aware neither of you are interested in more than my dick, but I'll be honest. I'm wicked attracted to both of you. I could sit and talk with you guys for hours and never get bored. Hell knows I lost lots of hours on the jobsite because I asked questions to keep you both nearby. Why the fuck I'm telling you all this, I have no clue. Guess I just wanted to be honest from the start so you know where I'm coming from.**

Fuck, did I love his openness. Talk about refreshing.

Me: **I didn't grow up in the system, but I might as well have for all the attention my parents gave me. Mads was the first person to love me unconditionally, and I put a ring on her finger as fast as I could.**

@CarpenterColt: **You're one lucky man.**

Me: **Don't I know it.**

@CarpenterColt: **Having unloaded my shit and my desires through cyberspace, are you still interested in getting together?**

I sipped my beer but didn't really need to consider his question.

Me: **Can you guard your heart?**

@CarpenterColt: **I want you both enough to try. You might not be on the menu, but having you watch me love on your wife? Yes, please, and I'll take fourths and fifths if you'll allow me access to Madeline's sweet curves and she's willing.**

She *would* be, no fucking doubt. I expected she'd want a couple of extra doses of him as well. As long as we were on the same page, I trusted myself to keep my hands off his body.

Me: **Have any plans this Friday?**

@CarpenterColt: **I do if you tell me where to be and when.**

A sense of satisfaction settled over me as I sent him a reply with those exact suggestions.

@CarpenterColt: **Looks like I'll be busy Friday night.**

I went on to explain a few other details—our requirement of consent and open communication, and he willingly agreed to it all.

Just for a taste of my sweet wife.

9

MADELINE

Rain slashed at the windows. Had it been the dead of winter, we would have had over a foot of snow by dinner. As it was, dreary darkness clung to the summer sky, and the power went out a few minutes before eight when our hookup for the night was set to arrive.

Hudson had found someone on Missing Link interested in the same thing as him—a bit of fun on a Friday night. Although my hormones weren't sold on having someone else's dick, hands, or mouth on me, excitement still stirred my blood.

Barefoot and clad only in my blue satin robe, I lit candles in the living room and bedroom since Hudson said it was too late to cancel. The flickering light would lend a more romantic feel, and I hoped the atmosphere might encourage more arousal once our date for the night arrived.

Fingers crossed I would at least find the guy somewhat attractive, I settled onto the couch beside my husband to wait. He entwined his fingers through mine and kissed the back of my hand, his whiskers soft on my skin.

"Nervous?" he asked.

"A bit. It's been a while."

"Over seven months," Hudson said, placing our clasped hands on his thigh, his thumb rubbing in circles. "Do you miss him?"

We didn't discuss Peter. Ever.

Heat rose in my chest at the memory of his innocent eyes and lying lips. "No. He can burn in hell for all I care," I bit the words out, needing to suppress the thoughts and rising emotions hearing Peter's name always brought to the surface.

Hudson chuckled. "Christ, I love your fire, Mads. Glad to see that flame still lives inside you."

"Anger always rouses when I think of that asshole," I muttered, working on smoothing out my furrowed brow.

"I hope tonight will rekindle the rest, love." Hudson brushed his lips over my hand again, helping to ease my annoyance with his steadiness.

"What if it doesn't?" I asked with a whisper. "It's been a fight sometimes to climax the past couple of weeks with a man I love."

"You aren't broken," Hudson reminded me, squeezing my fingers. "Tonight will help you better see that."

I chewed on my lower lip. "What if I'm not attracted to him?"

"You will be—I promise." Hudson chuckled.

Since I'd had no interest in being involved in setting up our date for the night, I hadn't asked anything. What he looked like. Not even his name.

None of that mattered to me. Our boy toy for the night was meant to be a jumpstart, nothing more. And I trusted Hudson in knowing what I liked since we tended to appreciate the same things in a man.

Headlights flashed through the bay window from a car

pulling into the driveway, and a shot of adrenaline set my nerves on edge regardless of my lack of arousal in that moment.

I swallowed hard. "What if he has bad body odor?"

"He won't."

"H-How can you be sure?"

A soft knock sounded, but Hudson didn't reply or get up to let him in.

"Answer the door, Mads." His tender smile, the assurance in his warm gaze gave me courage to take my first step toward more healing.

For Hudson—but perhaps a little bit for me too, I realized as a hint of desire finally whispered through my core.

My legs shook as I shuffled across the living room, and I paused, hand on the doorknob, and inhaled slowly to calm my fluttering heart. I couldn't find a smile, so I didn't bother.

I swung the door inward.

"Colton." His name was rasped as though ripped from my lungs along with my breath.

I stared at the gorgeous man dripping rain from the ends of the dark hair plastered to his forehead. He stared right back, and I could barely make out his long eyelashes in the lack of exterior lights that usually shone down from the porch overhead.

His slow smirk hit my core like a flare punched into flame. "Madeline." His greeting held a hint of huskiness and pure sex he'd never emitted when we'd spoken before.

A shudder rippled through me.

I squeezed my thighs together as a rush of elation lightened my chest which had felt heavy for far too long. "W-What are you doing here?" I asked, my voice nothing more than a squeak as rain pounded straight down behind him onto the paved walkway.

"Come on in, Colton," Hudson called from the couch behind me.

Colton's smirk dissolved. "You didn't tell her?" he asked my husband without taking his gaze off my face.

"Nope."

"You're—" I clamped my lips shut for a second to process. "You're not here for Harper's Construction?"

The corner of his lips quirked up. "Oh, I'm here to work, alright—if you're interested?"

Instinct had me stepping back without a word because I'd been interested from the first time I'd laid eyes on the man.

Colton stepped past me onto the tiled entryway, and I breathed deeply, my mouth watering over the scent I'd caught a dozen or so times when he'd built our back deck and I lingered in his space because he'd made me feel... good. Same as then, my nose caught a hint of soap and spice —definitely no bad body odor.

He smelled downright delicious, and I wanted to lick every inch of his body.

I swallowed a bit of drool and shut the door, leaving us in silence. Hands on my hips, I faced my husband. "Explain," I demanded without a trace of anger in my tone.

Hudson hadn't moved from the couch, his thick thighs spread and arms extended across the back of the cushions in his usual relaxed pose of confidence. "Missing Link matched us, and I recognized his profile image. I extended an invite, and Colton accepted."

"It's your call, Madeline," Colton stated quietly, pulling my focus from the cocky glint in my husband's eye, "but I'm really hoping you'll say yes so I can live out all those fantasies I created while watching you in the kitchen."

One of my eyebrows shot up. "You were checking me out?"

"Every chance I got. Couldn't keep my eyes off you—especially when you were in your element." The low tone of his voice tightened my nipples, and the slow once-over he began snagged on the hardened points beneath my thin robe. "I like to bake too, remember?" Colton whispered, leaning toward me as though telling a big secret. "But I got you talking because I don't just find your baby blues and lush curves gorgeous. You light up every cell in my body whenever you're near me."

A flutter winged through my belly as awareness of mutual attraction settled over my mind. Yes, I'd found him hot as hell all sweaty while working behind our house, but the shakiness inside his words brought on was something new I felt for him.

Something I'd experienced once before and recognized. The spark of a deeper connection in the making like the one Peter had broken, which had shifted Hudson's and my marriage onto a dark path.

A drawing beyond lust, the potential for more if given the chance to flourish. Like a rosebud at the rising sun's first kiss of rays.

Potent.

Dangerous regardless of its beauty.

I should have said no. Told Colton to leave, that my husband had made a mistake, but my body vibrated with a driving need I hadn't felt in months, hell, hadn't expected to *ever* feel again.

Yearning stung my eyes and the back of my throat.

Trusting Hudson as I'd done since the first day I'd met him at a mutual friend's home, I made my decision—for better or worse.

I nodded my answer, fingers crossed that my husband knew what he was doing because if not? A shiver slid over my skin at the thought.

"Take off your shoes," Hudson said, and Colton kicked his off without hesitation.

I could imagine the *good boy* on Hudson's lips, but he didn't speak his pleasure over Colton's compliance.

"Shirt."

Colton yanked his wet, black T-shirt off overhead, and I bit the inside of my lip to keep from sighing. Muscles. Ridges. Golden skin. Tight nipples. Tattoos. I soaked in the gorgeous sight of him, my fingers twitching and mouth watering. He held his shirt in hand, his dark eyes peering at me, waiting.

"Drop it," I whispered, a thrill shooting through me when he listened.

The T-shirt landed with a soft splat at his feet.

In order for Colton to have stepped through our door that night, he had to have agreed to the ground rules Hudson always laid down before playing in the past.

Consent to give and receive unless a "stop" or "slow down" uttered from any set of lips.

"Touch him, love," Hudson commanded, his low tone pebbling my skin.

Colton's eyes hooded as though sensing my excitement over Hudson's words, the cocky smirk revealing his dimple making my core pulse.

"Brat," I muttered.

He grinned. "I'm all yours," he whispered, arms spreading wide like a pair of dark angel's wings, lats popping and eight-pack abs rippling.

Swallowing hard, I stepped forward and filled my lungs with the warm scent of man and soap. "Arms down," I whispered, and he once more did as told. "Good boy," I murmured what Hudson had not.

Those bedroom eyes of Colton's widened slightly, his smile fading and lips parted. Pink flushed his high cheekbones.

One corner of my mouth quirked up over his response. Colton Payne had a praise kink—and Hudson and I enjoyed the hell out of giving in that way.

I traced Colton's lower lip with my thumb, keeping a foot's distance between our bodies. His chest rose on a sharp inhale.

My pulse thrummed as I dragged my fingertips over the scruff on his chin, down his neck to his collarbone. His pecs... I placed both of my palms atop them, and his muscles flexed at my touch. We shared ragged breaths already, and the night had just begun.

So. Much. Potential.

And sure trouble.

But trusting my husband, I readied myself to dive in without overthinking a damn thing.

10
———

COLTON

In the first twenty-four hours of switching my profile to looking for relationships, I'd gotten a shit ton of match notifications.

I hadn't put in sex preferences, so the list had included every color of the rainbow from a trans couple where the wife wanted a side dish to keep as a pet to a gay throuple wanting another boy to daddy.

Countless red hearts had revealed more pokes than I'd ever gotten in a day, and I'd scrolled through, grinning like a dork. It hadn't taken long for my smile to slowly fade along with my hope once I'd had a chance to sit over coffee break then lunch.

By the time I'd gotten home from work that night, washed up, and finished the steak bomb I'd picked up from the sub shop for dinner, I'd gone through all the pokes— and ended up not returning a single fucking one.

Again with the nothing clicking bullshit, no interest like I felt for the Youngs.

I hadn't experienced the same spark, the same draw to her sweet smile and his intense gaze. The way she'd spoiled me. The feel of his hand clasping around mine with just a hint of dominance that lit my insides right the fuck up. The way we'd easily connected through light conversations about nothing of importance, the mundane shit of daily living.

So what were the chances Missing Link would give me the opportunity of a goddamn lifetime? Sure, the Youngs didn't want anything serious, but being offered to touch and taste half of what I'd been dreaming about for over a month straight?

Five nights or one and done, every cell in my body had climbed aboard the whatever-the-fuck-you-want train when Hudson had invited me over for a Friday night fuck fest.

I was too damn hot for both Hudson and Madeline to not enjoy the hell out of every minute they offered me.

But I hadn't expected a punch to my solar plexus at her soft murmur of being a good boy. Like, what the fuck? And she couldn't be more than a handful of years older than me.

I might have mommy and daddy issues, but those goddamn words licked over my skin, delved deep into my chest, and lit me the hell up beyond what I'd felt watching them have sex through their screen door.

Thank fuck Hudson had laid down the law about not getting involved emotionally, letting me know up front not to expect more than satisfying my lust, because I would have fallen hard the moment she touched my lower lip. The breath ripped from my lungs, and every inch of my body vibrated with awareness of...something.

Could have been life-altering.

Fucking euphoria forever.

But I held tight to my emotions and anticipated plea-suring Madeline and loving every second of having access to her generous curves while her hot-as-fuck husband watched.

She palmed my pecs, and I inwardly groaned at the thought of her teeth scraping over my hardened nubs.

"Taste his skin, love."

My dick bucked in my jeans at Hudson's words, his low, rumbling tone that demanded action again. I wanted his commands too, damnit. Wanted him to take the reins and dictate my movements to ensure Madeline got what she needed. Not that I didn't trust my own instincts when it came to women, but Hudson knew his wife in ways I never would...and goddamnit, I found myself yearning to please them both.

Clenching my hands into fists at my sides, I held still—breath included—as Madeline leaned into me, placing a soft kiss against the base of my throat.

"Oh fuck." I gulped a needy sound, my head tipping back, my stare unseeing on their ceiling so she could put her mouth wherever she wished.

She trailed her lips down my sternum with sweet kisses that broke goose bumps along my arms. Soft, warm hands slid down to my sides, thumbs ghosting over the deep grooves of my V, every caress as though she stroked my dick. My abs flexed as she rubbed her cheek over my right pec. A flick of her tongue over my nipple leaked a hiss from between my lips.

"Wanna touch," I half-whined, fingernails digging into my palms.

I wasn't sure why I didn't. Hudson had stated anything was on the table unless Madeline said no, but I wanted her verbal consent—or maybe his verbal permission in person. I finally gave Hudson my attention for the first time since the door had opened to reveal the focus-stealing beauty of Madeline wrapped in blue silk.

His intense stare, lustful and so goddamn *in control* from where he sat sprawled out as though completely at ease did more funny shit to my insides. It was the same as when our eyes had met through the screen door what seemed ages ago.

"Please," I whispered, not sure if I begged for mercy or—

"Put your hands on my wife, Colton."

Pre-cum welled and smeared the inside of my jeans, and I didn't bother swallowing down my moan. I tried to say her name, still wanting her consent, but only the ending came out as a strangled "Lin?" that I liked the sound of way too fucking much.

She lifted her head, those bottomless blue eyes vulnerable. "Yes."

Like she'd done to me, I placed my thumb on her lower lip but dragged it to the side to part the soft flesh. So plump and pink...

Her hold tightened on my waist, and I stepped closer, leaving electrical-charged inches between us. I palmed her neck—gently—tipping her head slightly. Pupils swelled, she held my gaze.

"Wanna kiss you," I murmured with hardly any tone to my voice.

She fucking whimpered. Shuddered.

Needy—just like me.

I grasped her face in my hands and zeroed in on her mouth with no finesse whatsoever. I swept my tongue between her lips, and she sagged against me, all sensual curves and honeysuckle sweetness.

Fucking hell.

She clutched at my back, and I wound one hand into her

silken hair, my other sliding down her spine to grasp her backside, tugging her closer. My dick throbbed against her belly as our tongues dueled, moans feeding my need to devour every goddamn inch of the woman trembling all the fuck over my front.

"Christ." Hudson's voice registered in my buzzing brain, the lust in his tone ratcheting mine up another level.

I'd jerked off—twice—in preparation so I wouldn't blow early like a goddamn virgin the second I got my hands on Madeline, but the rumble of his curse as though affected by the thickness of the sexual tension between his wife and I took me higher.

My balls drew up tight against my groin, ready to unload.

I slowed the feasting between our mouths and eased back from the edge of nutting inside my jeans. Madeline stared at me wide-eyed, swollen lips parted, and red tinted her cheeks, attempting to cover the spattering of freckles over her nose I hadn't noticed before.

"You're so goddamn beautiful, Lin," I croaked out the words. "Your curves drive me wild. I want to explore and taste every inch of you."

She tore her focus off my face to glance at her husband.

"I told you you're free to play, love," he said, his tone warm and full of assurance.

Untangling herself from my lingering hold, Madeline returned her attention to me. Without a word, she took my hand and led me toward the darkness of the staircase. We moved past Hudson, and I glanced his way.

He lifted his gaze off my ass and raised one of his brows as though inviting me to call him out for staring at what he'd said he had no interest in.

I grinned instead.

Maybe he could be enticed to join in the fun.

We passed two open doors while silently shifting through shadows in the upstairs hallway. I glanced to the right rather than the left—a crib. Changing table and rocking chair. The scent of powder and flowers.

The Youngs didn't have children, but was Madeline pregnant? She didn't look it from what I could tell. Were they adopting?

Hudson had mentioned baggage. Loss.

Assuming never gained a man jack shit, but my mind went toward miscarriage or something rather than pregnancy, and that light feeling in my chest dissipated, leaving behind heaviness that pulled in my eyebrows. Unease crept in, and I questioned my reasons for Hudson wanting me there other than rekindling the fire in their marriage.

Filling a void?

Healing?

Distraction?

I'd never had a family of my own, never had a man and woman I could call Mom and Dad for real. I understood sorrow and heartache on a level most didn't. Hearing the words you've been desperate for your whole goddamn life only to have what you'd been promised ripped away.

I squeezed Madeline's hand as she led me into a room lit by two candles. Shadows danced over the bedroom walls from the flickering flames, and a soft golden glow radiated around her light brown hair as I followed her over the threshold. Her hand lay warm in mine but not limp or disinterested.

She almost...clung to me as though hope filled her chest, and she grew desperate to keep it close to her breast.

Footsteps sounded behind us as she stopped beside their bed and turned toward me.

Big blue eyes peered at me, open and vulnerable. Our breaths rose and fell in time together, slightly heightened, a little fast. Neither of us glanced over at Hudson as he entered our periphery and settled quietly into a chair against the wall off to the side, but awareness of his presence, his potent stare, caused goose bumps to erupt over my arms. Madeline's lips parted, and fuck waiting on orders, I leaned in and picked back up where we'd left off, diving into her mouth, pulling sighs and moans from her throat.

Cotton candy—that was what her tongue tasted like on mine. Pure, addictive sweetness, a shot of sugar straight into my bloodstream.

I tugged on her hair, tearing my lips from hers to lick over her neck, wanting to bite and suckle clear down to her toes. But no man would care for marks on his wife unless put there by himself. Keeping my teeth to myself, I trailed my lips to her ear, nipping on her lobe.

"I want to see you," I whispered, and she shivered, nodding.

The power suddenly flicked back on, bathing their bedroom with bright, blinding light.

"Perfect timing," I said, waggling my eyebrows as my pupils adjusted.

She laughed lightly, the glow of pink on her cheeks so damn beautiful my chest tightened.

Pulling back enough to watch her face, I tugged on the knot holding her robe closed. My damn fingers shook, but I still made quick work of unwrapping the gift of her, thankful as fuck for the brilliant glow from the overhead bulbs.

The blue silk parted from chest to thigh, teasing at the top and swelling over her full breasts but hiding her tight nipples. Soft belly, so damn beautiful, I wanted to rest my cheek on her and just sigh in contentment. Slight stretch marks assured me I had assumed correctly.

My throat went tight at the thought of their loss, but I forced my inner focus on the goddess in front of me and how I might gift her a night of passion and sated bliss.

Trimmed golden curls lay at the apex of her thighs, and my mouth fucking watered.

Madeline slid the robe off her shoulders, and it fell near silent in a swish of fabric to lay at her feet. Thick-as-honey thighs, shapely calves, and the cutest damn toes I'd ever seen got gobbled up by my focus, my groin swelling with lust to the aching point.

Her hands slid over her belly—hiding the silvery marks.

"You're stunning," I murmured, reaching out to caress her wrists.

"On the bed, love." Hudson's rumbled command moved his wife away from me until the foot of the bed kissed the back of her knees.

She sat. Slid over pale sheets.

The bed had been stripped of blankets, but her presence in the middle of the large mattress, leaning back on a bunch of pillows enticed me to fall down, face-first, and burrow in.

"Lose the jeans, boy."

Fucking. Hell.

I groaned, finally glancing over at Hudson for the first time since we'd entered the bedroom.

Fire flared in his steady gaze, his lips set in a firm line. He expected to be obeyed, and while I tended toward brat at times when bossed around, I didn't want anything in that moment but his praise.

Staring into his eyes, I flicked open my button, slid down my zipper, and shoved my jeans to the floor.

His gaze dropped to my dick as I straightened, kicking

my jeans off the rest of the way. He sat tensed, hands on the chair's arms as though calm, but nothing about his body suggested relaxation. I could sense the vibrations energizing his blood—could fucking feel it in my own.

Our gazes clashed. Held. My fucking breath dissipated, pulse pounding as I palmed my dick.

Want you too.

Fuck, did I ever.

His eyes narrowed. "Lick my wife's sweet pussy until she comes on your tongue."

My length twitched in my hold, and I swallowed another rush of saliva.

That man, that *fucking* man, pressed buttons I hadn't known existed in my head, and goddamn did I need more.

Hudson had warned me to not let myself get attached, and had I been smarter, I'd have yanked my jeans back up, stuffed my aching dick away, and gotten the hell out of there.

That sense of not being enough, of what a couple looked for, rose in the back of my mind.

But like the good boy I wanted to be, I listened to the man calling the shots, knowing my heart faced yet another jagged dagger's plunge.

11

HUDSON

I lusted to be her.

To be him.

Every cell in my body vibrated at high frequency, wanting to combust into flames.

Mads lay sprawled out like a waiting feast, the pink in her cheeks, the way she stared at Colton letting me know her body had remembered how to grow hot and desperate with abandon, exactly as I'd hoped for.

Colton climbed onto the bed on hands and knees, stalking forward, all lithe muscle I wanted to bend and own.

I'd hoped for sexual tension but hadn't expected lust so damn heavy in the air I could taste it. Smell it. Fucking feel it brushing over my skin and raising the hairs on my arms. Never had I ever experienced such a draw. Not even with—

I cut the thought off, focusing on Colton as he palmed my wife's thighs and spread her wide to make room for his shoulders.

I could tell by the way he had devoured Mads with his gaze that he truly appreciated her curves like I did. His gaze had caught on her soft stomach, and I wondered if he noticed the marks she'd tried to hide from him in a brief moment of insecurity.

There was no doubt he wanted to map out her body and taste her from lips to toes. But he listened like a good boy, diving right into her glistening pussy like I'd told him to.

She let out a hiss, her hands finding his dark head as her hips rotated, and satisfaction roared through me, offering contentment I'd missed. A fucking power trip, one that Mads loved to feed and benefit from. She'd been made for me. Accepted me. Loved me.

And I wanted her happy, unraveled, and put fully back together again.

Colton hummed an admonishment to her wiggling and clamped his forearm over her waist to hold her still.

Mads whimpered, a sound I'd been gifted a few times in the previous couple of weeks, and I sank into the chair, spreading my legs to make a bit of room for my aching cock. Like Colton, I'd gone commando, and I knew before the night ended, I'd have a wet spot darkening my jeans if not busted nuts and an absolute mess inside the denim.

The sounds of wet, lewd licking, suckling, and the releasing of flesh kept my dick in a constant state of throbbing, and I finally released my death grip on the chair to push down on my length. The pressure felt too fucking good, and I swallowed a curse.

Mads's head tipped back, her lower lip between her teeth. The pulse in her neck and the flush on her cheeks sent another shot of triumph through my mind. Arousal flooded her body for another man, reminding her she was far from broken. She was going to come on his tongue, exactly as I wanted to see. Fucking needed to soak in from a distance where I wouldn't get caught up.

Arm still banded over Mads's hips, Colton reached

between her thighs and lifted his focus to her face. Her back arched as he pressed fingers into her core.

"Oh damn," she whimpered, her head raising to watch him fuck into her pussy. Eyes glazed, she held his stare, her lips parting as she panted for breath.

"So warm and soft," Colton murmured, his rasped tone making my dick buck in its prison. "Sweet and wet for me." He rotated his arm, forearm flexing, the sopping sounds of finger fucking loud in the tensed silence of our bedroom.

Mads gasped, eyelids fluttering shut.

I could tell from her reaction that he'd found that roughened bit of flesh deep inside her body, and it would take all of three strokes before she climaxed like she'd done for me two nights before.

I had to press on my goddamn bulge again. "Suck her clit," I rasped.

Colton dove back in, growling like a hungry animal, his arm working. Two strokes...three—Mads came with a gasp, shuddering, her lips whispering curses that fell over my body like a cleansing rain.

Colton groaned, lapping and licking, his hips grinding into the mattress.

The boy was going to mess up our sheets, but I wanted to give him more than release against cotton. His bringing pleasure to Mads...

I stood, pulled a condom from my back pocket, and moved closer, my blood buzzing.

Mads stilled as Colton gently licked her clean.

Both looked at me as I paused beside the bed.

"Make her come on your dick." I tossed the condom beside Colton's shoulder, and he glanced up at her, the request in his dark eyes making me respect the hell out of him for always checking in for consent.

I'd already given mine to my wife, but she still looked my way.

I nodded and stood like an oak beside the bed, drinking in the sight of her splayed thighs, the swollen flesh between them as Colton sat back on his haunches. She would be hot and tight, the most luscious, silken sheath around his girth.

I took in his straining cock, the pearled bead of moisture at the top as he ripped the foil packet open.

"Wanna help?"

I jerked my focus to his face, the lustful glint in his eye, the smirk on his goddamn mouth, and my gaze narrowed. "No," I lied.

Glancing down at my bulge, he pushed, "Sure about that?"

Every muscle vibrated to leap onto Colton, but I bit my tongue to keep quiet and simply glared until he lifted his focus to my face and took the hint.

He shrugged as though unaffected by my steadfastness, but a flash of disappointment swept over his eyes and disappeared as he once more turned his attention to my wife.

"Can I kiss you while I fuck you?" he asked, planking on one arm over her body, the other hand on the base of his dick.

Mads's crooked smile lifted her lips as she reached around his back, thighs around his ass, and pulled him closer.

He sank into her lush body with one slow thrust, his ass flexing—and begging for my dick.

"Yes," she whispered, and I bit my groan back as more pre-cum smeared inside my jeans.

He gave her his full weight, their mouths coming together in languid movements, tasting and savoring as slowly as their gyrating lower bodies.

Same as he'd done through the screen while watching me and Mads, I got off on seeing him sink into my wife's body over and over again. Their soft moans and the heightened sounds of wet fucking took my tension to a level I struggled to contain.

My blood buzzed, pulse thrumming like a damn drum in my temples.

Colton shifted forward, drawing up onto his knees, the position offering me a view of his balls, taint, and waxed hole.

"Fuck," I choked on the word, caught up in staring as his ass worked to fuck deeper into Mads. I clenched my fists to keep from reaching for him.

He gave her his weight and grasped beneath her backside, lifting his own even higher.

I'd never known the meaning of the word temptation until that moment, but I couldn't cross that line and open myself up again.

Fucking little tease needed to have his cheeks reddened. My palms itched to leave marks all over his ass and thighs, to show him who was boss.

"You can touch me," he offered, his voice hovering on begging. So damn needy...fuck did I lust to give him what he wanted.

"I'm not on the menu," I reminded him, my tone far from firm as my entire body tightened in total opposition to my sense of self-preservation.

"Hud," Mads whispered, and I met her pupil-blown blue eyes. I wanted to pleasure her more than anything on the goddamn planet, but bending toward her request for a threesome was one thing I couldn't give her.

Colton and I had already connected on a surface level

while he'd worked for us, and the potential lay between us for an incredible dynamic and sexual combustion.

But I would never trust my heart to anyone but Mads ever again.

"No," I stated firmly.

Colton released one hand's hold on her ass and planked onto his elbow. "His loss," he murmured and captured my wife's lips in a kiss that attempted to sear the skin off my body.

My fingernails dug into my palms, and my jaw ached from clenching my teeth. The scent of sex flooded my nose, and I cursed at the unrelenting throb in my groin.

I needed my wife to come. Needed Colton to get the fuck out of my house. Needed to sink into Mads's body and find release outside his presence.

Moving closer toward their heads, I bumped the bed with my thighs.

Both Colton and Mads turned to look at me, panting, Colton's hips stalling out.

"Don't stop," I growled the words.

He moved without hesitation, and I couldn't help the next words to leave my lips.

"Such a good boy."

"Ah, fuck." He closed his eyes, head dipping so the tips of his hair caressed over Mads's forehead.

Her right breast lay toward her side, nipple hard and pink. I filled my hand with her flesh, angling the offering to Colton. "Suck," I ordered, and he shivered, his hips once more losing rhythm.

But he dove in, his lips closing over her hardened tip.

Mads let out a low moan, her eyelids falling shut and head tipping back. "Yes," she hissed, her back arching.

"Use your teeth," I stated through my own.

She gasped, arching again. "Harder—fuck me harder. Please—oh shit!"

Mads shuddered and came, her thighs holding tight to Colton as he pistoned between them into her lush pussy that had to be squeezing the life out of his dick.

"Fuck yeah," he groaned, grabbing her ass and thrusting deep. "So fucking good, Lin—goddamn...fuck, yes."

He snapped his hips and grunted.

Stepping back, I grabbed my bulge and squeezed, getting a better view of his balls pulsing cum into the condom. His hole contracted with his release, and my nostrils flared as I fought to breathe.

That ass would stretch all pretty and pink around my girth. Sucking me in. Squeezing me until I filled his hole with my cum. I could see it in my mind...dripping down his taint, over his balls, between my wife's thighs.

Marking him in such a way would create a bond I couldn't handle emotionally.

I swallowed hard, my entire body rigid and on the verge of exploding with the need to come.

Colton collapsed and moaned, stretching his legs out while staying buried inside my wife's body. "Even better than I'd dreamed," he murmured and laid a soft kiss on Mads's lips.

She sighed, her fingertips trailing down over his spine as they fell into a languid kiss, the type that made promises without words, connected hearts together.

Nope. None of that shit.

"Time to go, boy." I refrained from nudging Colton, knowing a simple brush of skin contact with him would send me into a fit of conquer and claim.

"Fuck." Colton slowly backed off my wife, holding the base of the condom. "You okay, sweet thing?" he asked her, drawing out a genuine smile on her lips from where she sprawled in what appeared to be satiated bliss.

"Better than okay." She glanced at me, the pure, relaxed happiness in her eyes hitting my chest like a goddamn axe and making my heart race.

Exactly the reaction from her I'd hoped for.

I'd expected another man's dick wouldn't heal her depression, but we'd made one hell of a step in the right direction of getting back the lives we'd lost.

"You can see yourself out," I told Colton as he climbed off the bed, knowing I sounded like the world's biggest asshole, but my patience had reached its end.

I needed to experience my wife's joy firsthand, to taste it on my lips, to feel her welcome me inside her without emotional restraint.

Colton eyed his wet shirt I'd brought along from the entryway as I ripped mine off overhead, my intent perfectly clear.

"Shit," he whispered while yanking up his jeans and mine pooled around my ankles. "Can I stay and watch?"

Mads stared at me, her pupils swelling as the heat inside me burned through my eyes. "No," she whispered the word on my tongue, as though feeling the exact same way I did.

I was going to fall on her—into her, and both of us knew combustion hovered ahead, one we hadn't thoroughly enjoyed in far too long. A coming together that required privacy, an intimate moment where no one else was required or allowed.

Tearing my gaze off my wife, I gave Colton my attention. "Thank you," I barely managed to speak.

"So that's it?" he asked, studying my face with dark eyes full of disappointment, and his shoulders sagged as he clutched at his shirt.

"That's it." I laid down the law that wouldn't be broken even though my healing heart yearned for more.

He glanced at Mads and nodded. "I wish you both the best."

I stared after him until he disappeared through the bedroom door, assuring myself I hadn't made a mistake in letting him go. Listened as the stairs creaked beneath his weight and the front door shut with finality that a deep part of me didn't want to accept.

Fucking tough shit.

Turning, I found Mads staring at me, her face still a gorgeous shade of pink, her nipples hard, cream smeared between her lax thighs. The memory of Colton's ass, his smooth taint and hole as he'd fucked into her rose in my mind, causing my dick to jerk in my hand.

I hadn't realized I held myself let alone smeared pre-cum all over my length with every slow tug.

"Give me your dick," Mads said and rolled onto her knees, her chest on the bed.

"Christ, Mads." I groaned, squeezing my base at the sight of her tight pucker.

"You won't allow yourself to enjoy his ass, so have mine to find your release."

"Fuck." I yanked open the bedside drawer and grabbed a bottle of lube. "I don't think I can be gentle," I warned her while climbing onto the bed between her thighs.

"I don't want you to be." She wiggled her hips, and I slapped her ass cheek with a crack meant only for noise effect.

She groaned, her back arching deeper. "Hurry up and stretch me with your thick fingers. I-I've missed them so damn much."

"Jesus." I dribbled lube down through her crack and

massaged her hole until she softened. She sighed as I pressed my middle finger in deep without resistance even though I hadn't touched her back door in almost a year.

"Mmm," she hummed, her eyelids fluttering shut. "More, Hud—give me more. Help me remember what it's like..."

I worked in a second, scissoring and thrusting.

My wife was a goddamn queen—and I told her as such.

"Then put your king-sized cock in my ass and own me with it."

A shudder ripped through me as her filthy mouth reemerged from its sleep. "Fuck, woman, the things you say."

I removed my fingers from her body and lubed my dick to the point it dripped onto the mattress.

The memory of Colton's hole flashed in my mind as I pressed against my wife's. "Sorry, love."

I shoved in deep, my eyelids slamming shut as silken heaven welcomed me home.

12

MADELINE

I had a shit ton of things to process, but the act of Hudson pushing fully into my ass with one thrust took dominated my mind. The stinging burn, the consuming air-stealing force of his claiming scattered all thoughts.

Pain wasn't my thing, but having Hudson lose control, being the conduit for his lust to reach release—that made me hotter than anything under the sun, exactly as it used to do. He'd been delicate with me for far too long, withholding his passion from unleashing, and I stuck my ass up, ready to *feel* again.

He didn't disappoint. He never did.

But I wouldn't come a third time. My body had spent itself around Colton's cock.

Something I would think about later...after my husband took out on me what he'd wanted to give that boy and had denied himself because of fear.

Hudson grunted with each push forward, slamming into me, his fingertips digging into my waist. I forced myself to relax since tensing up would only leave me a pile of aches and bruises in the morning.

Eyes closed, I kept my silence, not wanting to disturb whatever he imagined in his mind while railing my ass. I didn't doubt he saw Colton bent over for him, backside jiggling with every jolting slam of his hips. Just the thought of him doing that very thing twinged a bit of life back to my core, and I sank into the fantasy with my husband, thinking that perhaps I had another climax in me after all.

I imagined I observed from beside the bed, Colton grasping at the sheets, gasping at the feel of Hudson's dick stretching him beyond pleasure. He would enjoy that bit of pain, enjoy the bite of a slap or two from Hudson's palm.

As Colton's body relented to the intrusion, he would moan over the silken glide of my husband's lubed dick delving deep into his body, pegging his prostate with every thrust. Loosened, he would ask for more. Harder. Deeper. He'd beg Hudson for release, not touching his dripping dick until granted permission.

He would paint our sheets white while Hudson unloaded deep in his ass.

I moaned, realizing my pussy ached with need. Snaking my hand beneath my body, I found my lower lips slickened by fresh arousal. Tears of relief sprang to life in my eyes, and I buried my face in my pillow, flicking over my clit.

A throaty cry ripped from me as I came, my hole squeezing around Hudson.

He shouted—and heat burst inside my ass.

Fucking amazing...yes, oh my god, yes.

I gasped for oxygen, my body twitching even after Hudson went still. He sank against me, and I went onto my belly, loving how he blanketed me with his muscle, heat, and sweat. Panting against my ear, he groaned, one last flex of his backside attempting to bury his dick deeper into my body.

"Goddamn," he moaned, huffing and puffing to the point I giggled. "That sound..." He nosed along my neck, gentle bites along my skin sending goose bumps racing down my arms. "Love to hear you happy, Mads."

"I'm going to be okay," I whispered, a heavy sigh sinking me deeper into the mattress, my sadness at bay for the time being. "*We're* going to be okay."

Hudson hadn't allowed himself to play with Colton even though I'd been able to taste his lust as the younger man had fucked me. I'd been a bottled-up mess of arousal and hormones, ready to explode before Colton had even slid into my core.

Something about Colton had shifted things inside me—and not from his dick. Perfect in size, he'd filled me the same as Hudson did, stretching me deliciously with his thickness, but there was more...in the way he kissed. The way he moved. The way he worshiped my body with his hands as though grateful for the experience.

I'd always had a kink for exhibitionism and voyeurism, same as most of our poly friends, and the idea of exploring more with Colton definitely clicked all my buttons.

He'd flipped a switch inside me, somehow taking my mind beyond where it had been stuck.

I didn't dare to believe that meant depression and sorrow would no longer have a hold over my life, but I clung to hope I'd found my ability to move forward. We would continue with healing and experiencing happiness in ways I hadn't ever expected to again.

Evidence of that possibility remained etched on my face even after Hudson and I washed each other in the shower like we'd always done after a hookup. Once between fresh sheets, our gazes met as we cuddled close.

"How are you feeling?" he asked once we settled in after our evening of debauched fun.

"Deliciously sore but peaceful for the first time in far too long," I answered.

Hudson smoothed back my still-damp hair, trailing his knuckles over my cheek. "You were beautiful tonight falling apart on his tongue and fingers."

Arousal attempted to rise, but I willed it away, ready to discuss our night without sexual distraction.

"Why didn't you touch him when he offered himself to you?" I asked, searching Hudson's sated eyes.

"You know why."

"But you wanted to."

Hudson didn't bother refuting my claim.

"Did you imagine him while fucking me?" I asked, hoping for an affirmative.

"Yes."

I smirked, that flash of fantasy definitely wanting to warm my blood.

"Don't get any ideas, Mads."

"But think about how rough you could be." I lowered my voice, trailing a fingernail down his chest and over his pec. "Not having to restrain your passion, being able to unleash all that pent-up sexual aggression you rarely let out to play." I dragged my fingernail over his nipple, pulling a hiss from his lips.

He clasped his hand atop mine, pressing my palm to his heart. "You fulfilled that role tonight, love."

"But you still held a piece of yourself back, didn't you?" It hadn't felt like it—but I knew my husband.

"I won't hurt you."

I leaned in and kissed him softly, lingering long enough

that his heavy exhale filled my lungs with warmth and the scent of mint from our toothpaste.

"We needed this," I murmured, pulling away. "Thank you."

Hudson hugged me tight against his chest, crushing me to him. "Anything for you, love." He kissed the top of my head, and I closed my eyes, truly happy for the first time in too damn long.

———

Humidity near ninety percent made the outside air a stifling, sopping blanket the next day, and I sweated through my bra and tank top before crossing the grocery store's parking lot from car to entrance.

But not even my physical misery could erase the smile that still lingered on my lips.

While passing the nursery earlier in the morning had sent an ache twinging through my heart, I'd chosen to keep moving and not linger on the sense of sadness and loss the sight always brought.

My action hadn't been choosing to forget what we lost but rather an inner turning of focus on what I *did* have and the hope for more.

The automatic doors of the grocery store swished open, blasting my face with blessed coolness, and I sighed, plucking the front of my shirt away from my chest while retrieving a cart.

"Hi, Marsha," I called to the seventy-something bagger in lane one. She'd been working at the store for over twelve years, remembered everyone's names, and kept tabs on their lives too. She also knew how to pack groceries without smashing strawberries or bread like the younger kids did.

"Madeline! How are you, honey?" she replied, her smile wide and hazel eyes twinkling as always.

"Wonderful," I replied, feeling the truth of what I'd chosen as an anchor in the deepest parts of my soul. "I'll see you soon!"

I'd slept the night through—as had Hudson for the first time in months. Fully rested, we'd enjoyed our first cup of coffee before it grew too warm as the sun rose over our back deck. We had reminisced about our time with the man who'd changed our lives in under an hour.

While his leaving had felt abrupt, almost...cruel, Hudson had assured me Colton had been well aware of what we were and weren't looking for.

More than whatever it took to light the flame, which he'd more than helped accomplish with one single night of hot, sweaty sex.

I still wouldn't have minded a longer coming down time, a bit of snuggling while catching my breath, but Hudson had needed me. The ache in my backside with every step down the grocery aisle brought a secretive smile to my lips. Internal warmth licked at my cheeks clear to my toes whenever I remembered the sounds he'd made and the heat he'd flooded through me.

Reaching for a jar of salsa from the top shelf, I sighed, thinking about pushing Hudson for another night with Colton.

"Mads?"

The jar slipped from my hand, crashing and splattering across the aisle. My heart seized along with my lungs, and I closed my eyes, refusing to turn around as every good thing I'd clasped around my heart crumbled to dust.

"You no longer have the privilege to call me that," I whispered, my stomach churning.

A warm hand on my bare elbow sent me careening sideways to escape his touch.

"Don't touch me!" I fought for breath like I'd run a 5K, finally facing him.

Adulterer. Liar. Manipulator. Betrayer.

Peter.

Still runway model stunning even at his shorter height, he flashed his smile as though he had the right to approach me and chat like we were old friends.

His blue-green eyes took a slow run down over me, making me shiver and tempting bile up the back of my throat. "I miss you," he whispered with a boyish tone inflicted intentionally to stroke all my nurturing buttons.

I gagged and pulled my cart between us. "Tough shit. Go away." My legs trembled, but I hurried toward the aisle's end, desperate to escape him.

"Mads, wait! Please. I just want to talk." Peter followed on my heels. "Please! I've been texting and calling Hudson, but he won't answer—he won't give me the time of day. Can you tell him that I have some things to say he needs to hear?"

I spun abruptly, causing Peter to stumble into me in his haste to keep close.

His hands seared my elbows as he caught himself from falling, and it took every ounce of self-control inside me to not knee him in his balls. Or vomit. "Hudson doesn't want anything to do with you—neither do I, so I suggest you go back to whatever rock you crawled from beneath and enjoy the bed you made for yourself. You're no longer welcome in ours."

I abandoned the cart. Walked past Marsha without speaking a word and sucked in thick, muggy air while hurrying to my car.

Tears thickened my throat, and I swiped wetness from my eyes while attempting to drive home without the groceries I had written on my list.

Why did he have to show up and rip away the delicious feels I'd finally gotten to experience since he'd left us? Why approach me when Hudson had clearly spelled out the consequences of his actions?

I pulled into the driveway, relieved to see Hudson's truck gone. The aches in my body from the night before no longer enticed me to smile. I crawled like a weary person who'd gone without sustenance for a month into the house. The stairs proved as insurmountable as Mt. Everest, but I dragged my ass to the top and into the nursery with wetness in my eyes.

The rocking chair's cushion soothed my backside, and I took to steady movement, back and forth, back and forth, losing myself to the silent rhythm that had always quieted my mind with comforting darkness.

13

COLTON

I should have walked out before we'd even gotten started because I hadn't slept worth a shit Friday night. My goddamn emotions had gotten caught up exactly like I'd feared, that dagger digging into my chest like a mother-fucker. Touching Madeline, licking into her mouth while her hot pussy welcomed my dick, had been a life-altering event.

We hardly knew each other, but I'd felt something stir-ring between us, potent and fulfilling in the way I'd been hoping to find.

Saturday, I couldn't keep from thinking about Madeline and her sexy, bossy as fuck husband I wanted to suck on like a damn ice pop. Shit between him and I would be just as mind-altering as my too-short moments with his wife. The hunger radiating from him had been palpable.

The heat had settled in again, making for one miser-able-as-hell morning. At least I had off from the day job and had gotten some gym time in before the sun fully rose. But the rest of the long hours with nothing to do but work on my own home's latest project, which meant gutting out the half bath? I fantasized until I had to take a break and jerk off. Forced down dinner, remembering eating out Madeline's pussy. Showered and shoved a few fingers up my ass while thinking about Hudson's thick cock.

I lasted until seven at night when I finally poked him through Missing Link, asking how they were doing and if they wanted to meet up again.

He never got back to me.

Sunday went pretty much the same as the day before.

Hot.

Melancholic.

Continued the bathroom rehab. Rubbed my dick raw dreaming about Hudson being balls deep in my ass—or Madeline's while I thrust up into her tight pussy.

Another poke, another day of being ignored fed my insecurities and hatred of being rejected.

We'd connected from day one, and the sexual energy had been off the charts, so why the radio silence? Sure, Hudson had told me they only needed a jumpstart, and from what I'd seen before being sent on my way, he'd been hellbent on fucking her clear through the mattress.

What I wouldn't have given to sit and enjoy the show. Maybe run my hands over Hudson's backside as he thrust into his wife.

Or I could have tasted the sweetness on her tongue, swallowed her whimpers as he loved on her body.

That unquenchable thirst for a Youngs/Colton sandwich hit full fucking force by Monday morning, and a scowl settled firmly in place by the time I parked at the jobsite. Blake pulled in alongside me in his silver Ford, grinning through the opened passenger window.

I couldn't rouse my lips in response.

"Still haven't gotten laid?" Blake asked the second I climbed from my truck.

"Oh, I got some, alright," I muttered, shoving my seat forward to get my tool belt from the back, "but he'd been serious about that one and done shit."

"And you want more," Blake said, rounding his hood.

"Fuck yeah, I do." I slammed my truck's door shut and swung my belt around my waist, glancing over the condo project taking shape along the Merrimac River. We'd gotten the first part of the building framed out and planned to hang exterior panels starting that day.

I'd told Blake and Reid about the Missing Link app the week before, the off-the-wall chances of finding the Youngs, and the mix up that had ended up matching us. They'd both encouraged me to enjoy the hell out one last hookup before looking for love, so I'd jumped in, needing to satisfy those fantasies.

But fuck, did I lust for another taste, another chance to get Hudson to cave and touch me. Or let me worship his body with my tongue and hands—fucking *something*.

"What are you going to do?" Blake asked.

"Fuck if I know," I muttered. "It's not like I can just go knock on their door, drop to my knees, and beg."

"You never beg."

I shot Blake a glance, my lips firmed in a flat line. He had it right—I'd always enjoyed the fuck out of my sexual encounters. Called the shots. Left when I'd wanted. But this shit? Territory owned by Hudson? While the good boy in me salivated for more, I found myself unsteady. Unsure. Lost in my mind about how to move onto the next potential love match when the Youngs had given me Kool-Aid I wanted to guzzle every goddamn day.

"So do that," Blake suggested with a shrug. "Go knock on their door and beg for that silver fox's dick in your mouth."

"Fuck," I muttered, heat prickling over my skin from more than the mugginess of the swampy air around us. "He's a goddamn oak." At least, he'd stood beside their bed like one within touching distance while I'd fucked Madeline. His body had vibrated with tension and need I'd felt as real as his wife's skin pressed against me.

"So chop him down at the knees."

"How the fuck am I supposed to do that?"

"Be persistent. Don't give up."

"No means no, asshole," I muttered at him. "Didn't your mom ever tell you that?"

Blake barked out a laugh and slapped my shoulder. "Squeaky wheel gets the grease."

"And restraining orders," I grumbled, the sweat already dripping down my back deepening my scowl.

"One last attempt won't get that severe of an outcome," Blake said as we approached the other guys hanging outside the makeshift office.

He had a point. Hudson hadn't exactly said no to a second night—just that he didn't want to touch me, and that was it. Okay, so maybe a little more final than I could justify going against, but...

Maybe asking in person would be enough of an entice-ment that he'd fold to a second chance for me to weasel beneath his body—

"Romeo here is pining," Blake announced to the guys while nodding toward me, "so beware, unless you want your head bitten off."

"Asshole," I muttered while one of the newer workers—Jake I think his name was—said something about not minding teeth. I flipped him the bird even though he was hot as shit, and I'd have hit on him if he wasn't a Harper's Construction employee along with me.

Reid sidled up to me as Blake started dictating orders to all the guys for the day's work.

"How'd it go Friday?" Reid asked quietly.

"I want more," I muttered like a kid whose candy had been taken away.

"Dick or pussy?"

"I only got a taste of the second. Hudson refused to touch me."

"How come?"

I shrugged, his talk about baggage and healing probably all the answer I would ever get. "He's definitely not on the market—*they* aren't. He hadn't lied about that shit. Pretty much tossed me out on my ass the minute his wife and I finished."

"Shit."

"Yeah."

"So what are you gonna do?"

I glanced at the river on our left, once more thinking about its winding course and its final destination. "Guess I'm going to try to talk them into one more night and hopefully break down the wall that's closing him off from me."

"What about her?"

I glanced over at Reid, the concern in his dark eyes leveling out a bit of my unrest. I might not have family, but I had steady, sure friends who had my back. "We had a definite connection even before the sex," I stated quietly, blood wanting to head southward at the memory. "Given the chance, I really think it could be something more."

"Then go for it," Reid said, same as he'd done the week before when I'd told him and Blake about the app matching me with the Youngs.

I set my thoughts on one last attempt to create something real with them.

But the how escaped me—or maybe it was fear of further rejection that hindered my mind from coming up with a plan.

14

HUDSON

Peter had touched my wife and sent her spiraling hours after our breakthrough. I'd gone from elated to murderous rage, the swoop in emotions bottoming me out like the world's highest roller coaster without the elation of the fall. Nausea bubbled in my stomach like rancid acid.

I wanted to rip that fucker apart limb from limb. Slice off his twink-sized dick and shove it along his lying tongue deep into his throat until he choked to death. My blood boiled for it.

Thank fuck for self-control, or I'd have gone on a rampage and located the asshole who'd torn the newly blooming flower of life inside my wife's heart to shreds.

But I'd talked Mads into leaving the rocking chair for our bed Saturday night, and I'd wrapped myself around her, offering what comfort I could. Soothing touches. Gentle kisses on her face. Whispered words of edification and love.

By Sunday afternoon, she'd seemed a bit more at peace, and I'd kept her company in the kitchen while she made pink and blue macarons for a baby shower. I gave her space, allowing silence between us for her to process.

All while I burned inside, craving an outlet to take out my pent-up aggression and anger on.

Colton had reached out through Missing Link's messaging system, but I didn't reply even though he'd have been the perfect person to help me find release. But that reminder of Peter only doubled down my determination to keep other men at arm's length.

Colton had known the score going in, and we'd accomplished our task.

Or, at least, we had until Peter cut right through the fragile strands Mads and I had begun to weave around us again.

Monday, I went to work, needing to breathe even though humidity clogged the air. My muscles ached from the physical effort put in, but my mind didn't settle over the worry of having been set a step back. Sweat-drenched and covered in sawdust, I returned home in the evening to the scent of something savory when I had expected nothing.

"Mads?" I called from the entryway where I unlaced my boots.

"In the kitchen!" She sounded more like herself, thank fuck.

Some of the tension left my shoulders.

I found her pulling a roast from the oven, rising steam scenting the room with onions, carrots, and beef. My mouth watered, but it was the sight of Mads in a cute sundress, her hair damp from a shower and hanging over her bare shoulders that made me hungry.

She set the pan on the stovetop, and I wrapped my arms around her, burying my face in her warm neck. Usually, she allowed me to linger regardless of my state of filth, but she wiggled forward, putting distance between us.

"You stink."

I snickered at her lighthearted tone and backed away. "How soon until dinner's ready?"

"Now, but it'll wait until you shower." Sass had returned to her voice, and I dropped a quick kiss on her cheek and hurried upstairs, feeling more buoyant than I had all weekend.

The passing of time since the run-in with Peter on Saturday had eased her emotions a hell of a lot faster than it had mine, and the hope to get back to a new normal lessened my thoughts of violence toward the cheating prick. Putting his audacity on the back burner, as well as the memories of Friday night with Colton that plagued me more than I cared to admit, I quickly scrubbed the workday from my body. I pulled on shorts and a T-shirt before heading back downstairs.

Mads had set the dining room table. She'd even lit candles and poured wine.

Blood swelled my dick at the promise of her actions, and I stalked into the kitchen, my fingers itching to touch.

She washed a pan in the sink, and I crowded in close, my hands finding the hem of her dress. Sliding my palms up the outside of her thighs, I once more nuzzled her neck.

No panties kept my touch from her skin.

"Christ, woman," I groaned, my hands filled with the bare flesh of her backside. Eyes clenched shut, I squeezed and kneaded her soft ass, jiggling the mounds as she rinsed whatever she washed. I laid open-mouthed kisses over her throat, taking advantage of the tilt of her head, drinking in the soft sigh she released.

I ran my hands around to her front, my fingertips in her curls, dipping lower to find warm, damp folds.

My dick thickened against her lower back, and I groaned

at the thought of sinking into her pussy. "You drive me mad, love."

She moaned as I traced her slit with a teasing touch.

"I'm so damn hungry," I growled, more breath than tone against her ear—and backed off, slapping her ass on the way.

"Jerk!" she laughed.

Fucking *laughed*.

My throat went tight, but she tossed a handful of suds at my shirt, the light in her eyes hitting me like that goddamn axe again.

I smiled, excited to draw out the rightness that had returned. "Dinner smells amazing. Thanks for cooking for us."

"Well—" Mads rinsed off her hands and grabbed a towel "—I sat in the rocker remembering how perfect Friday night had been, the lack of depression and happiness I'd gotten to experience. It made me realize that I just needed to take another step forward, and that every bit of progress would leave the shit behind eventually. Even if just for a little. Grab the potatoes," she said, nodding toward a foil-covered bowl.

She retrieved a small platter and gravy boat, and I followed on her heels into the dining room. "I decided to forget about that little shit, shave my legs, slather on your favorite lotion, and spoil you rotten with your favorite meal," she said, and we set the food on the table.

"You're too good to me," I said, pulling out her chair.

She sat, her soft smile dazzling me, but a hint of sadness still lay in her eyes. I leaned down and pressed my lips to hers, lingering to soak in the sweet moment.

"Thank you," I whispered, the ache in my chest pure love and appreciation for the gift of her. "I see a full-body massage in your near future."

She shivered, and I took my seat, studying her across the table.

Pink flushed her cheeks, and the black of her pupils swelled a bit, eating at the sky blue of her eyes. "I love us."

A grin claimed my lips. "I do too."

"Eat," she ordered, handing me the platter with sliced roast beef. "Then we'll talk about further steps forward."

"What were you thinking?" I asked after filling my plate since I wasn't about to wait because I had plans for later.

"I want to play again."

I eyed her, slowly chewing my mouthful of tender beef, my pulse picking up slightly. "With?" I asked once I swallowed even though I already knew her answer would make me uncomfortable as fuck.

"Colton."

Just his name alone kicked lust into my groin regardless of how often I'd told myself I didn't want him, didn't just enjoy being in his company. "Why him?"

"Because we have great chemistry, and one taste wasn't nearly enough."

I had a greedy girl, but the thought of more Colton raised my hackles in a warning I couldn't ignore.

"I want him," I told her what she'd already figured out, "which is why we can't get involved."

"He's a good boy, Hud—nothing like Peter," she insisted, leaning forward the slightest bit.

A muscle ticked in my jaw.

"He's desperate for edification and affection," Mads continued.

"How can you possibly know that after one night?" I grumbled even though I'd caught hints of both from his tone and reactions to my bossing him around in our bed. His confession of his upbringing through our messages through Missing Link gave weight to her assumption. Made him even more of a temptation.

"He melted at every caress, and elation filled his eyes every time either of us offered words of praise," she answered with exactly what I'd seen. "I don't know his past, his family history, but it's obvious he's a lonely soul like you were."

Her statement hit hard, but she'd never been one to pull punches. It was one of the many things I adored about her. She'd found me when I'd been at my lowest, her attention and nurturing exactly what I'd needed in my life.

It was why I wanted to give her the world. It was why I'd agreed to try for a baby even though I'd have been an old first-time father when I'd never wanted to be.

But Colton?

"How about I look for another hookup on the app?" I suggested rather than explaining to her what Colton had shared with me about his upbringing. "Someone in tune with a few nights of fun without the mess of emotions."

"I want more."

Fuck.

I put down my fork and rubbed a hand over my whiskered jaw. She held my gaze with a stubbornness that usually made me rock hard.

"It's not that you aren't enough—"

"I know," I interjected.

"—I just want that hole Peter ripped open filled up. You said for years that we were meant for a third, and once I understood and got to experience the lifestyle, I realized you were right. I miss having another man to spoil. And Colton is..."

Her voice trailed off, but I got what she couldn't find words for.

Mads's motherly instinct always ran toward those in need of nurturing. Peter had been a much younger spoiled brat, his downtrodden spirit calling out to us both in different ways, but his immaturity had wrecked the beauty we had thought we'd found.

While Colton portrayed hints of brattiness, he was a man with a steady job. A hard worker. A seemingly sensitive soul.

I'd seen him take note of the empty crib when he and Mads had passed the nursery on the way to our bedroom Friday night. Noted his hesitancy in the following moments as though remembering via the app's messaging system I'd mentioned baggage and loss. And in the flickering of mere candlelight before the power had come back on, I'd caught the empathy in his dark eyes even as he hungered for my wife.

Peter hadn't even sent his condolences—not that we'd have accepted or appreciated them.

He'd been my darling boy, the younger man who'd owned half my heart—but had become a petulant little prick from the moment we'd found out Mads had finally conceived. His insecurities probably had him thinking he would be replaced in our lives.

In retaliation, he'd stupidly attempted to make us feel like he did. Replaceable. Unnecessary. Nothing but an extra appendage to discard once used up.

All he'd accomplished was to rip my insides to shreds and turn our seemingly solid foundation to rubble.

"I know how much you laid on the line when accepting Peter into our lives and that you aren't ready to get emotionally involved again," Mads said, "but at least give Colton the chance to prove himself. He's such a sweet boy."

"He's not much younger than you," I muttered, pushing

a potato along my fork.

"Age aside, he still calls out to that side of me that needs to pamper and love."

I'd seen it. Felt it.

How the fuck could I deny her?

Goddamn it all to fucking hell and back again. She had been my salvation, and she would be my undoing.

"A sex date only." I finally folded, meeting her gaze, my tone firm. "Nothing more—and please don't ask me to participate, Mads. It's a hard limit for me right now."

Probably for fucking ever. Once bitten and all that shit.

Disappointment pulled on the corners of her eyelids, but she nodded. "I'll respect your wishes."

I released a slow, unsteady exhale, refusing to think about that man in our bed again until he sprawled there. I also wouldn't dwell on the fact he already seemed emotionally invested.

"I'll contact Colton and set something up for later this week if he's available," I promised her while telling myself I wouldn't lay a finger on his body no matter how much want radiated between us.

Mads's wide smile settled some of my unease, and deciding to go with her plans of moving forward, I set my focus on the future beyond Colton rather than the next couple of hookups ahead.

If he would even agree.

I bit back a snort. Not even a herd of horses would keep that boy from running to our doorstep once I sent the invite because Mads had been right. Colton craved what she wanted to give him—what the deepest parts of me yearned to lavish out on his needy ass as well.

But I wouldn't be moved.

Peter had made sure of that.

15

MADELINE

A young woman named Tara sat beside me at support group on Wednesday night. Like me, she'd given birth to a stillborn child. But she hadn't hemorrhaged to the point she'd ended up in emergency surgery and lost the ability to carry a child again.

Tears rolled down her cheeks as she shared her story, and not knowing a thing about the woman, I reached for her hand and squeezed. She clung to me until finished with her tale of grief.

I wanted to wrap her up in my arms and encourage her that every day got better. That some moments hurt with sorrow as fresh as first learning of your loss, but they became fewer and further between with each passing month.

Her daughter's name had been Mia.

Ours had been Maya Joy.

Even after the group time ended, Tara and I lingered near the exit, exchanging numbers and making plans to meet for lunch on Saturday afternoon.

I had no friends who could fathom the darkness overshadowing me more days than not. While Hudson had grief of his own over the tragedy we'd faced together, he couldn't grasp the loss as a mother, the responsibility I'd felt to protect the child in my womb.

Understanding Tara's sense of failure and guilt, I wanted to offer solace, an ear for when her heart became too burdened.

She hugged me tight outside the library where the support group met on Wednesday nights. "You gave me hope tonight, Madeline," she whispered, her voice still wobbly from all of the emotional upheaval a first-timer usually experienced when sharing their story in the way she had. "Seeing your smile, hearing your encouragement that things will get better...I can't thank you enough."

"I'm glad I decided to come," I said as we stepped back from each other. "It was a pleasure meeting you, and I'm really looking forward to lunch. It'll be nice to have someone who understands."

"I agree." She smiled through a fresh welling of tears in her eyes. "Thanks again. Really."

Another quick hug and Tara moved off.

My heart felt full and peaceful as it often did after sharing in and taking part in others' grieving processes. Knowing we weren't alone, that others thoroughly empathized from their own experiences made coping that much easier.

Tara turned and waved, and I lifted my hand.

The second I lowered my arm, fingers slid over my palm and clasped hold of me before I could move away.

Peter.

He clung to my hand with both of his, his eyes wide. Tear-filled. His lower lip trembled, and for the briefest moment, instinct demanded I hug him.

My stomach heaved, and I stepped back, jerking my hand from between his. "What are you doing here?"

"I'm in trouble, Madeline," he whispered with a hoarse voice, glancing around and rubbing his palms down his jeans. Restless and clearly agitated, he couldn't stand still.

Thinner than normal—and the young man hadn't ever been muscular—he appeared fragile. Pale with worry.

I wanted to tell him he deserved whatever trouble he'd gotten himself into, but being mean wasn't in my nature. "I really have to go," I said, my voice nothing more than a ragged whisper. "Hudson is expecting me."

"Please." He reached for me but dropped his hand before making contact. "I'm sorry for grabbing hold of you like that, but you always held my hand when I was hurting, and I just..." A tear slid down his cheek, and he bit his lower lip.

My mind knew better than to give him the comfort he sought out even if my soft heart wanted to wrap him up and make all the bad things disappear.

"You always took such good care of me—you and Hudson both. I was a fool, Madeline. An immature, stupid idiot. I made the wrong choice, and now...now I'm suffering." His voice broke, his shoulders slumping. "I—I just need my safe place back. My home."

My throat tightened, but I refused to be drawn in by his manipulations. Taking a deep breath, I attempted to steady myself. "You betrayed us, Peter. Our home is no longer yours, and it's not a haven for you to hide in. If you've made even more bad decisions that have caused your circumstances to worsen, I'm afraid you're going to have to face them on your own. Hudson and I aren't emotionally available to you. Our time, the relationship we'd had, is gone because of what you did."

Puppy dog eyes wet with tears implored me for forgiveness. "I didn't love Ryan," he whispered.

"Then why fuck him?" I asked, my stomach clenching at the memory of walking in on Peter and the older man in our bed. The one where the three of us had vowed our commitment to each other two years earlier.

"I-I was feeling left out," he rushed to explain, swallowing quickly. "You and Hudson were so happy about the baby like you were in your own little world while I looked in from the outside."

"We never saw you anywhere but right beside us, Peter. It was your insecurity that led you to those emotions."

"You're trying to invalidate my feelings!" he cried, whining like a child, which only hardened my heart toward him.

A couple left the library, glancing our way before moving down the stairs, and I held my tongue until they passed from hearing.

"If you had communicated with us, kept that vow of honesty at all times we'd agreed on," I said to Peter, "things wouldn't have spiraled out of control. Hudson and I were not responsible for your responses, and had you just opened your mouth and shared—"

"But I was afraid Hudson would get mad!" Peter threw his hands up and bounced on his toes as though unable to stand still in his distress. "He's so much older than me, more mature—I didn't want him to think less of me."

"And you figured bringing Ryan Foley into our bed without our consent would make Hudson think highly of you?" I shot back, my stomach twisting. "Did you even stop to consider how betrayed he would feel by your actions?" I asked as someone approached on the sidewalk below. "That claiming you loved him more than life, then allowing another man to stick his dick in you—*in our bed*—would tear his heart in two?"

"I didn't mean to hurt either of you," Peter muttered, his long eyelashes fluttering closed. Twin tears leaked from beneath his eyelids as he shifted on his feet.

We'd seen Ryan a few times with Peter but hadn't ever been suspicious of their friendship. There hadn't even been any red flags to make us pause and question.

"I...I just wanted you both to understand what I was going through," Peter said.

Something a simple conversation would have taken care of.

But Peter had always been a little impulsive. Without having a daddy figure in his life, he'd run into trouble time and again as a teenager. When we'd met him at a friend's house, he'd been a homeless young twenty-year-old, lost and mangy as a stray kitten.

He'd ensnared both our empathy. Our hearts.

"You accomplished your goal," I said, all trace of feeling sorry for him long gone. "We understood how you might have felt left out, but my finally conceiving had nothing to do with your unfaithfulness and intentional lack of consent like your actions did. The three of us discussed having a child together for two years—two *years*, Peter. You shared in the decision-making. Not once did we go behind your back in attempts to get what we all desired."

"But I hadn't realized how a pregnancy would change our dynamic! You started to pay more attention to your swelling belly than you did me." More tears poured from his eyes—the type that enticed snot to dribble from his nose and drew the gazes of two young girls walking past the library.

Peter swiped his sleeve over his face.

God, the drama began to drain what little energy and patience I had left to deal with him.

"Peter—"

"And don't get me started on Hudson," he cut me off, sniffing harshly. "He snuggled you every night, forgetting about his good boy who would bend over backward to please him."

"So you went and found another dick," I stated the blunt truth, the memory in my mind ripping through my chest.

"I-I thought—"

"You *didn't* think," I cut off his contrite whisper, my own words ragged. "Bad choices bring about consequences, Peter, and unfortunately for you, that meant losing the trust of the two people who loved you the most."

He wailed, dropping to his knees and grasping at mine. "Please, Mads—you have to forgive me, I can't...I can't do this by myself!" Sobs ripped from his lips, tears and snot running once more.

I hated that my heart hurt for him, hated that my emotions would even consider feeling a little bit sorry for him.

At least no one shared the library stairs or sidewalk with us to double my discomfort.

Peter clutched at the hem of my shirt like a little child, trembling and peering up at me through his tears, his eyes full of innocence and sadness.

"I can't do this," I whispered, trying to pry his hands off me. "Leave me alone—let go."

"No!" He buried his face against my belly, sobbing. "I need you back. I'll do anything, I swear! I'm sorry for letting that man have me. Sorry for acting like a spoiled brat. Hudson can redden my ass until I can't sit down. I-I'll scrub the house from top to bottom for the rest of my life to make up for the mess I'd caused on our bedroom floor."

The bedroom floor...

Nausea erupted at the memory of the god-awful cramping, the blood. The doctor insisted it wasn't the shock, the instantaneous stress of finding our young lover—

"Let me go," I whispered, my own eyes welling as panic began to squeeze my chest. "Let me go!"

He pulled.

I pushed.

And I couldn't keep the whine of hysteria from rising up my throat.

I never should have acknowledged him. Shouldn't have allowed him to speak a single word to me.

Darkness closed in on my periphery as I fought to fill my compressed lungs.

"G-go...please..." I croaked out.

The ground seemed to rise up, swallowing me whole.

16

COLTON

Friday night at 7:00. Don't be late.

I read Hudson's message a dozen times since it had popped up Monday evening, and each scan of his command shot lust through my blood. I'd been logged into the app, still working out the words to use to beg for another chance. But how else would begging be interpreted? No matter how I worded my request, it would sound needy as fuck.

Which I was.

Then the ding had come through, offering me exactly what I'd wanted, and I'd responded with an immediate, **I'll be there**, before jerking off to fantasies about talking that man into joining in the fun.

The following two days of work had dragged, and I was jonesing for a hit of Youngs to the point my restlessness had Blake and Reid in stitches. They dragged me out for dinner right after work on Wednesday, and we bullshitted over a couple of beers to help pass the time.

They reminisced about the last woman they'd shared while I dreamed of doing the same with Hudson. But unlike my buddies who didn't cross the bromance lines when a woman lay between them, I wanted Hudson's hands all over me and vice versa.

Less than forty-eight hours, I told myself, glancing at my cell. My feet were antsy as fuck, and I couldn't sit still any longer.

"I'm heading out," I said and swallowed down the rest of my beer.

"It's only eight, and you've only had one beer," Blake said, flagging down our waitress. "Have another."

"Nah. I'm beat."

"More like you wanna go beat off to thoughts of Madeline and her daddy," Reid said.

I grabbed some kernels of popcorn from the bowl we'd shared and tossed them in Reid's laughing face. "He's not her daddy—it's not like that."

"But you wouldn't mind if he slapped your ass around a bit," Reid insisted, his dark eyes still twinkling.

I flipped him the bird. Getting drunk with them on Friday nights over the years and spilling all my kinks hadn't been some of my better choices. At least they weren't prudes or got insecure a pan guy worked with them. I'd caught a bit of shit when I'd admitted to Blake and Reid that I thought they were hot, but both were secure enough that no weirdness fucked up our long friendship.

Our other good friend Micah Fox owned Elite Escorts, and his brother preferred men, so he was cool with my sexual preferences too. It felt nice to have such open-minded buddies who wouldn't judge me like some of my foster families had done since I'd been aware of which way I swayed at an early age.

I knuckle-bumped both my favorite assholes before

heading out into the cooler air. A deep breath filled my lungs. Thank fuck the mugginess had finally relented. Since I'd only had one drink with my dinner in the three hours we'd been sitting there bullshitting, I didn't bother with an Uber.

Clearheaded, I grinned at the wind whipping through my truck as I headed south, windows open.

I was still anxious for Friday, but getting out with the guys had definitely helped me calm down. Exiting Route 1, I headed toward home, in a good enough mood I didn't bark at the Masshole who didn't know how to use a roundabout.

Veering from the circle at the first right, I glanced around the downtown where I'd bought my fixer-upper. While closer to Boston, it still had a small-town feel with its close brick buildings and wide sidewalks.

The massive library sat on the left.

Some young punk was on his knees, hanging onto a woman's shirt—

Madeline.

"The fuck?" I slowed as she attempted to pull away from the guy, and he grabbed her tighter, putting his head on her stomach.

Panic lined her face, and I jerked the wheel, angling into someone's driveway. I left my truck running and hopped out. Madeline's knees gave way, and she sank to the ground. The fucker who hadn't let her go caught her—but still.

A quick glance left and right, and I sprinted across the street, my stomach tight and brow furrowed.

The guy had laid her on her back and was patting her face as though frantic, tears all over his own.

"The fuck?" I growled, yanking him away from Madeline who lay boneless on the sidewalk. "Lin?" I dropped down beside her, pulling her limp body against my chest. "Hey, baby...wake up for me, huh?"

She grimaced, and I shot a glare at the blond kid slouched behind me.

"Who the fuck are you?" His words carried a harshness that didn't match the condition of his face and the penitent actions of him being on his knees and clutching at her seconds earlier. Manipulative little fucker—I'd seen my fair share like him.

"I'm a family friend," I snipped back, clutching Madeline closer and repeating his words. "Who the fuck are *you*?"

"I'm her boyfriend," the asshole sneered, his gaze dropping to my arms as I held her tight. His hands twitched.

I barked a laugh. "The fuck you are."

"Colton?" Madeline's soft voice tore my focus off the guy.

"Hey, baby. I've got you—you alright?"

"I—I think so..." She blinked, and I loosened my grasp on her a bit to let her sit up. Her attention flitted to the blond. "Go away, Peter," she whispered, blinking as tears welled in her eyes. "Just leave me alone."

"Mads—"

I jerked toward him, my scowl over the nickname he felt he had the right to use cutting off whatever he'd wanted to say. "Get the fuck outta here, *Peter*."

"This is public property, asshole," he shot back with a hoarse voice while pushing to his feet. The dude couldn't have been more than five and a half feet. A cute twenty-something twink but full of shit, which made him ugly as fuck. "I'm not done with you and Hudson," he told Madeline.

"Well we're done with you." Unsteady in words and movement, she started to push onto her feet, and I hopped up, cradling her elbow.

"Sure you're alright?" I murmured, trying to get a better look into her eyes she kept downcast while standing.

She swallowed hard and nodded, leaning on me. Her body trembled along with her lower lip.

"Tell Hudson—"

"Shut the fuck up, asshole," I spat at Peter to cut him off, clasping Madeline's arm so she wouldn't fall over again. "Come on." I started for the street, ignoring the sputtering of Peter—whoever he really was to the Youngs.

"I-I can walk," Madeline whispered, but she propped against me as though drained of energy.

"I got you, Lin. Gonna take you home to Hudson, okay?"

"My car..."

"You're a trembling fucking wreck. I'm not about to let you drive."

She didn't argue with my blunt conclusion, and I opened my passenger door, helping her inside my truck's cab. A shudder rippled over her, and the glassiness in her blue eyes tightened my chest.

"What happened?" I asked, leaning over her to grab the seatbelt since she sat, hands limp on her lap.

"Peter is our ex," she whispered, and a tear slid down her cheek.

Why the sadness?

She'd told him to go away, and from what I'd seen before she'd passed out, it looked like he'd begged on his knees. So who had dumped who and which heart had been broken?

I shut the door and hurried around the hood. A quick glance at the library and I noted Peter hadn't stuck around to watch us leave.

No matter what had gone down between the Youngs and him, I hated the fucker for causing her tears, for whatever words he'd vomited at her that had brought on such emotions.

I climbed into my truck, my jaw set.

Madeline stared out the windshield, empty hands still lax atop her thighs. No cell or keys for her car.

"Did you have a purse?"

"Hmm?" She shifted her head toward me with emotional weariness causing her entire body to sag.

"Purse?"

"Oh." Two blinks cleared her glassy eyes even though tears still leaked down her cheeks. "Shit." She craned her neck to look back at the library. "I had a small one with me when I left the meeting. I-I must have dropped it."

"Stay here." I hopped back out and retraced our steps to the front of the building.

Nothing.

And no sign of Peter who might have picked it up if someone else hadn't first.

"Shit." Lips in a thin line, I stalked back across the street, cursing the little fucker in my head.

"He probably took it," Madeline stated quietly as I got back in empty-handed, resting her head against the back of the seat. "Another excuse to talk to us."

"What the fuck did he want?" I asked while backing out of the borrowed driveway. It wasn't any of my business, but I found myself protective over the woman filling the cab with her delicious honeysuckle scent and sweet presence.

Madeline wiped at her eyes and exhaled a heavy sigh. "Another chance."

"No offense, but the guy's a lying asshole." I couldn't hold back my thoughts from seeing him acting like a repentant soul to calculating, manipulative prick in a blink.

"He is, but we found that out a little too late."

We were only a couple of blocks from the Youngs, not nearly enough time for the story I was dying to hear, so I kept my mouth shut from spewing questions.

"We were together for three years," Madeline said after a few seconds of silence between us. "Hudson and I came home from a dinner party and found him in our bed with another man when he'd claimed to be sick to get out of going with us."

My jaw clenched. That cheating asshole was the reason Hudson wasn't on the menu—no fucking doubt.

"I lost our baby that night," Madeline whispered, her voice choking on more tears.

I reached over and grabbed her hand, squeezing it tight. Swallowing hard, I tried to think of words to offer but fell short.

A shuddered inhale, and she continued. "That was seven months ago."

"I'm sorry," I finally said the only thing worth a shit.

"That's why I've been a bit depressed and Hudson got on Missing Link."

"Distraction," I murmured, hating the crash of disappointment that clarity brought. Cheated on, jaded, the Youngs wouldn't ever be open to more than having a plaything in their bed.

"No," Madeline stated as firmly as her wavering voice probably allowed. "To show me that I'm not broken, that taking steps toward living again would bring happiness into our lives we've been missing since Peter's affair."

I glanced over at her unsmiling face. "Did it work?"

She gave me a sad smile. "He told you to come over again on Friday night, didn't he?"

That hit of lust his command always brought when I read it shot through me. My skin pebbled over my arms. I cleared my throat. "Either it didn't really and you wanted to try again—or you felt what I did and wanted to explore the beginnings of a promising connection."

"The latter, Colton." Her soft tone, the assurance of her hand squeezing mine eased the part of me that still questioned if I did the right thing in agreeing to another night.

It also gave me hope. Two against one...

I steered into their driveway, noting Hudson's F-250.

Madeline released a heavy sigh. "He's going to be pissed."

Then I wasn't about to let her go in there alone and have him stir up more angst that might unintentionally drag her emotions back down to where they'd been moments earlier.

Shutting off my truck, I slid out and rounded the front to assist Madeline.

I grasped her elbow while she climbed down but didn't let go. A foot to the passenger door slammed it shut, and I kept hold of her while we moved across the paver walkway toward the front of the house.

Hudson must have seen me pull in, because he opened up the door the second we hit the stoop's first step.

"What happened?" His gaze flitted between me and Madeline, his question obviously meant for whoever spoke first.

"Peter," Madeline whispered.

"Fucking little cunt," Hudson spat, stepping back as I led his wife into the house. He slammed the door shut behind us. "What did he do, Mads?"

"Caught me outside the library when I was leaving support group."

"Did he touch you?" Hudson vibrated with red heat, hands fisted and eyes blazing. Even pissed off as hell and on the verge of violence, he hit all my goddamn buttons.

"Yes," I hissed in answer for Madeline who had hesitated but didn't shy away from her tensed husband. "He wouldn't let go. Got on his knees bawling like a little bitch, and whatever shit he spewed made Lin pass out."

"Fuck!" Hudson sent his fist into the wall.

17

HUDSON

Neither Colton nor Mads flinched at my rage. My wife sagged against Colton, and he held her upright, grasping her chin.

"Okay?" he asked quietly, subtly angling her away from me.

Fuck.

I ran my fingers through my hair, wanting to rip out the strands from the roots. Mads knew I would never raise a hand to her, but Colton didn't know shit about my character. He put his back to me to protect my wife.

Peter never would have done such a thing.

"Why don't you go upstairs and take a nice hot shower. Wash the feel of him off you, okay?" Colton suggested, slowly releasing his hold on her. "I'll fill Hudson in on the details, and once you're done, he'll have calmed down to talk to you without *losing his shit*."

Those last three words of his held a hint of warning for me even though he didn't face or acknowledge me.

Mads glanced over his shoulder to meet my gaze.

The last fucking thing I wanted to do was upset her further. "Go on," I rasped, nodding toward the stairs. "I'll be up in a bit."

Colton and I both stood in silence as she walked up the stairs.

I yearned to go after her, but she needed space, and there was someone else available to give me answers without falling further into depression.

"What the fuck happened?" I bit the words out quietly the second our bedroom door shut behind her.

Colton still stared up the stairs, his back to me. "Your ex was begging her for another chance."

I cursed, wanting to smash the wall again regardless of the throb in my knuckles.

"I was driving by and didn't hear what was said, but he wouldn't let her go when she tried to pry his hands off her." Colton turned toward me, studying my face with unsettled dark eyes as I fought to keep from behaving like a goddamn lunatic. "When I parked and ran across the road, he'd upset her enough she passed out. The little shit at least caught her from hitting the ground."

I should have felt at least a tiny bit of gratitude, but zero trace entered my heated blood.

"I yanked him away," Colton continued, "picked her up, and she came to pretty quickly. She told him to leave. He went from apologetic to cold in a blink."

A jaw muscle twitched my whiskers. "He's a manipulative little cunt."

"I figured that out pretty quick."

I met Colton's steady gaze, appreciating his firm stance and going to my wife's rescue. "Thank you for intervening and bringing her back here."

"She was too upset to drive."

I nodded, easily imagining that truth considering how emotional she'd been when she got home Saturday after Peter had approached her in the grocery store.

Colton shoved his hands in his pockets. "Lin said the two of you walked in on him fucking another guy."

A muscle ticked in my jaw again. "Ryan Foley," I bit the name out, my hatred for that man almost as palatable as what I felt for Peter.

"Is that what caused her to lose the baby?"

Memories flooded my brain—the satisfaction on Peter's face when mine had drained of color at finding him on his knees for that asshole Ryan. Mads had doubled over in pain, and the blood...I'd lost our supposed good boy, my baby girl, and almost my precious wife.

She had survived the hemorrhaging, but our Maya Joy and Mads's womb hadn't. I'd been too exhausted to deal with Peter when I'd finally gotten home from the hospital. He'd been smart enough to keep his mouth shut and leave when I'd told him to.

Seven months of silence...I should have known he would return once things settled. The kid had always been a relentless little shit.

"That night is none of your concern," I muttered to Colton, ready to send him on his way even though I'd have preferred to shove him against the wall and unleash the aggression still racing through my blood.

"Gonna have to disagree with you on that one, Hudson. You allowed me into your lives—"

"Bed," I corrected him, pinning him in place with my stare. "We let you into our bed, boy. You have no right to our personal shit." Each word launched off my tongue like a snapping whip.

He took a step closer as though unafraid of my anger, his eyes darkening as his hands slid out of his pockets to fist at his sides. "The fuck I don't. Lin touched a part of me deep inside I never knew existed before. Something instinctive. Protective. You aren't the only one who hungers to tear Peter limb from limb. Learning he hurt the two of you makes me want to feed him his own goddamn dick."

"Fuck." I rubbed my shaking hands over my face, my insides still tensed. I did *not* want to get involved with Colton, let alone like him anymore than I'd already did regardless of my intent not to.

The shit Peter had stirred up since Saturday had only hardened my resolve.

"I'm not going to just slink away and disappear because you've got trust issues."

I shot Colton a glare.

"I understand he hurt you—"

"You don't understand *shit*," I spat, hating that I couldn't stop from trembling from the adrenaline still swamping my bloodstream.

"—but that doesn't give you the right to make assumptions about a man you barely know."

I held his steady stare, those dark eyes of his seeming to easily read clear through to my aching soul. Peter had made me so goddamn weak...a fucking emotional basket case, and I couldn't stomach the thought of getting involved with another man "I have no interest in knowing you."

Colton stood less than three feet from me, and energy like a live wire flooded with antagonism and hunger zapped between our vibrating bodies regardless of my cruel words tossed out in self-preservation.

"You're full of shit, Hudson," Colton stated quietly. Calmly. His head tipped to the side as he studied my face. "I think you want me. Lust to sink into my ass and call *me* your good boy."

Jesus Christ.

"And that truth scares the shit out of you," he continued, taking one step closer, lessening the charged space between us.

One command would send him to his knees—I could feel his desire to submit, had tasted it the night he'd loved on Mads's lush body and gave her pleasure. But fucking hell, he'd called me out. Fear *did* rule my mind, my ability to make the choice to give him what we both craved.

My stomach hardened even as it churned with that bitter, rancid acid again. Full-on tremors owned my muscles.

"You need to leave," I rasped, every cell in my body screaming to unleash on his willing body. "Now."

Colton stared at me in silence long enough that I fucking shivered from head to toe, goose bumps breaking out over my entire body.

Straightening my shoulders, I reached behind me for the doorknob, yanking it open.

He eyed the outside before giving me his attention again. "Don't upset her," he stated quietly, and I almost laughed even while appreciating his balls.

"I'm not going to."

"Friday night?" A hint of hope laced his tone, but I wasn't in the right headspace to promise shit.

I needed to check in with Mads. Figure out if I could handle having Colton under my control again without losing my shit. I'd stood up to the pull the previous handful of minutes, but...doubtful.

"I don't think that's a good idea."

He narrowed his gaze, leaning toward me. "Don't deny your wife just because you're a chickenshit."

I bared my teeth, and he smirked.

Tempting...oh so fucking tempting.

"This ends right here, right now." I bit out the words, wishing I could let loose on his ass for being such a brat.

Colton didn't attempt to touch me while passing me by —*thank fuck*—and stepped out into the night. "Oh—" Colton spun to face me on the top stair "—Lin dropped her purse outside the library, and I couldn't find it when I went back to look. It's possible that piece of shit might have picked it up. If he comes knocking and you need help—or an alibi—I'm your man."

Goddamn his persistent and perfect ass to hell and back again.

I shut the door in his face before I could yank him against me and rested my forehead on the cool wood.

I lusted to taste his tongue. Tell him to get on his knees and swallow what I gave him. Bend him over the couch. Command him to open his ass up for me until his hole gaped and he begged for me to fill him up.

But I also wanted to lie him out on our bed and oil his body until he melted beneath my touch while I showered my appreciation for taking care of my wife over every inch of his skin.

"Fuck." My hand still hurt like a bitch, and the ache in my groin wasn't much better. On the verge of painful. How the hell could I be on a high after what Mads had gone through? It had been empathy that had drawn me to Peter, but it was lust, pure and simple, that had me craving to lower my walls and enjoy a taste of Colton.

No.

No fucking way could I allow that type of vulnerability in our lives again. It had damn near ruined our marriage. I wouldn't give another outside force the power to break our hearts again.

Colton had been such a good boy, listening to what I'd told him to do on Friday night—I hoped he obeyed that final command I'd issued for him to leave us alone.

18

MADELINE

Numbness had begun to creep in as I climbed the stairs. Without much thought, I turned on the shower, but I hesitated before stripping down as the few minutes I'd spent inside our entryway replayed like a flash in my head.

Hudson had been livid as I'd expected.

And Colton attempted to shield me from his wrath even though there had been no need.

Would my husband take out his aggression on the sweet man who wanted to protect me? My legs still shook, but I hurried across our bedroom and cracked open the door, too curious to wait for Hudson to join me.

He and Colton argued, but I heard more sexual tension than anger in their voices. Yes, Hudson was good and truly pissed, but I knew he wouldn't hit another man. He'd kept his hands to himself when finally confronting Peter all those months ago, and if anyone had deserved a broken nose, it was that lying sack of shit.

Their voices lowered as Colton asked about the Friday night date Hudson had set up. Hudson's roundabout way of saying no disappointed me, but Colton telling him to not deny me because he was a chickenshit stole my breath and made me want to laugh at the same time.

No one called Hudson out.

Ever.

I strained my ears, waiting...hoping for a bang that meant Hudson had finally put Colton up against the wall to ease his sexual tension.

"This ends right here, right now."

My chest went heavy at Hudson's firm tone, and I slipped back into the bathroom, my eyes stinging.

He joined me a few minutes later, climbing into the shower stall with me. Without a word, he pulled me against him, and even though I didn't want to sag against him for ending things with Colton, my body denied me.

His strong arms held me with tenderness that started up my tears again.

"Did he hurt you?" Hudson asked, his voice calmer than I'd expected.

"Not physically, no."

"What did he say?"

"Nothing of importance," I mumbled, having zero wish to relive the conversation. "Colton left?"

"Yeah. He's...uh, not coming over Friday night."

Annoyance flared even though I'd already known that bit of information. "Why not?"

"We're too much drama."

I stiffened against him, and he ran a hand down my spine as though attempting to soothe my disappointment.

But the feeling straightening me upright wasn't from Colton's "thoughts" toward us.

Hudson had lied to me. Outright fucking lied, something I'd never heard from him before. What he'd done was no different than withholding his feelings like Peter had from both of us.

Needing space, I stepped away, my throat too tight to get into an argument.

"Mads?" Hudson questioned as I opened the glass door.

"I already washed," I whispered. "I just want to rest." Both truths—but I didn't expound on the reason I'd moved away from him. Too much hurt cracked through my heart, and I couldn't find the words nor did I have the energy.

Colton had called out my husband, and Hudson had done exactly as Colton had expected. Pulled a chickenshit move because he was afraid.

But emotional exhaustion insisted I save that quarrel for another day.

"Anything for you, love," Hudson had whispered to me Friday night after finding his release inside my ass, and I knew he'd meant every word. He would lay the world at my feet if given the opportunity.

Yet he allowed fear to hold him back from vulnerability, from the possibility of finding someone else to take Peter's place in our lives.

I couldn't help the anger his lie had flared inside me, but I understood where he came from. Having a solid foundation and a loving set of parents who supported me made being open to love easier. Shielding myself from potential hurt wasn't a natural instinct for me like it was for Hudson who didn't have the best upbringing.

His homophobic parents were both gone thanks to a bad heart and cancer, but they'd shaped his younger years with toxicity and negativity. He'd escaped their overbearing authority at eighteen and struggled for years to find himself, only doing so after cutting them from his life completely at age forty when he'd met me. He'd told me countless times in our years together that having my love, my attention, and the way I mothered him on occasion filled that emptiness inside him. His desire to be a father figure and lavish love on a needy younger man had been met by Peter.

He'd claimed he'd been at peace. Felt complete.

Then Peter had cracked the foundation of our lives.

I understood Hudson's need to protect himself, but that didn't mean I had to just sit back and let him wander down the path Peter's choice had veered him onto.

He wanted to make me happy, which meant keeping Colton in our lives for a little longer. Perhaps indefinitely if things were allowed to progress in the way I could feel as clearly as my hand tucked beneath my cheek.

I lay in bed, waiting for sleep to drag me under as the shower continued to run in the bathroom.

It would be smart to give Hudson some time to calm down, and put the latest Peter episode behind us—then I would take a step forward once more and push for what I wanted.

A simple request would be better rather than an elaborate dinner he might see as manipulation for me to get him to cave to my wishes.

Hudson might not be able to be honest with himself or me in a moment of emotional upheaval, but I would choose truth.

Eventually, he would relax back into the motions of our new normal, then I would see how far he really would go to give me the desires of my heart.

I wanted Colton again. I longed to see him under my husband. And maybe someday, he would gain the trust of Hudson to the point he would lower his walls enough to let Colton show him how it felt to be loved on by another man again.

Hudson had offered himself to Peter, something I hadn't ever expected in our relationship, but Peter had been emotionally fragile, needing reassurance. Hudson had bent over backward to make him smile again.

I didn't remember the circumstances that had led to Hudson's act of submitting his body to our boy, but I relived the scene in my mind in vivid color. Peter had been weeping with thankfulness, words of love spilling from his lips as he'd sunk into Hudson's body.

My husband had given that lying, betraying ass his trust, allowed intimacy beyond what he'd ever expressed interest in. I feared his stubbornness would keep him from finding love again in the way I knew he craved with a younger man.

I could have been a manipulative bitch, playing my husband to get exactly what I wanted—Colton in our bed—but I refused to lower myself to the ways of Peter.

Closing my eyes and slowly exhaling my lungs to emptiness, I vowed to lead by example. Move forward. Open myself to the future regardless of what it might look like. I would be honest as we had vowed to do when agreeing to a relationship, then the triad we'd enjoyed for almost three years.

Honesty. Consent. Love would come first.

And I would trust Hudson to see the beauty available to us both, the truth that I would stand by his side and cling to his hand no matter his fear or insecurity. I'd done so once before without coercion. I took hope in believing he could get there again.

19

COLTON

Even though Hudson had been an ass to me on Wednesday night, I strangely didn't have a scowl etched in stone on my face the next day. No one asked what bug had crawled up my ass and died. Blake didn't call me into the office to help me get my head straightened out before I snapped on a co-worker.

Friday went much the same, but my brain got to working over Madeline's missing purse and if that asshole Peter had ever ended up taking it to their home. I trusted Hudson to watch over her, expected the poor woman probably wouldn't be going out anywhere on her own for a while.

He'd claimed their lives weren't my business, but I stuck by my argument. Regardless of his wanting me to stay away, he couldn't keep my heart from being invested.

And it was. Thoroughly.

I dreamed about them both. Thought of them constantly. Checked the ML app dozens of times every day, hoping that Hudson would reach out to me.

With how Madeline had insisted she too was invested in

what we'd begun the weekend before, I was sure she would talk him into trying again.

But the days continued to pass without Hudson sending a message, and nothing bothered me more than being ghosted. The weekend came and went the same as the last. I was ignored and wallowed in rejection like I had as a kid.

At least depression got the better of me rather than anger like the kind I'd felt for Peter. I wondered if I could somehow look him up and threaten the shit out of him if he ever approached Madeline again.

Not my business.

I stared at the PB&J sandwich in my hand, that damn saying whispering in my head.

"You okay?"

Reid had been sent to another jobsite around ten, so just Blake and I sat on the tailgate of his truck for lunch break.

"Yeah," I lied to my boss and bit into my boring sandwich while shoving my cell into my pocket for good—or at least until I went back to work.

"Youngs on the brain?" he asked as a gold BMW i8 pulled through the jobsite entrance gate.

"Yeah." I eyed the sweet car. "Isn't that Micah's new ride?"

"Looks like it," Blake said, checking out the shiny vehicle entering a dust zone. "He's dropping off some plans for his office remodel. Probably gonna bitch about getting his baby dirty."

I snorted and bit into my sandwich again, wishing for chicken salad with grapes.

"How's my favorite pimp?" Blake asked with a grin as Micah strode toward us in slacks and button-down, a folder in his hands.

"Fuck off, Harper," Micah said and nodded at me. "How's it going, Payne?"

"What's up, Fox?" I spoke around my mouthful.

"I got your text about stopping by. Are those the plans?" Blake asked.

Micah handed over the folder. "I was going to send them over via email but was up this way and figured you'd be here. You guys are making good progress."

Blake glanced over the condos he and I faced. "This place is going to be gorgeous when we're done."

"Sucks for the people on the other side of the road," Micah said. "Did you have any problems getting the permits to build?"

"Lots of squawkers didn't want their view of the river cut off, but the town cares more about having more residents to tax than pleasing three homeowners," Blake answered and glanced through the file Micah had brought.

"Speaking of homeowners across the street," I said, "did Wren cave to your charms?"

I learned that a pretty little dark-haired woman lived across from the jobsite and had caught Blake's eye.

"Who's Wren?" Micah asked.

"Blake's latest conquest. Can you believe she had the gall to say no when he asked her out Monday during break? Turned him down flat," I said.

"I figured I would take her coffee every morning when she gets home from her night shift at the pharmacy," Blake explained. "She'll fold eventually."

"Maybe at that point of her day she doesn't want caffeine," I said with a snicker. "Try offering to sing her lullabies or some shit."

Micah snorted. "Fucker can't carry a tune."

"Fuck off," Blake shot back although there wasn't a speck of anger in his dark blue eyes. "I'm a goddamn canary."

I shared a look with Micah before we both burst into laughter.

"I tried again Tuesday, but she shut me down," Blake mumbled.

"And you got to the jobsite too late this morning to bug her with a cup of coffee she probably doesn't want anyway."

"If you need any help getting someone under you," Micah said, "I'm your man."

"I don't do dick," Blake reminded him, his tone bland as he studied the blueprints for Micah's office.

Micah punched his shoulder, and Blake tipped into me with exaggeration, dropping the file to hold his offended arm. "That hurt, you prick."

"Did not," Micah scoffed. "Back to business. I'm always looking for men on my team." He glanced at me, an eyebrow raised.

I shook my head, same as the last ten times he'd bugged me to be one of his escorts. Shoving another bite of my sandwich into my mouth shut down the conversation of why. My reasons had changed from not interested to looking for real love and the situation I'd landed in because of it.

The lack of communication, the not knowing, was doing weird things to my brain and giving me indigestion or some shit. I'd been pretty confident that Madeline would be able to reason with Hudson and an invitation for another night together would come through.

When I'd fished while driving her home from the altercation with their asshole ex, she'd outright told me she'd had feelings for me too and wanted to hook up again. And how she'd leaned on me, allowed me to comfort her even after we'd gotten to their house and Hudson stood mere feet away—there was no doubt in my mind she trusted me with her emotions.

Surely Hudson had seen that? He'd definitely noted the way I'd made myself available to her. He'd thanked me for fuck's sake.

Goddamn stubborn ass.

Maybe I should have slammed him into the wall and taken charge since he'd been too much of a chickenshit to make a move. I'd gotten all up in his space. Tempted him to command me to my knees like his eyes told me he'd wanted to do.

But I got the door shut in my face instead of the taste I'd been salivating for. Guess the wooden barrier gave the coward the strength to let me go.

"The plans are pretty straightforward," Blake said as I popped the last bite of my lunch in my mouth out of habit rather than hunger. "I can have an estimate over to you sometime tonight."

"Sounds good, but the job is yours," Micah told him. "Money isn't a problem, and I trust you to be fair."

"The escort business is going that well, huh?" Blake asked, putting the folder aside and picking back up his own ham on a fat Kaiser roll.

I eyed my second sandwich. *Maybe I ought to start spoiling myself.* I knew how to make chicken salad. I could even grab grapes and cut them up into tiny pieces for that burst of sweetness.

"I'm seriously looking to hire a couple more guys," Micah said, and I shook my head before he asked *again*, my mind once more going back to Madeline and how she'd made me muffins, cookies, lemonade...god, what a sweet, thoughtful woman. And that ass. Those plump breasts perfect for resting my head on. Her lips and tongue I couldn't stop dreaming about tasting once more.

Clearing my throat, I hopped off Blake's tailgate and headed back to work where I could take out some aggression since there was no place on the site to empty my balls. Somehow, I managed to not check the app for a whole ten minutes.

It felt like ten goddamn months.

20

HUDSON

Nine days after I punched the wall, my hand still wasn't back to normal. I had trouble grasping a chainsaw, so I left that work to my employees. Raking up the smaller shit from the trees falling to break apart on the ground proved easier, and I popped on my headphones to block out the noise and set to my task.

Too often, my mind wandered to the dark-haired carpenter I'd sent away. Longing deep inside me to touch, to taste, to connect continued to mess with my brain. But I couldn't relent. Couldn't allow the walls I'd built around my heart to lower.

I'd experienced hurt almost my entire life by not being given love from the two people who should have. Having Peter looking at me like I was his hero, his savior, had knitted together parts of my soul my parents had ignored. His betrayal had laid waste to my ability to trust. To love outside the rock of my wife.

But fuck, how my body yearned, burned to enjoy that kind of bond again. Another man to fill the void Peter had left.

The war continued. Daily. And I attempted to keep myself busy enough to escape thoughts of Colton.

We were clearing a partial lot for our customer's new addition and had been working there for a couple of days. The job was bigger than my usual, but I had the manpower and equipment to get it done. A lower bid had landed me the job on the rocky acreage across town from home. Not that I needed any leads for the next six months at least, but I still stuck Young's Tree Service signs out along the road in front of their house to advertise.

We'd finished for the day, and I stood with the homeowner in his driveway to discuss final payment when a car I recognized pulled alongside my sign.

Peter's brand new Camry I'd bought him for Christmas the year before.

I'd been waiting for him to contact me about Mads's purse and had about given up thinking he'd been the one to take it from outside the library.

He climbed from his car with her bag in his hand. His blond hair had grown a bit longer, and he wore his usual tight skinny jeans and a green shirt to make his eyes pop— my favorite look on him.

"Shit," I muttered, the sight of him punching my gut with a dose of sadness and rage.

And the thought that Colton was ten times the man Peter could ever hope to be.

"You know him?" the homeowner asked.

"Yeah and not exactly someone I want to talk to." My stomach clenched along with every muscle in my body.

"Want me to take care of it?" The man I'd been working for was a local police officer and had probably noted my instant tension.

"I'll handle him—but this might get...a little ugly words-wise. How about I swing by tomorrow to pick up the check?"

"Sounds good. I'll be right inside, so just holler if you need me to intervene in any way."

I nodded, shook his hand, and turned to find Peter stopped a few feet from me. Large, doe-like eyes peered up at me through lowered lashes, his pupils pinned from the bright sunlight.

I crossed my arms to keep my fists tucked away, spread my feet wider, and held his stare until he glanced at the driveway. His act of submission lacked the power to rush arousal through my blood like it would have the year before.

The sound of the cop's front door closing settled heavily between us, and I forced my focus to stay in the present rather than meandering to the way Colton had obeyed my every command with no argument.

"Mads dropped her purse." Peter clutched it to his narrow chest, his voice hoarse as though longing to keep it as a prized possession.

"And it took you nine days to return it." I didn't need an explanation as to why. Just like with her body and her clothing, he'd found comfort in holding it close since she'd denied him on the library steps.

"I've been wanting to talk to you," he whispered so I barely heard.

"Well I have nothing to say to you." I held out my hand. "Give me the purse."

He toyed with the strap, his slender fingers shaky. "I will after I state my mind."

"You'll hand it over now, or I'll take it."

His gaze shot up at my threatening tone. "You wouldn't hurt me," he barely breathed the words.

"After what you did?" I shook my head, hardening my stare to match the granite in my heart. "You're playing with fire seeking me out like this, Peter."

"I was wrong."

"Goddamn right, you were." I didn't bother trying to hide my harsh tone or keep it from rising along with the heat flushing through my body.

"I made a mistake."

He'd said the same thing the night I threw him out of our house, and same as then, anger lay ready to unleash on his scrawny ass. At least the initial heartache I'd experienced no longer ripped across my chest. "What's your point?" I bit out the question, ready for our conversation to be over so I could get away from the mere sight of him.

"I want another chance."

My head shook before he even finished speaking. "No way in hell."

Those big eyes of his welled, and he shifted toward me like a scared, innocent lamb in need of protection.

But I had become the big bad wolf who wanted to rip his head off, not some friendly lumberjack who would wrap him in my arms like I used to do.

"Don't come any closer to me," I said, my low rumble shivering over him with deadly intent lacing every word.

His lips parted, and tears slid down his cheeks. "I miss you. Miss our Mads."

"She's no longer yours," I reminded him, my tone cutting. "You gave up that right the night you offered your body to another man. You come near her one more time, and I swear to fucking God—"

"One mistake can't ruin what we have, Hudson!" His voice raised as his lower lip trembled. "Three years of absolute heaven, and you would let one wrong choice keep us from finding happiness again?"

I dug my fingernails into my palms where they buried beneath my armpits so I wouldn't grab him and shake some sense into his pea-sized brain.

"It's been seven months," I hissed through my teeth, bending toward him—but the little shit didn't cower. His hint of stubborn brat I recognized was something...more than what it used to be.

Without the blinders of love, I saw it for what it was.

"Why are you really here, Peter?" I asked, stepping closer, my arms uncrossing.

He still held his ground.

"Hmm?" I pushed for an answer when he didn't offer one. "Did whatever sugar daddy you found after I kicked you out realize what a manipulative little whore you are and tell you to get lost too? Are you having to live out of the car I was kind enough to not come after and reclaim?"

Peter lifted his chin, but his gaze flitted away. "It simply took me this long to realize what I'd given up."

"Bullshit." I spat at his feet, my body starting to buzz with the need to throttle his ass. "Want to hear how I know you're lying?" I didn't give him a chance to answer. "Your mouth is open."

His brow furrowed with darkness I'd never seen before.

"What?" I asked. "Don't like to hear the pathetic truth?"

"Shut up!" Tears no longer filled his eyes, but anger flushed his cheeks. "Just shut up!"

I towered over him, goading him into attacking so I could *defend* myself. "You're nothing but a needy little bitch who will say and do anything to get what you want. Free rent. Free food. Money in your bank account. A fucking new car!" I hollered, waving my hand toward the Camry.

"Shut up!" Peter shrieked and swung the purse at my head.

Grinning, I grabbed it before it made contact and yanked, pulling him against my chest when he didn't release his hold. "Stay the fuck out of our lives, Peter. You're no longer welcome," I hissed the words and shoved to get him away. Had we been anywhere except a cop's driveway, I'd have planted my fist into his nose.

Peter tumbled backward, lost his hold on the purse, and fell to the driveway. I stepped in to loom over him as he cried out, clutching his head that had snapped back to hit the blacktop. "Ow!" He rolled into a fetal position, and I noted the blood on his hands but had zero fucks to give.

"You come near my wife again," I warned him, my voice low and shaking, "and I'll end you. Understand?"

"Hudson!"

Shit.

I turned to find the cop hurrying toward us, eyeing me warily. "Step away from the boy."

I did as told, my hands in the air, purse dangling from my right fist.

"Are you okay?" he asked, kneeling down beside Peter.

The waterworks started up, his face crumpling. "I-I was j-just bringing his wife's purse back to him," Peter all but wailed.

I rolled my eyes over his theatrics. "He's full of shit," I stated over his whining, but the cop shot me a glare.

Knowing the manipulative little prick, I suddenly realized how much shit he could rain down on me. A niggle of worry slid through my bloodstream, cooling me instantly.

"Stay put and be quiet," the cop told me. "I'll deal with you in a minute."

Shit. What had gone down couldn't have looked good for me.

The cop checked over Peter's head, and I rifled through Mads's purse for a pack of tissues.

"Here." I tossed it onto the ground.

The cop pressed a tissue to the wound that Peter cried over like I'd hit him with a goddamn axe rather than simply shoving him to get him.

"You're going to be fine," the cop assured him. "It's just a small cut, but head wounds always bleed a lot. You don't even need stitches."

Peter continued to wail, his cries like fingernails on a damn chalkboard. "I-I want to p-press charges! He-he shoved me, and I d-didn't do anything but give him her p-purse! He threatened to k-kill me if I didn't g-get away from him!"

"Calm down, son." The cop tried to shush Peter who glanced up at me through his tears. Calculation lit, and I readied for what I knew was coming next.

"But Hudson," he said, "we can sit down tonight like a family and figure this out. You'll give me another chance, and I won't get you into trouble, okay?"

There was no hesitation in his voice, no stumble or stutter over words when seconds ago he'd been full of it.

The cop had seen me shove the little shit unprovoked physically, and I doubted not wanting him in my personal space would be reason enough to *make* someone step back.

The fucker.

I nodded an agreement to Peter's bullshit suggestion because what else could I do while a goddamn cop knelt between the two of us, giving the piece of shit his phone number if Peter changed his mind about pressing charges?

Peter would show up at our house. We would sit, and I would let him talk. But there would be no second chances.

Lucky for him, he now had a cop in his back pocket if things went to shit. I had to keep my hands to myself no matter how badly I wanted to break his pretty face.

21

MADELINE

Tara and I sat down for lunch together for the second time since I'd met her at support group the week before. Saturday had been four hours of both of us sharing our stories over salads with grilled chicken and two glasses of wine each.

I'd even told her about the mess with Colton, which made my chest ache with longing.

She didn't judge Hudson or me for our lifestyle and admitted to enjoying a little pain with her pleasure, how her husband sometimes shared her with another couple who played at a BDSM club in downtown Boston.

I invited her over the following Friday for lunch since she was off work, and I had no baking orders to fill.

It was five o'clock somewhere, so I mixed up a couple of margaritas to go with the fish tacos I'd made. After lunch, I took her upstairs to the nursery.

We stood in silence just inside the doorway.

"I used to spend a lot of time in that rocking chair," I said, my chest heavy but no tears in my eyes. "I try not to think about the what-ifs, but it's so damn hard some days."

Tara took my hand and squeezed. "We hadn't done more than paint the nursery for Mia, but I sit in the middle of the empty room and do the same. I struggle with creating a new space. It..." She swallowed audibly when her voice broke. "I'm afraid that if we fill that place with something else, I'll forget about her. It'll be one less memory, you know?"

"I do," I whispered, my eyes welling. "But maybe someday, you can prepare that room for another child."

She nodded and rubbed the wetness from her cheek with her free hand. "We're already trying, but I refuse to get my hopes up or even dream. It hurts too much."

Hollowness resided in my lower abdomen rather than an ache where my womb used to be.

"At least you have the choice to try again," I whispered, my throat going tight.

"Oh, Madeline." Tara threw her arms around me, and we shared tears of sorrow few others would ever truly understand.

She left a couple of hours later, and I sat in the rocker, eyeing the pink walls. The butterflies on the small quilt hanging over the crib's side bar. The mobile of fireflies silent and still. Stacks of newborn diapers and spit cloths on the changing table's first open shelf.

Dozens of outfits lay folded in the drawers below.

Everything was going to waste sitting in a bedroom that would never hear a newborn's cries.

My chest went heavy, and the darkness began to close in.

But I didn't want to wallow anymore. I was tired of tears and heartache. Sadness and feeling sorry for myself.

I needed to live. Breathe again. Experience intimacy that had fallen once more to the wayside since Hudson's lie the week before. I hadn't spoken a word, and we'd reverted into the rut of going through the motions.

No meaningful discussions.

No affectionate touches.

No sex.

I had made the decision to lead by example but hadn't been able to find the strength to choose a different course when faced with the opportunity to initiate.

But Tara had. She'd decided to try for another baby with her husband regardless of fear of losing another child. That kind of heartache and pain would be ten times worse than Hudson and I fighting through the issues that had arisen from his damn stubbornness since meeting Colton.

I pulled open Maya Joy's closet door without realizing I'd gotten to my feet. Bins of diapers from our baby shower stood stacked on the floor. Boxes of wipes, bottles of baby wash and powder filled a basket atop the shelf. Over a dozen blankets sat folded and waiting for use—and I was done holding onto goods when someone else might need them.

Like I'd shed a heavy cloak, the weight lifted off my shoulders as I settled my mind into being proactive and went downstairs to grab a couple of trash bags from beneath the kitchen sink.

A quick glance out the window to the deck beyond reminded me of Colton. His smirk, the light in his eyes whenever I'd handed him a snack or cool drink and he would blurt out questions to make me linger outside with him to chat about mundane things. The feel of his lips. His tongue between my thighs. The way he'd held my gaze when thrusting into my body, as though trying to burrow into my heart and soul.

Arousal licked down my spine, and I turned away, focusing on the steps I could take on my own to move forward.

Hudson arrived home late from work by the time I'd

emptied Maya Joy's closet, changing table, and small dresser. I had even stripped the crib and packed up the sheets and blankets along with the pink curtain hung above the room's lone window.

That sense of lightness, of relief, remained, spurring me onward in making change even though I'd shed a few tears while working.

"Mads." Hudson stood in the doorway. Shoulders hunched and scowl denting his brow, he glanced around the room, seemingly pissed at what I'd chosen to do.

He'd been pushing me for months to pack up the room...

"You're mad."

He turned toward me, shaking his head. "No," he rasped out. Wetness welled in his eyes, and he hurried across the room to pull me against his chest.

His heart thrummed beneath my ear, his muscles quivering.

"What's wrong?"

"Peter."

My hackles raised. "What did he do now?"

"Showed up at the jobsite to give me your purse back."

But that wasn't all he'd done. Once Hudson filled me in on the events of the previous hour, I too vibrated with rage.

"He's coming *here*?" I barely kept my voice from a shriek.

"I didn't have a choice, Mads. It was either agree or have possible charges brought up against me. The cop saw everything."

"You shouldn't have shoved him!"

Hudson didn't speak, but his whiskers twitched as though he'd clenched his jaw.

"Sorry." I swallowed hard and grabbed his hand, my

insides a trembling mess. "Let's go downstairs and get something to eat for dinner. Maybe have a drink or three."

"No alcohol for me," Hudson said, following me out of our spare bedroom. "I need to be in complete control for when that little shit shows up here and tries to manipulate us into letting him into our bed again."

"That's not going to happen," I snipped, grasping onto anger instead of the fear twisting my stomach.

"Agreed. But we have to at least hear him out without getting pissed and make him realize he stands no chance of getting back what he threw away."

"There's going to be tears," I warned, shivering at the memory of how he'd clung to my knees outside the library.

"He can cry a river for all I care."

"What if he gets violent?" I asked, following Hudson down the stairs.

"Then you call the cops."

I'd never seen Hudson take down a man, but Peter? "Do you think you can keep your fists to yourself?"

"I'm sure as fuck going to try."

I paused in the living room's entrance, wringing my hands. "It'll be better if we're in the dining room so there's a table between us."

"Good thinking."

"I'm going to set up my cell phone to record too in case he decides to somehow frame you for hurting him."

"I wouldn't put it past him," Hudson muttered. "Come on." He nudged me toward the kitchen. "Do we have any leftovers?"

"Oh...I made the most delicious fish tacos today for me and Tara and have a couple left in the fridge."

"I'm glad you've found a good friend, love."

I smiled even though my stomach still churned over the

night ahead. "Me too. Are you sure you don't want a margarita?"

Hudson declined, but I mixed up an extra strong one for myself. My emotions had about tapped out for the day, and I'd rather be buzzed than sober when facing Peter because I had zero doubt things would get ugly.

Perhaps I would set up Hudson's cell to record from a second angle.

Just in case.

22

COLTON

I continued to honor Hudson's request to leave them alone but couldn't keep from checking out the app like a lovesick fool waiting on a knight in shining armor who had no intention of reaching out to save my hurting heart.

"What's up with you?" Micah elbowed me.

I shoved my cell back in my pocket, trying yet again to focus on the fact I sat in a bar with my buddies on a Friday night and was supposed to be having fun. "Sorry," I muttered and picked back up my beer.

"You look like someone stole your puppy," Micah continued.

Blake snorted a laugh from across the table, damn near losing his mouthful of beer.

"He's pining over a married couple." Reid sat on my left and answered for me. "A daddy and mommy he can call his own."

"You're lucky I like you, Sullivan, or I would pound you to shit," I grumbled at the same time Blake called him an asshole.

Reid chuckled and sipped his beer.

"What happened?" Micah asked, angling on his barstool at our high table to face me fully. The guy had an intense stare and gave off the same sort of protective daddy vibes as Hudson. And while hot as fuck with his perfectly mussed blond hair and baby blues, Micah didn't turn me on like Madeline's husband did.

I offered Micah a quick rundown, everything of which Blake and Reid had already heard.

"Still think you need to try again," Blake said, shaking his head, his bottle of beer hovering near his lips.

"No means no," Micah stated his firm stance when it came to consent.

"That's why I'm sitting here with your sorry asses and not over at their house begging for another chance," I muttered, peeling at my sweaty beer bottle's label.

Micah pulled his buzzing cell from his back pocket, swiped the screen to life, and frowned. "Fuck." His fingers flew while texting. He stopped and waited, his focus on the screen. "One of my guys is puking his guts up and had to cancel tonight. Goddamnit." He started texting again, groaned, and scanned around our small table, his gaze landing on each of us one at a time.

"No. Nope." Reid slammed down the rest of his beer. "I've got plans."

"What plans?" Micah asked.

Micah had been after Reid to join Elite Escorts for months too, but he didn't want to fuck for money any more than I did.

"See that little blonde over there?" Reid nodded toward the bar while sliding off his stool. "She's an old hookup from a few weeks ago and has been giving me eyes all night. I'll see you losers later."

"Asshole!" Blake called after him.

Reid flicked Blake off over his shoulder.

"Colton?" Micah asked. "All you gotta do is sit and watch. It's a married couple who are newly into exploring their kinky sides, which is pretty much just exhibition but in the privacy of their own home. Less than an hour—I'll give you two hundred cash."

Married couple.

The idea of watching anyone but Hudson and Madeline getting it on soured my stomach. "Sorry, no can do."

"Blake—"

"No fucking way." Blake shook his head.

"Come on! I'm desperate over here!"

"I'm stuck on this little bird who lives across the street from the condo project," Blake said, "and she's everything I've ever wanted."

"All you gotta do is watch," Micah pushed. "No touch, no taste, no nothing but keeping your eyes open and enjoying the show."

"Thought you said no means no?"

Micah snorted. "This isn't the same thing, and you know it."

They went back and forth a bit, but I tuned them out, my mind traveling to the couple who'd stolen my attention with a stubbornness that wouldn't relent. It had been two weeks since I'd gotten a taste of Madeline. Fourteen long as fuck days filled with longing, highs, and lows.

I was getting tired of waiting.

"Please, Blake. I'm fucking begging. I'll owe you one."

Blake eyed Micah, his eyes narrowed in consideration. "You'll owe me two."

"Deal." Micah stuck out his hand without hesitation.

"You might regret this," Blake warned, clasping his hand.

"Doubt it. I'll call you an Uber."

"I've only had a couple beers," Blake argued. "I'm not even buzzed." He slid off his stool and pulled a hundred-dollar bill from a wad of cash he had in his pocket. "Send me the address."

Seconds later, I stared at my half-empty beer bottle, my shoulders slouched.

"You've got it bad," Micah said.

"No shit."

"Maybe one last confrontation, one last attempt, wouldn't be the wrong route."

I glanced up at Micah. "No means no."

"He said things ended right there in their entryway."

I nodded, confirming what I'd told him earlier.

"Did Madeline consent to the same?"

"She was upstairs in the shower."

"Then maybe you and she ought to gang up on his ass and talk him into giving you another shot."

"He's a chickenshit." I sipped my beer, barely able to choke it down from the tightness in my throat.

"Then be brave for him."

"What the fuck does that look like?" I asked, not wanting to hope only to have my heart stabbed again.

"Show up vulnerable as fuck and ask for another night. Let him see what it takes to bare yourself to possible hurt because there's an equal chance for reward too."

Lead by example.

I doubted Hudson would ever allow someone else to hold the reins.

I also doubted my simply laying it all out there for him to stomp on would make much difference either. Hudson didn't know my whole past, the rejection I'd felt that had crushed my heart. I hadn't been cheated on, but I understood the type of emotional pain that caused a man to shut down to protect himself, and that made me want to at least try one last time.

Offering Micah my thanks, I headed out, his good luck ringing in my ears.

Driving back toward town, I considered what to say and how. Not wanting to come off as a manipulative needy brat like Peter, I decided on straightforward. No bullshit. I'd fucked around with enough couples to know no polyamorous relationship would survive without open, honest communication.

Still, when I finally arrived at the Youngs and parked across the street, I couldn't make my antsy backside and restless feet take me out of the car. My pulse thrummed, adrenaline crashing all through me like a nor'easter. Made me want to curl in on myself and keep warm against the chill of possible rejection.

I eyed their house, the lights in the living room leaking around the lowered blinds.

Did they sit snuggled on the couch?

Entertain someone else?

My focus jerked to the driveway. One truck, one car.

Alone, then.

I released a heavy exhale, stretching my neck from side to side.

"You got this," I murmured to myself even though I didn't feel like I did, and fear made me want to drive away.

Car lights rounded the corner and flashed into my cab, blinding me momentarily. The vehicle passed me and pulled into the Youngs' driveway behind Hudson's truck.

That little blond shit from the library hopped out and

slammed his door with his hip since he held flowers and a bottle of wine in his hands.

"The fuck?" I scowled, watching Peter prance up their sidewalk with confidence in every step—as though expected.

Wanted.

Teeth gritted, I watched as he fumbled his gifts to free a hand and knocked.

The door pulled inward as though Hudson had been waiting for his arrival.

Peter pushed to his toes, grabbed Hudson's neck, and their lips met.

"Jesus *fucking* Christ." I jerked my head forward, glaring out my windshield, sickened in a flash. My hands clutched the steering wheel in a death grip as my stomach swooped and rolled. "The fuck?" Turning back to make sure I hadn't been seeing things, I caught the door closing behind Peter's tight ass in his skinny jeans.

Hudson had definitely kissed him.

Invited him in.

"Fucking little cunt," I muttered, wondering how the fuck Peter had talked Hudson and Mads into giving him a second chance.

Pain shot through my chest along with a sense of betrayal.

Peter had fucking cheated on them—and they still wanted him in their lives. I'd been nothing but kind. Attentive. Respectful and helpful. A *good* fucking boy.

And they'd rejected me.

Teeth clenched, I willed away the tightening in my throat and forced myself to start my truck back up.

The Youngs didn't want me, so what was the point of sticking around?

At least I was old enough that the state couldn't uproot my life and send me elsewhere.

One good thing about independence—I could choose on my own where to rest my broken heart.

23

HUDSON

Peter caught me off guard.

After the talking I'd given myself to be a goddamn brick wall that couldn't be moved, he still managed to take control of my body for three goddamn seconds before I regained control over my surprise.

Soft palm on my nape, he'd pulled my head down a fraction, just enough for his lips to press against mine.

I jerked back rather than giving him the opportunity to shove his tongue into my mouth where it would have gotten bitten off.

"Come in," I stated through clenched teeth, every cell in my body vibrating with the need to punch his nose clear through his skull.

"Do I smell brownies?" Peter called, his tone as radiant as his smile even though his voice sounded like he'd been screaming at a concert all damn night.

Was the fucking kid unhinged?

Not bothering to kick off his shoes like he knew Mads preferred, he hurried toward the kitchen, flowers and wine in hand.

"Peter," I heard Mads greet him, none too kindly.

"You made me brownies! I could kiss you!" His excited speech grated on my last fucking nerve. It was too bad he hadn't lost his voice doing whatever he'd been up to before knocking on our door.

"Don't."

I hurried forward, finding Mads's hand on Peter's chest to keep him at bay. Fire flashed in her eyes, but she attempted a kind smile at the young man who stood with his back to me.

"Yes, I made you brownies," my wife said. "They're still warm, and I'm getting you some milk too."

"Oh." I could hear the tears in Peter's voice. He turned to set his gifts on the counter, and Mads once more held out her hand to keep him from throwing his arms around her. "You're the best, Mads. Seriously. I couldn't love you any more if I tried."

She forced another smile, her gaze flitting to me.

I nodded toward the dining room and headed that way.

"Why don't you go sit with Hudson, hmm?" Mads suggested. "I'll bring in our snack."

"Okay." Peter used his soft voice, the one that exuded charm and innocence.

Little shit.

I sat at the head of the table, hands resting atop its polished surface.

Grinning, a pink flush on his cheeks, Peter took the seat on my right.

Clobbering him with my dominant fist wouldn't be an easy feat. Still, I shoved my hands beneath my thighs to keep from going all violent on his ass.

"Thank you for allowing me to come over tonight, Hudson." His eyes shone with brightness as he lightly touched my arm. His fingertip trailed from my bicep to my elbow before dropping away.

Clearing my throat, I nodded.

How to placate him and yet make his delusional mind understand that we were done escaped me. Mads and I had been discussing what to do all evening, and beyond physically hurting Peter to the point he couldn't bother us anymore, I hadn't planned jack shit.

His backside shifted with restless energy I'd never seen from him before.

"You wanted to talk," I said, my tone surprisingly calm considering the stormy turmoil inside me, "so talk."

"I'll wait for Mads." He winked, his gaze flitting toward the kitchen. "She baked me brownies," he murmured a second time, his face absolutely glowing.

Perhaps doing so hadn't been the best idea, but Mads had wanted Peter to be relaxed, willing to spill his guts.

Her spoiling Peter had always made him feel loved and safe enough to be vulnerable.

Fuck.

I swallowed hard, hating that he and I had that in common. At least he'd hurt me badly enough that I wouldn't ever be swayed into pitying him or agreeing to let him into our bed ever again.

Mads entered the dining room with a tray loaded with three glasses of milk and three plates with two brownies a piece.

I didn't touch mine but thanked her all the same as she served us with slightly shaking hands.

"Thank you, Mads," Peter said quietly, feigning shy and sweet. "You spoil me."

Mads made a noise beneath her breath—could have

been an agreement, could have been an internal curse over his soul.

I expected the latter.

She sat but didn't touch her brownie as Peter dug in.

"Oh my god," he moaned the words around his mouthful. "I've missed your sweet treats so damn much. So warm and gooey—just how I like them."

Mads didn't bother with a smile in return that time. "I believe my husband asked you to share what brings you here tonight, Peter." She used her firm tone that had often lowered Peter's gaze whenever he'd annoyed her.

I studied his blond head, the swoop of hair over his forehead, the pout on his lips as he shifted his attention to his plate.

What the fuck had Mads and I ever seen in him? Our protective instincts had risen hard and fast, and we'd dove in, heedless of any red flags he must have waved. We'd been blinded by his sweetness, his innocence, his need for stability and a home.

And he'd lavished love on us in return, a bright sparkling firecracker that hadn't allowed either of us to age in the three years we'd been together.

But we hadn't noticed the immaturity, the insecurities, until it had been too late.

An image of Colton laboring over our deck flashed through my mind, hitting me like a punch to the gut. Sweaty and focused on work, he was ten times the man Peter was and didn't have a whiney bone in his hot body—

"I've been an absolute ass," Peter said, licking a brownie crumb from his pinkie.

I snorted, and he shot a glare at me. "Go on," I stated firmly, my attention back where it needed to be. Daydreaming about a man I wanted but refused to allow myself to enjoy—all thanks to the punk-ass bitch sitting beside me—needed to stop.

Lips pursed, he stared at me an extra few seconds, as though trying to read how to break me down.

He wouldn't.

As though recognizing that fact, he turned toward Mads. "I made a mistake."

"Of the worse sort," she stated before he could blather on.

He nodded, taking interest in the second untouched brownie before him. "I-I realize that I must have hurt you both terribly. I can't...can't even imagine your emotional responses when you walked into our bedroom. He meant nothing to me." Peter's voice cracked, but neither Mads nor I made a move to comfort him like we would have done before.

"I acted in childishness. Out of insecurity. It was wrong of me to behave in such a manner and try to make you understand how I felt when a simple conversation would have been more than enough." His hoarse voice broke as though on the edge of tears.

I rolled my eyes, shaking my head when Mads glanced at me. The idiot could have at least come up with something more persuasive.

But not even dropping to his knees and sticking out his tongue for my cum or shoving down his skintight jeans and bending over the table in front of me would have moved me toward forgiveness. Those actions wouldn't have interested my dick in the way Colton's had.

I clenched my jaw, once more setting aside thoughts of the carpenter with the tight ass and how protective he'd been of Mads.

It was Peter's fault Colton had become forbidden fruit.

"I'm sorry for manipulating the circumstances, Hudson," Peter murmured, glancing up at me through his lashes as though hoping to woo me. I'd rather have mangled his pretty face. "I'd been desperate and took advantage of the cop being there...the blood." He touched the back of his head. "I'm fine, by the way."

I didn't give a shit but nodded as though I did.

"This place..." he trailed his focus around the room to the kitchen beyond, shifting on the chair again. "This is home to me. I felt it the first time you invited me in the front door. Warmth. Acceptance. Hope. And to think I almost fucked it all up," he murmured while shaking his head.

"You did," I corrected, crossing my arms since my hands had begun to fall asleep beneath my thighs.

Peter blinked up at me with puppy dog eyes that glazed over with wetness again.

Surely he remembered I wasn't moved by tears like Mads had always been.

As though seeing my inner coldness in my gaze, he turned once more toward Mads. "I've been staying with...a friend, but he started doing drugs a few months ago." Peter swallowed hard, a tear spilling down his cheek. "I-I snorted coke with him. Just the once, I swear! I didn't like it—don't want to do it anymore, but now he's all up in my space, trying to pressure me into partying with him and the friends who are always there."

I didn't give a flying fuck if he started shooting that shit into his veins.

The indifference on Mads face faded. She had a cousin who'd gotten tangled up with the wrong sort of friends and ended up paying for it with her life—and the little fucker giving her those big, pleading eyes knew that fact.

"I really have to get out of there." Peter rubbed his lips

together and smiled at my wife through his watery eyes as his nose began to run. "I have no place that's safe. Nowhere else to go. I—I need help."

Mads glanced at me, but I shook my head as he continued to blather on.

No. Fucking. Way.

"Peter." Mads smiled, cutting him off mid-sentence about how he hoped to escape his friend's apartment. "Hudson and I need some time to discuss this."

"How long?" he whispered, his lower lip trembling.

I wanted to smash it against his teeth while asking Mads what the fuck she was thinking. We needed him out the door. Gone from our lives for good. Not to drag this shit on.

"Not long," she answered kindly, her voice motherly. "I'll give you a call once we've come to a decision."

"O-Okay." He nodded, swallowed hard again, and glanced at his brownie. "I guess I can stay locked up in my room for a few more days—but my roommate is seriously persistent. I-I'm afraid..."

Mads stood and rounded the table behind me to squat down beside Peter.

My lungs seized at her show of concern.

"Hang in there, Peter," she whispered. "You're so strong inside. I have faith in you to make the right decision this time around. Hud and I will discuss a possible second chance, but you have to be patient, okay?"

He nodded quickly, scooting back his chair to wrap his arms around her.

Foreheads pressed together, they shared air while I fought off the desire to grab the back of his head and smash it against the table we'd shared too many meals at.

I ground my teeth. Swallowed the growl wanting to radiate up from my guts to ask Mads what the fuck!

Mads pulled away and stood. "Let me wrap up the rest of the brownies, and I'll walk you out."

Unable to move, I watched Peter scamper after her into the kitchen like a little kid. Twenty-five and he still acted like a spoiled brat, and not the good kind. But Mads led him into her domain, their quiet murmurs reaching my ears—but not their words.

Why had she gone soft toward him? Why allow him to press his forehead to hers? Why use that sweet tone that always revealed she relented?

Had she truly given into his bullshit, his obvious playing on her emotions?

Tension kept my shoulders up near my ears. My wife had a heart of gold. Forgiving. Loving. Tender. Had Peter actually gotten under her skin with his tale plainly stated to play on her protective nature?

I couldn't fucking move.

Couldn't face the truth that she and I had some serious shit to discuss the second she got his lying ass out the door.

24

MADELINE

Peter had played the perfect contrite spirit that would have at one time made both of our hearts sing out the desire to praise him for being such a good boy.

My stomach churned on the edge of hurling. I couldn't even stand the sweet scent of the brownies I'd baked for him. I'd done so because the chocolate in the air would get him into the house less on edge than Hudson and I had both expected. We'd agreed to keep things quiet. Allow him his say before shutting him down.

But something about Peter's shining eyes, the wildness of his expression regardless of his put together outfit and styled hair raised the hairs on my nape. He wasn't sober. He also wasn't stable.

I'd put both of our cell phones in the dining room like we'd discussed, but there was no way Peter would be leaving that night without some sort of ugly altercation. I could taste the tension in the air, feel it vibrating off Hudson.

Shit would go down. Ugly.

So I took the reins the second I saw an opening, sharing the words Peter needed to hear. Promising to discuss the possibility of a second chance. Anything to give him hope to get his ass out the door so Hudson and I could seek some legal advice on what to do about him.

Whatever shit he'd gotten himself into wasn't good.

He'd lost weight, something I hadn't noticed in the two times we'd run into each other around town. Dark circles clung beneath his eyelashes. Red streaks shot through the whites of his eyes.

All I could think about was my cousin and how one wrong choice had led her down a path that ended with her death. While I despised Peter, I didn't want his life to spiral into addiction—I didn't wish that pain on anyone.

Hudson stayed put at the dining room table when I took Peter to the kitchen. A good choice, since I could feel his vibrating anger at both Peter and me from a room away.

Peter seemed ignorant of the fact my husband wanted to flatten him into a pancake.

My skin crawled as Peter clung to my arm once in the kitchen. My shaking hands packaged up the rest of the brownies.

"You don't know what this means to me, Mads," he said, his voice as husky as my cousin's had become. His pinned pupils almost disappeared in his sea-glass eyes, and a sad smile curved my lips upward.

He had been Hudson's good boy once upon a time. So sweet and loving. Submissive and a complete attention slut in the best way possible.

My heart ached for him regardless of the pain he'd caused us.

"Come along." I laced my fingers through his and led him toward the entryway, instantly nauseous at his touch.

"When will you call me?" he asked, his tone barely above a whisper. "I-I can't stand the thought of going back there." A shiver wracked through his slender body, but I disentangled my hand from his to open the front door.

"Everything is going to be just fine, Peter," I assured him even though I doubted my words. He'd never had a strong constitution and had only ever truly flourished beneath our care.

He threw his arms around me, nuzzling my breasts with a soft sigh.

Bile gurgled in my stomach, but I gave him a few seconds before stepping back. "Go on," I motioned toward the door. "We'll be in touch soon."

"Promise?" he asked, those pleading eyes of his no longer able to sway my heart.

"Promise."

Peter scampered down the stoop and across the walkway, and I forced myself to stand there watching like a mother hen until he climbed in his car, waved, and pulled away.

The second the taillights disappeared, I swallowed against the urge to vomit and quietly shut the door.

I bypassed the dining room for the kitchen.

Stomped the trash bin's foot to open the lid. Tossed in the wilted grocery store bouquet Peter had brought.

Hands still shaking, I twisted off the cheap wine bottle's lid, dumping the contents down the drain. My gaze lifted toward the darkened backyard, the deck Colton had built for us.

An ache swept through my chest, desire atop the mess of emotions already rattling around inside me. My throat tightened as I attempted to push all the feelings down, but they rose regardless, choking and mind consuming.

Too. Much.

And the latest bout of emotional upheaval had started

up over one little lie carelessly tossed out because my husband feared trying again.

Colton was nothing like Peter—they were polar opposites in every way and yet he was a possible perfect fit. At least worth looking into. Hudson had brought him into our lives beyond Harper's Construction, and his insecurities, his inability to be vulnerable again, had slammed down walls where a meandering path could have led us toward something beautiful.

Anger stirred deeper than the rest of the feelings screaming inside me, and I clutched the sink's edge with one hand, remembering Colton's smile whenever I'd taken him muffins or lemonade. His light laughter, his carefree nature, how we'd carried on conversations as though knowing one another for years. Our shared love of the Red Sox. His hatred for raw tomatoes. My enjoyment found in baking— the connection of his spending his free hours in the kitchen in the same way I did.

I hadn't noticed while he'd been working on the deck that we'd connected so effortlessly. I'd been too caught up in my depression, my mind sheltered from possibilities I'd gotten a taste of—

"What the fuck, Mads?" Hudson's barely suppressed anger matched the churn in my stomach. "I thought we were on the same page and yet you drop on your knees like you want to wrap him up in your arms!"

"He's full of shit," I spat, my brain back in the mess of my reality.

"Exactly! So why the fuck lead him into thinking we would consider taking him back?"

I rounded on Hudson, empty wine bottle in hand. "Do you really believe I would let that piece of trash into our lives again? Do you even know me, Hudson? Have you paid even the slightest bit of attention to my depression lately?" He had, but the swell of shit inside me released like a torrential downpour, unhindered and spilling ugliness I couldn't contain.

"Then what the fuck were you doing giving him hope!" Hudson hollered, something he rarely did toward me.

Rather than cowering at his rage that matched my own, I turned toward the recycle bin sitting by the slider. I tossed the empty bottle without rinsing it first, the shatter and clanking of glass not nearly satisfying enough to ease some of my anger.

"So. Many. Damned. Lies," I hissed, feeding off the fire inside me so I wouldn't break down yet again.

"He's full of shit!"

"*You're* full of shit!" I rounded on Hudson, hands on my hips to hide how badly they shook.

He blinked, rearing back as though I'd slapped him. "What?"

"We've always agreed on honesty. Open communication!" Riled up, my mind went toward what I should have confronted days earlier and hadn't. I'd made a mistake in letting it slide but was past the point of being kind to either of us.

"*Exactly.*" His eyes spat fire, arms crossed over his chest as though calling me out for whatever bullshit he thought I was pulling when all I'd been desperate to do was get Peter booted from our house by any means necessary.

For the first time in my life, I wanted to growl at my husband. Hiss like a cat and lash at him with anger. We'd disagreed plenty over the years but never to the point of combustion.

"I overheard your conversation with Colton the other night!" I shot out, my voice on the verge of a scream. "You lied to me about why he'd left, why he wasn't coming over to play again!"

"Mads—"

"He barely knows you and yet offered to have your back, and you just shut him down without giving him a chance!"

Hudson didn't bother arguing that fact or even opening his mouth to make excuses.

Colton had wanted to be there for him.

And Hudson had denied us all.

Wetness glazed over my eyes. I hated—*loathed* that tears got the best of me whenever anger took control. "I am so damn tired, Hudson. Exhausted! There are too many emotions crowding in my head—there have been for months, and to hear you outright lie when you *knew* I was ready to move forward, that I wanted it with Colton...God!"

He visibly sagged, murmuring, "I'm sorry," but I wasn't done.

"Then Peter had to come in here and act in a way that would make me want to break down and wrap him up in my arms." My voice caught. "That lying little *fuck*." I spat the word out, my limbs trembling.

"Let me hold you, love," Hudson whispered, although his hands fisted like he wanted to tear down a wall.

"No!" I shook my head vehemently, my eyes wide to keep tears from spilling. I wasn't about to sag and let sorrow reign supreme again. I'd had enough of that shit. "Absolutely fucking not! I can't even..." Shaking my head, I pushed past him, needing solitude. Quiet. "I'm going to bed—and I want to be alone."

Hudson muttered a curse as I stormed toward the stairs. "Mads!"

"No!" I hollered back. "You made your bed on the

goddamn couch by choosing to lie to me, Hudson Young! You can sleep on it!"

My feet stomped on every tread taking me to the second floor, the thumps not nearly as satisfying in my anger as I'd hoped for.

We were a fucking mess—and I didn't know what to do, didn't have the capacity in that moment to make things right.

25

COLTON

My aching heart didn't want to go home and attempt to relax in bed. I couldn't bring myself to head to the north side of town to the empty house waiting for me, the silence that would make me go insane.

I drove around, still antsy as fuck, my insides quivering. The how, the why of their choice made no fucking sense whatsoever, and the lack of answers wouldn't let my head stop from spinning.

As a kid, I'd never gotten the chance to call out foster families who ended up rejecting me, sending me on to the next house because of something I did or didn't do. Eventually, I learned to be on my best behavior, but that hadn't panned out either. I'd been promised a forever home twice in my "good" years, only to have that rug ripped from beneath me because of stupid choices I'd made.

While Hudson and Madeline had given no such promises, I'd felt one hell of a connection, had been sure we could have created something better than just a fun fuck fest.

Knowing I wouldn't sleep, that every hour of every

goddamn day would suck until I put shit to rest like I'd been unable to do as a kid, I gritted my teeth and turned back toward the Youngs.

A quick question, an acceptable answer, and I would go curl up somewhere to lick my wounds. I would leave them to reap the consequences of giving that little shit another chance.

Even if their words sucked, I would accept their truth and walk away. I would move on.

I lied to myself though. Seeing how Hudson had allowed Peter back into their lives, that he'd chosen that piece of shit over his wife's emotions riled me the fuck up. What the hell was he thinking? Why would he force even more bullshit onto Madeline when he knew she couldn't stand that guy's hands on her?

She'd passed out in front of the library for fuck's sake, had been so overcome with too many negative feelings her body couldn't fucking *deal*.

And he'd put his mouth on the kid. Let him inside their home as though forgetting about his betrayal—or at least forgiving, which the asshole didn't deserve.

My jaw ached from clenching, my stomach twisted up tight in a hard knot.

Had Madeline been aware of what Hudson planned, or had he withheld information from her like he'd done when setting up our night together?

If that was the truth, what was the sick fuck thinking?

Pulse pounding and driving a little too fast, I pulled up onto the sidewalk in front of their house. Adrenaline coursed through me, steadily shoving me forward. I threw my truck into park, hopped from the cab, and strode across their front yard.

Peter's car no longer sat in their driveway, but that fact

didn't lessen my hurt or my determination to confront Hudson on why he'd allowed that shithead access to Madeline—to his *mouth* when he'd denied me.

Their shared history had jack to do with it. I knew Hudson wanted to smash the kid's face in as much as I did, so what the fuck?

I skipped up the three stairs to the stoop's landing and rapped three times without hesitation, hard enough my knuckles stung. Jitters coursed through my insides, but I lifted my chin, jaw muscles tight.

The door pulled in—yanked, more like it—and Hudson stared me down with a shit ton of emotions in his eyes.

Surprise.

Anger.

Fire.

My dick perked up so damn fast I swore I heard the *boing!*. I stepped forward without an invite, crowding him enough that he backed into the entryway, stumbling on the rug.

I kicked the door shut with my foot, not taking my eyes off his. "The fuck, Hudson?" I growled the words, demanding an answer.

His hands fisted at his sides, to keep from punching me for barreling in uninvited or grabbing hold of me I couldn't tell. Too much energy radiated between us, a slew of hunger and pissiness that only fed both feelings inside me to the point of blowing the fuck up.

And he smelled so goddamn delicious that my mouth drooled.

Fuck.

"I saw you," I spat out, poking him on his hard chest, the warmth of his skin reaching through his black T-shirt. He didn't flinch, so I poked a second time, desperate to get my hands on him in any way I could. "Putting your mouth on that pretty boy you called a cunt. What. The. Fuck!"

Hudson grabbed my wrist to keep me from poking again, twisting my arm away but not letting go. His grip singed through my skin, clear into my blood, heating me from the inside out.

"Did you fuck him? Hmm?" I seethed through my teeth, not about to pull away from his hold—it felt too fucking good, sending even more restless energy crackling up my arm and straight to my groin. "Bend him over the couch and shove your dick up his tight little ass?"

"Jealous?" Hudson asked, his voice strangely calm considering the accusations I'd spewed and the wildness in his eyes.

"Fucking right I am! And here's some more honesty to show you how that shit ought to be done—it fucking *hurt* that you would give that cheating whore a taste of your mouth when you'd denied me. That you would let him into your house again after how he tried to manipulate and emotionally hurt your wife. And here I am, wanting to support you and shit—and you fucking reject me!"

My nostrils flared as I attempted to suck air into my lungs before continuing on. He didn't utter a word, simply stared at me, the fire in his eyes intensifying to the point I wanted to fight and fall to my knees at the same time.

"You're no different than any other family I thought I might find a home with," I spewed, my chest aching. "Not that I'm looking for a daddy—fuck that shit—"

Hudson grabbed hold of my neck and slammed me against the door. He leaned in, his hazel eyes glinting. "I didn't touch him." His low voice rumbled with barely restrained passion, kicking through me like an adrenaline shot to the balls.

"Bullshit," I rasped, holding onto his wrist with my free hand since he'd pinned the other to the door at my waist.

I could easily have broken free. Shoved him back. Attempted to dominate him physically as I'd done verbally, but I lusted for him to prove me wrong. Make me eat my words. Give in to what he wanted, what I could see raging in his blown pupils.

I leaned into his palm, stealing more of my own air to tempt him past the point of giving a shit about his fear. "You. Kissed. Him. And yet you refuse to let me in when I know every piece of you wants to—fucking longs for it." Pressing my hips forward, I found exactly what I'd expected.

One hell of a boner trapped inside his jeans.

Shit...he was so fucking ready. For me.

I grinned, feeling like a goddamn maniac when he didn't back off—but he didn't grind against me either. "Give me your mouth, Hudson. Let me the fuck *in* like your hard cock tells me you want to."

"No."

He had to go and bite out that fucking word, one I had to respect regardless of how his lying to himself broke my heart.

"Goddamn you," I hissed, wrenching away from his hold as what was left in my chest tore completely in two.

I turned to rip open the door and escape, but he grabbed me by the scruff of the neck, growling like a goddamn animal, and that weakened my knees before I could suck in a breath. He wrenched me toward the living room, and I stumbled beneath his grasp, my feet moving to keep me from falling.

Fuck yes, my mind crowed, tingles sweeping through my body as I allowed him to take the lead. *Let loose, old man, and make me proud. Show me what you got.*

26

HUDSON

R *elentless fucking brat.*

He'd goaded me past the point of giving a fuck about more than showing him...what, exactly? He'd spoken truth, and there was no denying his honesty. Although I hadn't exactly kissed Peter, Colton must have seen the moment the fucker had captured me unaware, pressing his lips to mine.

I burned inside at the thought of him watching. Lusted to show him that I didn't want Peter in the way I did him.

Even pissed and hurting, Colton had gotten hard as fuck from our confrontation, and my dick grew tired of being denied when he'd pressed his groin against mine.

He wanted a good pounding, a taste of me? He could have it and walk away bowlegged and sore. Because that was all the fuck he would get from me.

I shoved him forward into the living room, releasing his neck and causing him to stumble. Colton grasped the edge of the couch to keep from sprawling forward onto the cushions.

Without giving him a chance to spin, I crowded against

him, my nose against the soft skin of his neck, my hands going for the button on his jeans.

He smelled slightly of hops, lust, and virile man in desperate need of being bent over and taken without mercy.

"Want this?" I ground my aching cock against his ass while yanking his zipper down.

"Fuck yes," he groaned, pushing back against me. "Give it to me."

"You aren't calling the shots here," I whispered harshly against his ear, yanking his jeans and boxers down to his thighs. "My house, my rules, and you're going to take my dick like a good little boy without complaint."

"Christ," he rasped, a hard shudder ripping through him.

"Now bend the fuck over the armrest and spread yourself for me."

I dropped to my knees, yanking his jeans to his ankles with me while he did as told.

He gripped his ass cheeks, pulling them apart, offering me his smooth puckered hole.

So fucking pretty—I wanted to burrow in and wreck him from the inside out.

My cock bucked, and I shoved my face into his crack, groaning deeply as his musk filled my nose. I worked my length loose of its prison while licking and probing at Colton's ass, wanting so damn deep inside him that he lost his breath while hollering my name.

"Fucking hell, Hudson," he moaned, another shudder rippling through his body.

I smeared pre-cum over my length, tugging and edging myself while eating his ass, drinking down his curses and mutterings.

"So good," he whimpered, lifting his backside like a

bitch in heat, his chest and face on the cushion. "Need more —give me more."

Squeezing the base of my dick, I rimmed him with a fingertip, smearing saliva around his clenching hole. Without warning, I shoved in deep to the knuckle, taking Colton up onto his toes.

"Fuck!"

"Mmm," I hummed under my breath, leaning forward again to lick around my finger, feeling up his silken walls. His insides burned with heat I craved to have wrapped around my cock.

Another droplet of pre-cum oozed from me, and I spread it down my length, working myself in time with my finger fucking Colton's ass.

Needed inside. Deep.

A creak on the stairs sounded—Madeline no doubt had heard us and came to investigate—but I didn't give a fuck. She would be nothing but a puddle of arousal once she caught sight of what went down.

I would deal with her *I told you sos* later.

Dropping my dick, I went for Colton's, reaching between his legs and the couch to find him steel-like and sticky.

"Leaking for me already?" I asked against his cheek, nipping hard enough he gasped.

"Fuck, yes." He moved back a bit, offering me room. A few strokes over and inside him, and he panted. "Wanna come—let me come."

"No." My voice didn't allow for argument, but he moaned like a needy little slut, working against my thrusting finger.

"Give me another."

I didn't bother with spitting, just shoved a second finger into his ass.

"Jesus fucking Christ!" He bucked forward, but I followed, my forearm flexing to reach deep into his ass.

"Hudson," Mads whispered, but I ignored her.

"You like that?" I taunted Colton, rubbing over his prostate.

"Shit yeah." He shuddered, collapsing his chest onto the cushion once more, grabbing hold of my wrist that jerked him off. "Feels so fucking good."

"Like a little pain with the pleasure of someone stroking deep inside you, huh?"

"Hell yes," he groaned, his back arching again.

"Bet if I shoved my bare dick up your asshole right now, you'd shoot your load all over our couch before I painted your insides with mine."

He whimpered, and I worked a third finger in, twisting and thrusting, so goddamn hard for him.

"Don't hurt him," Mads stated quietly, the break in her voice pure lust. She moved into my periphery, close enough to touch, close enough to see how I owned that boy's ass with just my fingers.

"I want it, Lin," Colton said, turning his head. Sweat dotted his forehead, and pink stained his cheeks. "Want his dick raw inside me. Want to feel him for fucking days, his cum leaking out of my body."

"Hudson," my wife whispered, looking for my usual control. Consent.

"Is it safe for me to take you like this?" I asked, hissing as his asshole clenched around my probing fingers. "Because I promise you have nothing to worry about on our end."

We'd made doubly sure of that after Peter's betrayal.

"Yes—swear to fucking Christ—I'm on PrEP, and 'll show you the picture on my cell of my test results from before I even met you two if you want. Please give me your dick. Fucking *need* it."

I pulled away from him abruptly enough he winced and cursed, but Mads stepped in, grabbing hold of my cock before I could.

Cool wetness smeared over me.

I turned to find her face flushed and lips parted, a bottle of lube in her other hand along with an ignored condom. Pupils blown, her nipples furled beneath her silk robe, she stared at the small distance between Colton's backside and my throbbing dick.

"You knew," I stated, and she lifted her gaze.

The silent hunger in her eyes only heightened my need for him. "I heard every word and guessed where you would both end up."

"You hoped I would fuck him." I didn't bother asking. I could see the truth spelled out in her widened eyes and the pulse thrumming in her neck.

"Yes—but don't be an animal about it, Hudson. Hurt him, but only in a good way."

I stepped forward when she tugged. She reached out for Colton's hip with her other hand, her focus moving to his face as he peered over his shoulder at us.

"I need him," he told her before glancing at me. "Be as rough as you want, Hudson."

My stomach tightened, restless energy demanding I slam inside him and rip a few curses from his lips.

"Bear down and let him in," Mads murmured, teasing the tip of my dick over Colton's hole.

Colton obeyed.

"Ah, fuck," I muttered as his ring clasped around the head of my cock.

"I want to watch you take all of my husband's dick," Mads said while backing off.

Colton groaned, and I grabbed hold of his waist.

"Hope you're ready—" I yanked him toward me as I thrust.

He let out a string of curses, hands grasping at the cushions, but I plowed in until his hips hit the armrest.

Madeline whimpered a delicious sound that tightened my groin even further.

Buried deep, I paused, my dick throbbing at the heat inside his body squeezing around me. I had to fucking pause to appreciate how he clasped at me, the warmth of him attempting to suck me deeper. The heat of Mads's gaze flared fire through me.

I groaned, gyrating my hips to work in farther even though my balls already rubbed over his taint. "Such a sweet little hole."

"Such a big fucking cock," Colton gasped out as I flexed my hips, shivers pebbling the skin on his forearms.

Leaning over him, I rumbled my approval of his appreciative tone. I'd wanted a fast, hard fuck, but he felt so goddamn good. I wanted to savor him this one time I allowed myself to enjoy what I'd lusted for since the first day I'd laid eyes on the man.

Shifting my hips back, I dragged from his silken clasp, thankful Mads had brought lube downstairs. His hole was sloppy wet, so goddamn *luscious* around my cock.

"Goddamn, boy, you feel so fucking good," I moaned through clenched teeth.

Rather than stabbing into him, I slid forward, enjoying the slick glide, the way his asshole gobbled up my dick like it was his last meal. My drawn up balls rested against his, and I rubbed us together.

"Hudson," he whispered, once more looking over his shoulder. Dark eyes overrun by the blackest pupils. Fathomless wells, wanting to suck in and bewitch my soul.

It wasn't supposed to be that perfect. I wasn't supposed to crave submission to his need. And I sure as fuck wasn't supposed to lust for his mouth, his parted lips begging for my tongue and teeth.

Hard fucking limit.

Turning my attention on where I penetrated his pliant body, I backed out, groaning once more at how he squeezed around me as though attempting to keep me forever.

Never that—not ever again.

But I would enjoy the fuck out of his hot ass and make him paint our floor with his cum. Drink up his cries before finding my own pent-up release and filling him with my load.

27

MADELINE

I'd heard the rap on the door and peeked out the blinds. My heart had sped at seeing Colton's truck.

Then the raised voices, rich with lust and want, anger and hurt drew my attention.

Already riled from Peter and our argument, Hudson would be on edge. It would only take a few well-placed words from Colton to get him where he wanted to be. Either on his knees or ass up for my husband.

And my body burned for the same to the point I went breathless before hurrying to the bedside table for condoms and lube. There was no way in hell I was taking a chance things would hopefully make their way upstairs before their sanity came down a few notches and Hudson ended up denying what he wanted yet again.

My pulse raced as I scurried across the floor, the heat in Hudson's rumbled tone from downstairs tightening my nipples to hard points. Warmth spread through me, rushing arousal through me.

I reached the top of the stairs, so damn turned on that I

trembled at the sight of Hudson grabbing hold of Colton's neck and shoving him toward the living room.

Gulping, I started down on shaking legs, keeping quiet until I absolutely needed to interfere.

"Want this?" I heard Hudson growl just outside of my line of sight.

Colton rasped out a command for Hudson to give it to him.

In typical Hudson form, he reminded Colton who was in charge, whose house he was in. "...you're going to take my dick like a good little boy without complaint."

My core pulsed at his words, remembering how much Colton had enjoyed being called that on our one night together.

I crept farther down the stairs, desperate to see, to watch without interruption unless necessary.

The living room came into sight, and I paused, my breath catching at the sight of Hudson's face buried between Colton's ass cheeks. Their combined groans rose, and I bit my lip to keep from whimpering.

Hudson pushed his thick finger into Colton's hole without lube. I grimaced as Colton went up onto his toes with a curse.

My husband was out to make a point so Colton knew who he messed with, but I refused to let him hurt the younger man.

Another step released a creak from the stair I stepped on, but neither man paused or turned. Hudson continued to finger fuck Colton's ass and began to jerk him off.

Hudson shoved in another finger alongside the first, and I hurried down the stairs.

I whispered my husband's name, moving toward them as Colton admitted to liking the discomfort.

When Hudson worked in a third finger, I whispered, "Don't hurt him."

Those dark, bedroom eyes met mine, and I swallowed a moan at the need, the lack of fear in Colton's expression. "I want it, Lin."

The pain...and Hudson bare.

"Hudson," I murmured, needing absolute honesty and consent for what was about to go down between the two men.

He asked for my permission.

I gave it—and physically brought the two men together.

Both of them cursed as Hudson thrust forward, trapping Colton against the side of the couch.

Most wives would turn jealous, but I only burned with the need for more. Staring and silent, I parted my lips in an attempt to fill my lungs as Hudson's glistening dick slid in and out of Colton's hole.

"Knew it," Colton moaned. "Fucking knew you would feel this good inside me."

Hudson murmured an agreement, his wide hands grasping tight to Colton's hips.

"I'm so close...fucking hell, Hudson."

"Wait," my husband stated firmly but didn't give the whining man beneath him pause to collect himself.

The wet sounds of fucking and the slap of skin on skin heightened my desire until I panted, my entire body itching for physical touch.

I stepped behind Hudson and grabbed his ass cheeks, feeling them as they flexed, giving his dick to Colton in harsh thrusts. Taut and muscular, Hudson's backside begged for my teeth, but I lusted for more.

"Feed him your pussy, love," Hudson grunted the words at the same time I imagined the same.

A quick shimmy rid me of my panties, and I climbed onto the couch.

Colton planked onto his hands, his back deeply arched, jolting from every slam of Hudson's hips. His dark eyes held mine captive, a gorgeous pink flush over his cheeks.

Skin pebbling, I shifted my lower half beneath him on the couch, his hand on my hip helping to maneuver me where he wanted. One leg slung upward over the back of the couch, the other on the floor.

"Right there..." His gaze slid down over my shivering form while my robe gaped open to reveal my belly and wet pussy. "Goddamn, Lin."

Hudson held still, his hands rubbing up beneath Colton's T-shirt over his back. "Make my wife come, then you can too."

"Aw fuck." Colton swallowed hard and settled in to feast.

My hips rose up at the swipe of his warm tongue, and I grasped his hair. "Oh God," I moaned, head tipping back as the energy and lust in the room overrode my senses.

The sounds of flesh slapping—sucking—my whimpers and the men's groans filled my ears. Musk and masculine bodywash scented the air. A lapping tongue moved over my pussy, Colton's hot breath on my core. Heat flushed through me, and I licked at the dryness on my lips.

Tingles spread through my toes, creeping upward.

"Give her your fingers," Hudson said, his voice ragged and on the edge. "Stroke her G, and she'll cream all over your face."

Colton groaned against my pussy lips and did as told, quickly filling me with two fingers. A twist of his wrist, and he found the sure way to send me rushing into climax.

"Yes," I hissed, clasping his head tight and shoving my hips upward.

Only two strokes, and I came with a gasp, my core spasming around his fingers.

A deep groan ripped from Colton, one I recognized from our night together—he'd shot his cum down the side of our couch, but I had no fucks to give in that moment.

"That's it." Hudson's deep rumble sent another pulse through me. "Squeeze my dick, boy. Fuck!"

A shudder relaxed me on the couch, and I peeled my eyelids open. Colton nuzzled my pussy as Hudson's head tipped back, tendons rising in his neck. He hissed, bucked forward, and held still, filling Colton with his cum.

Colton moaned against my wet flesh, his body lax over the couch's arm, his hands grasping my backside to pull me farther beneath him. Panting, he rested his cheek on my belly as Hudson finished inside him.

Gasped breaths, heavy with satisfaction, whispered through the living room.

I caressed Colton's mussed hair, the thick, wavy strands smooth as silk. His breath ghosted over my stomach, and I lifted my focus to find Hudson watching us come down from our high. A soft smile quirked up one side of my mouth, and his eyes warmed, full of love. Elation swept through my chest as I recognized the satisfaction, the apology in his gaze.

Hope sprang up inside my chest.

Hudson had finally given in.

28

COLTON

Talk about sensory overload. Being used by Hudson, giving pleasure to Madeline—that was where I wanted to be twenty-four-fucking-seven.

My ass ached along with my tongue from eating out the sweetest pussy on the planet. And the softness of her belly beneath my cheek... A shuddering sigh rippled through me, and I couldn't help the grin on my face.

"Someone's happy," Madeline murmured, and I hugged her waist tight.

"Goddamn right I am."

She ran her fingers through my hair, scratching at my scalp, almost sending me into shutdown mode.

But Hudson backed away, leaving my ass gaping.

My mind started to spin about the fucked up situation, but Hudson groaned, keeping my thoughts firmly in place.

"Fuck, that's hot," he rimmed a finger around my hole, and I clenched, causing his cum to drip out.

I'd made a mess on the couch, Madeline had made a mess on my face, and Hudson...yeah. I could feel his cum oozing and sliding down my inner thigh.

Eyes closed, I slowly released a heavy exhale. The shit we needed to discuss could wait for morning—but one thing needed put to rest in my head first.

"*He* kissed *you*," I stated but with a hint of question in my voice.

"Yes." Hudson's firm tone eased shit in my head, and he used something—probably his shirt to wipe between my legs. Just a quick swipe rather than full-on cleaning. "Fucker caught me off guard," Hudson all but grunted the words.

I shouldn't have looked away as quickly as I had or I would have caught Hudson's action. But, I couldn't change the past.

Time to focus on the future.

"Come on," Madeline whispered, tugging on my hair.

Groaning, I pushed upright, clenching my hole again to see how sore I was going to be. Wasn't too bad considering what I'd expected. While I enjoyed a bit of pain, Hudson had one hell of a cock that wouldn't have felt too good thrusting in on spit alone. Thank fuck for lube and plenty of it.

Madeline climbed off the couch and wrapped her robe back around her lush body. She reached for my hand, pulling, but I still had my pants around my ankles.

Chuckling, I yanked them up one-handed to the tops of my thighs and trailed after her toward the stairs. I glanced over my shoulder.

Hudson locked up the front door and shut off the lights, offering me a brief nod as if to say he was okay with where his wife wanted me to go.

My heart thumped an extra beat—they were taking me to their bed. There'd been no discussion, but the two of them must have had some sort of brainwave chatting going on.

I wasn't about to question.

Or argue.

Madeline turned on dimmer lights and led me across their bedroom. She shed her robe, sending the silk to swish at her pretty feet. I stared at her ass as she crawled onto the bed, swaying hips and tits twinging life in my groin. Turning and smiling, she patted the mattress beside her—the fucking *middle* of the bed.

A Hudson, Colton, and Madeline sandwich?

Fuck yeah.

I shucked my clothes quick as fuck, kicking off my shoes and damn near tripping in my haste to join her.

She giggled, the sound so light and carefree I wanted to hear it every day.

I should have asked to shower or at least visit the bathroom to better clean up my slick hole and crack, but fuck it. For the first time in my life, I'd been bred—and by the hot-as-fuck silver fox I'd been lusting over for weeks. I wanted that feeling to linger as long as possible.

And I wasn't about to wait to snuggle the hell out of her before her husband changed his mind.

Madeline plastered herself against me, all warm, soft flesh and sweet curves. "Did he hurt you," she whispered as I wound my arms around her waist, drawing her groin against mine.

Couldn't get close enough.

I shook my head in answer to her question and ran my nose along hers, Eskimo kissing the hell out of her.

"He would have if I hadn't brought down that lube," Madeline said.

"Thank you." I gave her a chaste smooch, my lips lingering on hers while I took advantage of her backside being bare and inches below where I held her. So goddamn squishy and jiggly. I groaned, running my palms over her generous backside. "Fuck, you've got a great ass."

She giggled again, and I drank that shit up.

Hudson entered the room, flicked off the lights, and rustled around.

He stripped, I imagined, and a thread of arousal slid through my blood again. I'd yet to see the man in his birthday suit glory, and the thought of gray on his chest and groin tempted me to turn. But he'd stolen the opportunity from me.

Silence settled, and I continued to gently caress Madeline's back while waiting.

Wondering what the fuck Hudson was doing.

Had he engulfed us in darkness because he hated the sight of me like an octopus over his wife's gorgeous body? Was he trying to figure out how to tell me he'd changed his mind and that I had to leave?

Well fuck him if that was the case.

Madeline had invited me, he'd nodded, and I wasn't going anywhere if he decided to go chickenshit again on our asses. He could kiss mine.

The memory of his beard between my thighs, his probing tongue, and deep groans while eating at my hole thickened my dick, but I pushed the sight in my mind away.

Make a move, old man.

The bed dipped as though he'd heard my thought.

I held my breath, and the air left in a rush as he crowded up against my backside, all hard muscle, hairy chest, and thick thigh sliding between mine. His hot, drawn out exhale teased the back of my head, and I went boneless, a fucking pile of warm jelly.

Hudson wrapped an arm around me, grasped his wife's

hip, and settled in even closer. Their heartbeats thumped against my chest and back.

The rushing sense of rightness swelled throughout my body, tingling and yet relaxing at the same time.

A Youngs and Colton sandwich...fucking finally.

Fifty times better than boring PB&J. Chicken salad and grapes? That sweet and savory meal didn't even come close to comparing to the feel of Madeline and Hudson being my bread. I'd found the most goddamn fulfilling slice of heaven in their bed.

And they could have fun prying me out if either of them changed their minds—I was there to stay.

No pillow talk broke the peaceful stillness around us.

Hudson's breaths evened out first, and Madeline soon followed.

Me?

I snuggled in deeper, rubbing my cheek on whoever's pillow cradled my head, contentment ripe on my face in a lingering grin.

I had to work the following day, but that didn't keep me from fantasizing about waking up to a smorgasbord of flesh and sex, then coffee on the deck while the sun rose. Sounded damn near perfect. Madeline would make muffins like she'd done every morning when I'd worked for them, though I would have helped her if I didn't have to go swing a hammer all day long. I imagined Hudson would sit and watch the two of us seamlessly moving around the kitchen, his gaze just as heated as always.

He would order me to touch her once we finished baking.

Tell me to get between his spread thighs and finally fill my mouth with his cock.

A shiver slid down my spine, lingering in my tailbone

and ass. He could choke me, fuck my throat, and I would thank him.

Fucking goner.

Hopefully, they were on the same page and I would find myself wrapped up in a tasty burrito again the next night.

29

HUDSON

I woke a couple of hours before the sun, same as always. But unlike our normal the previous seven or so months, Madeline didn't seek me out as her body pillow during her deep sleep pattern.

Instead, I spooned cut muscle while a bubble butt cradled my too-early morning wood.

My wife's shallow breaths on the other side of Colton let me know she still dreamed, but I wasn't surprised. Mads loved to sleep—and the lucky woman conked out like the dead unlike me who jolted at every creak of our old house.

The young man tucked between us lay quiet, his heart in slow, steady rhythm beneath my palm. I breathed in the scent of herbal shampoo. Not sweet like Mads but mouth-watering all the same.

He felt good pressed all along my front, and the memory of how he'd taken me so well the night before turned my blood warmer than the contentment I'd found myself floating on in the darkness. I hadn't wanted to like or desire Colton, but I did, goddamnit.

Just seeing him snuggling with my wife the night before

had twisted me up with conflicting feelings. But the sight of him and her tangled together on our bed had proven too much. His dark to her light. His savory to her sweet. His hardness to her soft flesh.

Yin and yang—opposites yet powerful forces enough to draw me forward without thought of consequences to my poor heart.

I'd crawled into bed while telling myself to just enjoy the moment, that we could figure shit out in the morning. I was sure Colton still had questions about what had gone down with Peter, and I needed to decide once and for all what to do with the man in my arms.

Not seconds after closing my eyes, the stress from the day had caught up to me, and I'd passed out as though my body and mind understood the safety of being swaddled up with the two of them beneath our blankets.

That sense of ease lingered in the pre-dawn hour as I rubbed my thumb in light circles over the muscular chest I held.

Colton was no young punk like Peter. A spattering of black hair lay across his pecs, and Colton stood taller than me. Not my usual but impossible to resist.

And that ass, winking globs of white once I'd finished...
Fuck.

My cock bucked, and I shifted in the darkness, smearing my early morning wood's pre-cum along his crack.

Colton didn't move, but the thump of his heart beneath my hand kicked up a notch, letting me know he, at least, was awake.

Madeline breathed deeply in sleep.

I continued to rut against Colton's ass, my movement slow but steady. Insistent. Enough slickness continued to ooze from my slit that the back of my length slid deeper through his crack.

Since I enjoyed our playthings messy, I hadn't fully wiped him up the night before. That action paid off as remnants of lube and cum still coated the skin nearer his hole but not enough for what I wanted.

With quick twist of my body, I fumbled in the dark for the bottle I'd left on my bedside table. My entire length coated with slickness, I returned, pressing against Colton.

"Mmm," I growled low in my throat, flexing my ass to glide up through his crack again.

Mads didn't twitch a muscle, but Colton shifted back in an invite that flared fire through my blood.

I worked my swollen head through his crack until it caught on the rim of his ass.

He arched. Bore down.

And I glided right into his loose hole, the only sounds in the still bedroom our hastened breaths. A shudder rippled through both of us, and I once more grabbed hold of his chest, pulling him tight against me.

"You're such a little cock slut," I whispered against his ear while grinding my hips against him, desperate to get deeper.

Colton didn't argue, simply lacing his fingers through mine atop his heart.

"Couldn't help myself," I told him, loving how his pulse thrummed beneath my palm. "Wanted to feel how hot and tight you are around my cock."

I pulled out to the head and slowly sank back into him. Too fucking good...I had to bite back a deep groan.

Mads wouldn't care I fucked him again, but I had no wish to disturb her sleep. Recounting my actions would rile her up later in the day after the sun shone, and I could sit back and enjoy Colton satisfying her arousal like I would his.

"Be a good boy and squeeze around me," I whispered against his hair, my eyes closing as I focused on the perfection of his silken insides.

He did as told, his ring of muscle clenching at my girth.

I grunted a curse as my balls tightened. Holding still, I soaked in the moment, etching the feel of him, the combined scents of him and my wife, into my mind. The wall I'd allowed to lower between us the night before settled closer to the ground as I considered giving a triad another chance.

Peter would have to be dealt with sooner or later, but could the sure loss of him in our lives—fucking peace— create an allowance I could accept and submit my emotions to?

Colton tightened his ass around my cock, and I groaned, my dick trying to jerk inside his sheath.

"Again," I murmured, hissing when he listened. "Fuck— I could come without a single thrust."

Colton set to prove my statement true, intentionally pulsing his ring around my dick, not bothering to slide our hands down to his groin to ease his own aching cock. Such a sweet, selfless lover, but I wasn't in the mood to be as kind as him even if he'd wanted to stroke into my grip while I owned his ass.

"You want me to fill you with my cum?"

"Fuck yeah," he whispered, releasing my hand and reaching around my hip to grab hold of my ass. "Just stay right there—" his ass strangled my girth again "—and give it to me."

"Ah, fuck." Cum ripped up through my length, shooting deep inside his body. I bit his shoulder to keep from hollering as his ass milked me, squeezing every last drop from my balls.

Nostrils flared to fill my lungs, I heaved against his back, sucking wind like I had sprinted a few blocks. My heart raced. Ears rang.

"Christ, Colton," I murmured, still buried and holding him against me. "Not pulling out—gonna keep you plugged up while you drift back to sleep."

He shivered and grasped my ass tighter as though he wanted the same goddamn thing.

I briefly wondered if he would ever suckle on my cock, keep me warm that way while in bed. Something to think about later.

Absently, I rubbed my thumb over his chest, moving closer to his nipple with each pass.

He moaned as the edge of my finger brushed over his tight nub.

"You like that?"

"Mmm," he hummed in agreement.

I thumbed over his nipple, dragging the edge of my fingernail over his hard flesh.

"Fuck," he whispered harshly and swallowed. "More."

So damn responsive...I could feel his ass clenching down on my semi with every pass of my finger over his sensitive nub.

"I'm gonna make a mess on the sheets," he warned with a whisper, his fingers digging into my ass to hold me against him.

"Without touching yourself?" I asked, sure I misunderstood him.

"Fuck yeah."

My dick attempted to swell at the lust in his voice, the idea he would shoot his load just from nipple play.

I set out to make it happen, tweaking and tugging until he writhed, his ass still clenching around me as though desperate to keep me inside his body.

"Fuck, Hudson...Jesus." He gasped and lifted his head slightly as though wanting to see his cock erupt in the darkness—and his hole spasmed. "Fuck..." He groaned. Gulped. Cursed quietly, all the while his pulsing ass enticing my dick back to life.

Easier to plug him with.

Colton shuddered and went limp, whispering a few more curses.

"Did you make a mess?" I asked against his ear and sucked his lobe between my lips.

"Mmm," he murmured an affirmative, loosening his grip on my backside.

"Good boy," I whispered and nipped at his shoulder.

A full-on body shudder ripped through him.

"Now go back to sleep."

30

MADELINE

Somehow, I woke before the men, and smiling, I enjoyed the sight of them snuggled up tight, Colton wrapped in Hudson's possessive arms. Tenderness welled inside me, stinging my eyes. With my hand beneath my cheek, I studied Colton's face.

No lines dented his brow, the dark slashes of his eyebrows easily seen in the morning light filtering around our blinds. Pink stained over his nose like he'd been working out in the sun without his hat the day before. Full lips parted, he breathed deeply.

A good foot and a half separated me from the men, but I felt no jealousy inside. They were too beautiful together for me to be envious. Besides, I trusted Hudson's love, and there was no doubt in my mind that given the chance, Colton and I could find something almost as special as I and my husband shared.

Excitement stirred in my blood, warming my core and face.

I considered scooting closer, my knee shifting high

enough to help me along, but dampness smeared over my skin. Pulling my leg back, I slid my hand over the sheets in search of what I'd felt.

A puddle of cum, dried around the edges but still wet and sticky at the center.

With how Hudson played big spoon to Colton, I expected I knew what had happened.

And I'd missed it.

Sighing, I slid from the bed, quietly finding my robe. I didn't doubt Hudson attempted to plug Colton's ass full of his cum. A snicker escaped me on a puffed exhale, and shaking my head, I turned away.

It appeared as though my husband was back to his pre-heartbreak self and willing to try again, thank goodness.

Peace surrounded my heart and mind. Depression held no sway over my emotions that morning as I crept down the stairs for the kitchen. Within fifteen minutes, I had coffee brewing and blueberry muffins in the oven since Colton had admitted to enjoying those the most of all that I'd made while he'd worked on our deck.

I noted movement in my periphery while I gathered up the baking ingredients to put them where they belonged.

Naked arms wrapped around my center just like Hudson's always did, but the short scruff on my neck scratched and sent shivers down my spine rather than soothing with the softness of Hudson's beard. My skin pebbled as Colton smooched on my neck like I was his last meal with lip smacking and moaned appreciation of my taste.

The can of baking powder slipped from my hand, and I clasped his atop my belly, my head falling back and to the side. With how he loved on my skin, that boy could have free access any time of the damned day.

"Morning," he rumbled against my ear while sliding a hand inside my robe.

"Morning," I whispered as he caressed over my breast, settling its weight in his palm. "You're so goddamn delicious, Lin."

My nipple pebbled against his palm, and I squeezed my thighs together at the aching emptiness. I couldn't remember being so damn horny, wanting dick all the time since Hudson and I had first gotten together.

Talk about an addictive rush I hadn't expected to ever experience again.

Soft lips continued to trail over my neck, and I sighed, sinking against Colton's hard chest. He spun me and hefted me up into his arms, depositing me on the counter before I could squeak a protest about being too heavy.

"Don't even," he growled as though knowing I was about to chide him for lifting my weight up like that. "You're the best kind of woman, and I wouldn't change anything about your gorgeous body. If I ever hear you utter one negative word about this warm flesh—" he nosed my robe open and smooshed his face in my breasts "—I'll spank your ass red," he said, his voice muffled.

I laughed, grabbing hold of his head to pull him away.

His dark eyes hinted at amusement and arousal yet were still sleepy. Bedroom eyes, they would be classified as, the most beautiful things I'd ever seen.

"I don't like to have my ass slapped," I told him while smirking.

"Damn, woman, you don't know what you're missing." He feigned a sigh and pressed back in between my thighs, angling better to lose himself in my chest. "Mmm," he hummed his happiness. "So sweet and soft. Best. Pillow. Ever."

More laughter escaped me.

I'd never had someone enjoy my girls as much as he did without the sucking and plucking of nipples. He seemed to take real joy from my skin and the beat of my heart beneath his ear.

I slid my fingers through his thick hair like I'd done the night before, causing him to nuzzle against me. A sweet heaviness spread through my chest...almost possessive, definitely beyond the need to care for him.

"Did you sleep okay?"

"Mmm," he hummed. "Best night I've had ever, I swear."

I loved hearing he'd relaxed fully between us.

"Do you have to work today?"

Colton exhaled loudly and pulled away from my breasts, settling his arms around my waist and his forehead against mine. "Yeah, but I don't want to."

"We're not going anywhere."

He shifted back to meet my eyes, searching for how much truth I might have stated. "I don't want to talk details, but Peter is gone for good, right?"

"From our hearts, yes."

"Good."

"But it might take a while to convince him of that truth."

Colton pressed a chaste kiss to my lips, lingering long enough that I wrapped my arms around his neck. "I don't have much time this morning."

"Then let me get you some coffee while these muffins finish baking."

"Mmm." Another smooch and he stepped back—reluctantly, his dimple popping and causing my stomach to dip to the floor.

Colton Payne was stunning. Drop-dead gorgeous regardless of the fact he'd just crawled from bed, his hair mussed to hell, his eyes still half-lidded.

"Are you working on your own or with a crew today?" I asked, turning to get him a mug.

"Crew."

"You might want to take a quick shower. You smell like sex."

"Shit." He chuckled.

I nodded toward the stairs. "Take a quickie. I'll have breakfast for you before it's time to—"

The doorbell rang, cutting me off.

I glanced toward the entryway. "Why don't you go shower, and I'll get that."

Frowning, I hurried toward the door, rewrapping my robe tightly around me. Since Hudson had locked the upper chain before bed, I twisted the knob and peeked through the crack.

Peter.

His face lit up, all flushed and wide eyed. "I'm home!"

Shit.

"We weren't expecting you," I fumbled the words, my heart erupting into full-speed gallops at the sight of two duffle bags in his hands. "Um...Peter, I thought we said we would be in contact."

His face fell. "And I told you I needed to come back, Mads. That place isn't safe for me anymore. Surely you don't want me to stay there."

I inhaled slowly, attempting to gather my thoughts and nerves which had peaked at panic mode. The night before, I'd been ready for the confrontation. Hudson and I had planned. I'd worked through scenarios in order to keep my adrenaline from taking over.

But his showing up, unannounced, as though completely disregarding or forgetting our conversation?

My chest tightened as I fought for words—and my voice to call for Hudson.

31

COLTON

eter, I heard Madeline say.

"The fuck?" I muttered, glancing toward the stairs to see if Hudson hurried down.

He had still been passed out when I'd detached my body from his and grabbed my jeans off the floor. He hadn't stirred while I'd cleaned up in the bathroom either, my nose sniffing at the rising scent of coffee.

No footfalls sounded from overhead, and I wasn't about to leave Madeline to deal with that little fucker alone.

I stalked toward the front of the house, a trickle of adrenaline heating my blood and fisting my hands.

Madeline had the door cracked open, the top chain keeping it from swinging inward any farther. White knuckles clutched at the door handle, and the hem of her robe shook as though her body shivered while she attempted to pull it tighter around her with one hand.

Lips in a grim line, I stepped in close behind her.

"I'm here, baby," I whispered, pushing the door shut.

"P-Peter is—" She gasped, trembling as I slipped the chain free. "Wh-what are you d-doing?"

"Do you trust me?" I whispered against her ear, clutching her back against my chest as I grasped her hand atop the doorknob.

"Yes."

I opened the door wide. Grinning at the blinking ass on the stoop, I wrapped Madeline in a possessive hold, resting my chin on her shoulder.

"So you're the moron who threw away the best thing you ever had." I made a tsking noise while glancing down over his thin form since I hadn't gotten the opportunity to check the little shit out fully that night on the library steps. "Sorry to say—actually, no. I'm not." I grinned wider. "I'm *not* sorry to say it at all—that place you gave up in their bed has been filled by yours truly, so why don't you take your bags and get the hell out of here before I call my Uncle Sully. Chief of Police Sullivan...I'm sure you've heard of him."

More like the guy was Reid's uncle, but Peter wouldn't know that.

Red flooded Peter's cheeks, his eyes—pupils dilated as fuck—filled with piss and vinegar.

Recognizing he was high as a fucking kite, I gently shifted Madeline off to my side, tucking her behind me and straightening to stand in the doorway. My grin faded, and I crossed my arms, creating a wall Peter would never pass.

"Hudson and Mads are mine," he spat, and I had to bite back a laugh at the kitten wanting to take on a lion.

"When something belongs to you, you don't turn your back on it and chuck it in the trash. That's what cheating is, Peter. Betraying love. Tossing another's emotions in the garbage like they have no meaning to you."

"I didn't cheat!" he shrieked, bags dropping to the ground like he readied to go a few rounds.

Little prick wouldn't last ten seconds with my fists—fuck knew I'd had plenty of practice losing my shit as a kid.

I narrowed my gaze. "What do you call putting your ass into the air like a bitch in heat for another man to rail you into next week? *That*, kid, is cheating. His bed, your bed, doesn't matter where."

His chin lifted as he attempted to look down his nose at me. A slow perusal gave him an eyeful of me in jeans that weren't buttoned or zipped and probably revealed the root of my dick. "You really think Hudson will want *you*?" He sneered. "You're too tall. Too hairy. Too muscular."

I snorted. "His cum is still dripping out of my ass, so I'm gonna say yeah."

A low growl rose up Peter's throat, and I didn't bother holding back my laugh that time.

"In fact, he was so damn horny for me that he fucked me twice last night, filled my hole up with his cum, and plugged me so it wouldn't slip out while we slept. Yeah, that's right," I said, leaning forward as his eyes widened, "I slept in their bed. Between my silver fox Hudson and his sweet, soft wife."

Peter sputtered, trying to glance behind me to where Madeline laid her hand on my lower back.

I moved into his line of sight again, refusing to let him get an eyeful of her silk-clad curves. He had no rights to them anymore.

"It's time for you to leave, Peter," I stated quietly, my tone firm as fuck—and with every ounce of lethal warning I could inflict. "And if you ever show up here again, I'll make your life even more miserable than it already is."

He eyed me, wariness in his irises and tight pupils.

The guy was flying high on something.

I narrowed my gaze, ready to call him out, but he tore his

focus from my face to grab his bags. "This isn't over." He hissed like a snake.

"The fuck it isn't," I shot right back. "But if you want to play Russian roulette with a man you don't know, by all means..." I let my threat hang in the air, as unmoving as an oak on the threshold. I didn't even bother uncrossing my arms and spreading them wide, allowing him to take the first swing.

The twink had no power to affect me physically or verbally.

He'd lost out.

And it was my turn to bring a little happiness to the Youngs' lives.

"This isn't over," he repeated.

"Get the fuck off this property," I said, stepping out onto the stoop and sending him scuttling down the stairs. "You don't belong here anymore. This isn't your home, and Hudson and Madeline aren't your lovers. You fucked up. End of. Grow some balls, own your mistake, and leave before I make shit even messier."

He shuffled sideways down the walkway, tossing his bags into the car. His jaw opened as though he wanted to promise me one more time he wasn't done—but I was.

Pointing down the road, I stalked forward, my free hand fisted at my side. No words. Just a glare promising sure pain should he make a stupid ass decision yet again.

He lit out, engine revving like he'd attempted to squeal the tires of his Camry.

Stupid fuck.

I waited until he disappeared around the corner before turning.

Madeline stood in the doorway, arms tucked tight beneath her breasts, her face pale. Eyes haunted.

"Hey." I ran up the steps, picked her up in my arms, and kicked the door shut. "It's okay—he's gone. I won't let him near you again, swear to fucking Christ, Lin."

She shuddered hard, swallowing with just as much force, a whined whimper following the action.

"Shh." I set her on her feet, keeping her against me, my hands smoothing down her back.

A creak on the stairs lifted my focus.

Hudson descended, his lips set, eyes thunderous.

"He's gone."

"I heard." He moved in behind Madeline, wrapping one arm around her body to grasp my hip, the other holding onto her shoulder in a possessive grip. "Breathe, love," he murmured against her temple, his eyes on mine. "We have you."

I didn't know the man much beyond the physical and light conversations, but we shared silent communication as well as if we'd spoken the words.

Thank you.

Any fucking time.

I'd told him I had his back—and I'd meant it with every fiber of my being.

32

HUDSON

I'd been lazing in bed, replaying the night before and giving Mads and Colton a little alone time downstairs. The scent of coffee and muffins tempted me to the point of getting my aching bones out of bed, but it was the doorbell that had gotten me moving.

The second I recognized the two male voices rising from the first floor, I paused in descending the stairs.

I could see Colton from the waist down, hugging my wife, and since I was one breath away from blowing a fucking gasket, I'd made myself stay put. He'd said he had my back, so I let him take the reins, trusting him to watch over my wife.

It had been a good decision.

He'd pushed Mads behind him, taking up residency in our doorway like a goddamn wall who refused Peter access to our home.

I'd listened as Colton taunted Peter with stories of fucking, plugging, and cum dripping.

Fucking bravo.

I'd huffed a chuckle as Peter sputtered and tried to make Colton cave by stating shit wasn't over.

The kid was fucking delusional, the same as he'd been the night before. Definitely on something.

An engine had roared, and Colton returned, kicking the door shut.

He'd pulled Mads in close, murmuring assurances, offering soft touches to calm her.

I hadn't been able to stay away any longer.

He'd caught my gaze as I'd descended the stairs, his dark eyes full of anger, lust, and a protective instinct I recognized all too well.

I hugged my wife, grabbing hold of his hip to keep her tight between us where no one and nothing could hurt her. My eyes held Colton's, and I hoped he read the appreciation in my gaze.

We stood in silence for a few minutes until Mads's breathing regulated.

I wanted to kiss Colton for sending that asshole away without any issues other than threats, but a pinprick of... something dug into me, annoying like a crease in your sweaty socks stuffed into boots a size too small.

A sense of being off, but I couldn't put my finger on what it was.

Wariness brought back on from Peter's arrival? The light of day with the lack of hormones raging for a fuck to release tension?

"You have to get to work." I stated the only thing I could think of at that moment to give me the breathing room I hadn't needed until that second.

A frown flitted over Colton's brow, but he nodded. "Yeah."

Madeline straightened and released a heavy sigh. "We won't keep you," she said, her voice quiet.

"Lin—"

"You have to go." Her smile wobbled as she shoved Colton toward the stairs. "Take that quick shower while I get your coffee and muffin."

He hesitated and grasped her chin, studying her eyes.

"I'm okay," she whispered, her lips trembling.

He kissed her gently then nodded. "Be right back." A quick clasp to my shoulder and he ran up the stairs, skipping every other step.

Oh to be young again, I mused, watching his ass until he disappeared from view.

Turning, I found Mads doing the same. "Sure you're alright, love?" I asked, tucking her beneath one arm and leading her toward the kitchen.

"Yeah. Peter just caught me off guard. I really should have asked who it was through the door."

"I'm going to get one of those peephole things so you don't have to." I squeezed her tight and released her, heading toward the coffeepot as she went for the oven. "Muffins smell great."

"Blueberry," she murmured.

"Colton's favorite, you'd said," I mentioned while retrieving the pot to fill the two mugs and travel cup she'd pulled out.

"Yeah."

I sat with my coffee and Mads's at the breakfast nook, angled away from the table to watch as she set aside two muffins with a to-go cup for Colton. "Come here," I stated quietly, holding out a hand.

She settled onto my thigh, and I handed her a mug of coffee. Smoothing golden brown strands of hair over her shoulder, I studied her face. No lines dented her forehead, so she'd calmed considerably from the ruckus of the morning. Baring her neck revealed a hint of purple.

"Was Colton loving on you this morning?" I asked while trailing my finger over the slight mark.

Pink flushed her cheeks, and her eyelashes fluttered as she glanced down at the cup in her hands.

I'd thought I might be ready to let go and try again after our night together, but my stomach tightened with that hint of unease once more.

"Colton's mark looks good on you," I whispered the truth even though reservations held tight in my head.

"Would you mind if he came over after he gets off work?" she asked, giving me her crystalline eyes. No evidence of worry lingered, no hint of the unsettled feelings Peter's unexpectedly showing up must have slammed into her to make her shiver and shake like she'd done as Colton and I had held her.

His arrival had definitely set me on edge.

Getting caught up in something new would be a great way to ignore shit that had to be dealt with—because I knew Peter wasn't done with us even though we were with him. But trusting another man and welcoming him into our lives wasn't going to come easy.

I'd enjoyed the fuck out of Colton's body and got off on how he had no problems bringing my wife to climax, but I'd imagined my walls lowering too far for comfort the night before. Dawn and the unwanted arrival of our ex had brought clarity back damn quick.

"We can't rush this, the moving on, when shit is still lingering," I told her, needing honesty more than ever. "It's just too much for me right now."

Mads traced a fingertip over my eyebrow, smoothing

down wayward hairs that came with age. "I really feel a connection with Colton."

"He's been a great distraction." I tugged her closer on my lap, my hands lacing at her hip. "But I want you all to myself tonight, love."

Disappointment lit in her eyes but only briefly. "Okay." She set aside her mug and wrapped her arms around my neck. Our lips met, a soft taste, a promise of more to come.

Finally, I felt we'd gotten almost back to our normal from before the heartbreak and hemorrhage that had ruined her dreams of bearing children. Hope rose inside me, and while I knew inner healing couldn't come from another person's arrival in our lives, Colton definitely had some responsibility in lighting a path through the darkness we'd been stuck inside.

"Would you be alright with him helping me bake all those cupcakes tomorrow for the Webber boy's birthday party?" Mads asked.

I considered her words, thinking about watching how Colton would interact with her and I during the day where no drama imposed, no heated arguments leaving room for fucking in rage then sliding into bed completely wiped out.

Keeping things with him on a purely physical plane would be best, but the want in Mads's eyes, her excitement for something new...I couldn't deny her.

"And yoga," she rushed to tack on before I could agree.

"Yoga?" I grimaced at the thought.

She squeezed my shoulder. "It'll be good for your joints, and I need to get back into my old routine of caring for my body too."

I exhaled slowly. We had to start doing more things together, creating new traditions going forward.

"Okay." I agreed, knowing that I'd also given in to

spending time with Colton outside the bedroom where connections and feelings might grow. While I wasn't exactly comfortable with that fact, she deserved the world.

Her smile dazzled, her mouth on mine giving me a sense of life I'd only experienced with her. "Love you," she murmured against my lips.

"Love you more," I promised her, grasping her neck to keep her in place so I could show her exactly how much.

———

I saw Colton out to his truck a few minutes later. He didn't say much, but neither did I until we stood beside his opened door.

Hands shoved in my pockets, I waited for him to set his mug in the holder and the napkin-wrapped muffins on his dash.

He turned, his gaze slightly wary and full of questions.

"Mads wants you to come over tomorrow."

"What do *you* want?" he asked, probably hearing the hesitation in my voice.

"Physically? You," I freely admitted. "But I warned you we had shit to deal with. Baggage. And you got a taste of that this morning. And I'll be honest because that's what we need right now, I'm very hesitant about bringing someone else into our marriage outside the bedroom."

"Understandable," Colton agreed with a nod.

"I am open to the possibility of more, but right now..."

His slow smirk and the light in his dark eyes swept warmth through me, but I tamped it down. "So, tomorrow?" He pushed for those answers I could imagine filling his brain.

"Mads has some cupcake orders to work on. If you want—"

"Yes."

I narrowed my gaze at his sheepish grin. "You didn't let me finish."

"You have to know by now that I'll take whatever you're willing to give me."

The boy had fallen hard. I could see it in his eyes, had recognized his emotions while he had loved on my wife the night before and how he'd so willingly let me hold him. Plug him up. I'd warned him to keep himself in check, but he hadn't listened.

Not that my actions had helped any.

"I can't promise anything but yoga—" I grimaced again "—and spending the day in the kitchen."

"I'm not asking for anything more."

I raised an eyebrow at his statement.

"I'm not, old man." He clasped my shoulder before I could growl at him, the warmth of his palm immediately sinking through my T-shirt to singe my skin.

I'd never felt such chemistry with another man, and I couldn't decide if I hated or loved the draw.

"I'll see you tomorrow," he said while climbing into the truck.

I nodded and stepped back so he could head to work.

Until Colton raised red flags, I would allow him access to a sliver of our lives.

As for that love I knew he longed for?

The ball was in his court to prove his worth and earn my trust.

33

MADELINE

Hudson and I went on a date Saturday night for the first time in too long. We got dressed up, sat in candlelight, and shared a bottle of wine with our pasta dishes. The atmosphere of the Italian restaurant lent to a sexy mood, and my body remained warm from the night before and memories of Colton.

When Hudson stripped me down later in the privacy of our bedroom, everything but him fled from my mind as he worshiped me from lips to thighs. Even his kissing over my stretch marks didn't cause discomfort to twinge through me like it used to do.

Healing had begun, and I gloried in the sense of lightness inside my chest.

With every stroke of his length, Hudson took me higher, made my skin burn and my pulse thrum. We felt...new. Restarted on the course we'd begun prior to Peter and the loss of our daughter. The thought of her would always bring sorrow, but I finally felt ready to enjoy life as we had before.

Hudson woke me in the morning with his head between my thighs, his beard soft on my skin, his warm mouth and probing tongue cleaning the mess he'd made the night before.

"Filthy man," I whispered with a smile, my eyes closed as I held his head in place.

He rumbled an agreement and slid two fingers into my pussy as he closed his lips over my clit. He played me like a fine-tuned instrument, same as always, and my climax swept over me like a gentle wave, leaving me tingling and lax. Sated and happy.

His whiskers tickled as he dragged his mouth up over my belly and breasts.

I tasted myself on his lips and tongue, sighing as he settled his weight atop me. "Want me to take care of that?" I murmured about his hard length against my thigh.

"I'm good."

"Mmm," I agreed, running my hands along his spine, the softest skin over muscle. "That you are."

He chuckled, pecked a quick kiss on my lips, and rolled off me.

Stretching, I watched him shuffle to the bathroom. My sexy silver fox. I'd been lucky to catch his eye that day at our shared acquaintance's house. His wide shoulders had looked like they could carry the weight of the world. His hands, weathered and rough, promised the man was like my daddy and wouldn't shy away from work. His hazel eyes had been kind. Soft. And his smile had dropped my heart to my toes.

We didn't have much in common, but somehow we'd just...fit.

Hudson worshiped me, and I spoiled him. An easy give and take, a relationship built on honesty and trust easily earned within a matter of months spent dating. Some days, I was a bitch. Others, he was an asshole, but he was *my* asshole, and I wouldn't have my life any other way.

The shower turned on, and rather than lay there and be lazy like I tended to do in the mornings, I climbed out of bed and joined my husband, washing him with as much focused attention as he'd shown my body the night before.

He'd told me he had invited Colton over for the day, and I looked forward to having them both with me while reintroducing yoga back into my life and spending the afternoon in the kitchen. Wandering hands and stolen kisses between baking and icing cupcakes sounded like the perfect way to get the order filled.

Even though Hudson had loved on me well the previous twelve hours, I remained warmed and primed, aroused over thoughts of the day ahead.

Hudson and I ate breakfast we'd made together, discussing limits for Colton's visit.

I would play if Colton wanted—which I didn't doubt he would.

But Hudson had no wish to interact. Unlike Friday night, he was completely closed off to all physical touch.

Annoyance prickled through me at his declaration.

"What happened between almost taking Colton without lube until now?" I asked, unable to help my frown.

He studied his empty coffee mug clasped tight in his hands. "I'm thrilled that you're ready to move on so quickly —hadn't expected that—but there's something..." Lips pursed, he shook his head.

I reached over to grasp his wrist. "I appreciate your caution, but please don't allow fear to cloud your judgment. Colton is just as protective of me as you are. You heard him —saw him face off with Peter. He's a hard worker just like you. Blunt and honest like you. Perhaps you're a bit too similar for your tastes?"

Hudson shook his head. "I don't want to like him."

"But you do." I didn't ask a question since he'd already admitted as much days earlier.

"I'm afraid."

I squeezed his wrist, adoring him all the more for his openness. "Then we take things one step at a time. Yes, we jumped right into the fun, but there's so much potential with him, and I would really like to explore something more."

Hudson released a slow, steady exhale. "I'm willing to give Colton a chance to prove himself, but he's gone at the first sign of a red flag."

I patted his hand and stood to gather up our breakfast dishes. "As long as said flag isn't a figment of your imagination because of your sense of self-preservation."

"Isn't that what gut instincts are?"

Plates in hand, I stood peering down at my husband as he studied my face. "Perhaps, but make sure it isn't a preconceived opinion that shuts down what could be a good thing. Ask questions. Discuss what you're feeling and why."

"It's not that easy to trust, Mads."

"You mean it's not so easy to allow vulnerability. I experienced the same thing you did with Peter. But I want to live again, Hudson, and more than just the two of us getting back to what we had before him. We agreed to this lifestyle, and I still want it. I'm not offering you an ultimatum—I never would—I'm just asking you to please consider finding that sense of rightness again and being open with all lines of communication."

Hudson hesitated for a few seconds, long enough to churn my stomach, but he eventually nodded.

"Thank you." I leaned down and kissed his forehead, my insides settling once more.

"Want help with the dishes?"

"I'd rather you got those estimates done you said you had to do today so you can spend the rest of the day with me and Colton once he gets here."

"I'm not getting involved in anything physical," he reminded me.

"Today isn't going to be about just sex," I told him. "Yoga, remember?"

His nose wrinkled.

"Then time in the kitchen where we can get to know Colton better."

His lips stretched in a thin line as though he wasn't super thrilled.

Colton would prove himself, I had no doubt. I just hoped my husband managed to allow some vulnerability to give the younger man a chance.

Hudson got up from the table and hugged me from behind at the sink. Kissing over the mark Colton had left the morning before, he murmured an agreement to my plans for the day before disappearing into the office.

The doorbell rang right at ten o'clock when Hudson had messaged Colton to come over.

Hudson was in the bathroom, so I glanced out the living room window before answering the door.

White truck—Harper's Construction sign on the passenger door.

Colton.

Adrenaline rushed through my body as I pulled the door open. "Hi," I breathed.

"Hey, beautiful." Colton stalked forward, and I stepped

back, loving how his eyes danced down over my long T-shirt and yoga pants. "You look delicious enough to eat."

Heat flooded my face.

Colton glanced around. "Hudson?"

"Bathroom."

"Can I kiss you?"

"He gave me permission to mess around if that's what you're hoping for."

Colton grabbed hold of me and yanked me against his hard muscles. He swallowed down my gasp as I clutched at his pecs. He smelled spicy and warm, and I melted into him like butter.

"Definitely delicious," he murmured against my lips before pulling back. "So. Yoga, huh?"

"Yep," I stated firmly, expecting we would be laughing at one another more than gaining much for attempting to contort our bodies into graceful poses.

"Then cupcakes?"

"Chocolate peanut butter," I told him, attempting to steady my shaky legs and thrumming pulse as he continued to hold me.

"Frosting?"

"Peanut butter—with mini Reese's on top."

"Holy fuck, my mouth is watering. Can I lick the bowl?"

I smacked his arm lightly since as a baker, he knew the consumption of raw eggs wasn't a good idea. "How about we do up a double batch, and you take the extras to work tomorrow for all the guys?"

Colton pursed his lips as though deep in thought, his smirk and dimple still popping enough I wanted to swoon. "And what happens if they get demanding and want more?"

I leaned into him, nipping at his lower lip. "Then we'll

just have to make this Sunday yoga/baking thing a new tradition."

"Mmm." His hand slid down to my ass and squeezed. "I could live with that."

So could I, I realized, loving how easy it was just being with him. I hoped my husband would be on board.

"Hey, just a quick heads-up," I said quietly, "Hudson is... well, he's physically off-limits today."

Colton studied my face. "He already let me know. Is everything okay?"

"You didn't do anything wrong, and he'll be fine." It wasn't my place to say anything more about Hudson's feelings. I would leave that up to him to communicate if he wanted. "Come on. Let's drag Hudson's ass to the basement and attempt to find our center."

"Our what?" Colton asked with a chuckle.

"I'll explain in a bit."

The men didn't hug and kiss like Colton and I had done, but warmth resided in Hudson's eyes at the sight of our boy.

Said boy got plenty of praise from me while trying to twist and hold still in a triangle pose about fifteen minutes into our session. They had been chatting about the Red Sox's season nonstop, and I realized I would never get the same effects from yoga if the boys continued to join me.

Perhaps we would keep Sundays for baking in the kitchen, and I could get my self-care done earlier in the morning.

Hudson didn't attempt half of what Colton and I did. He sat on the mat, eyeing Colton through every movement, watching how he extended and bent, trying for relaxation when all we did was talk rather than focus on inwardly centering ourselves.

When Colton stuck his ass up in downward dog, Hudson's groan had Colton wiggling his backside.

My pulse leapt—but my husband stayed put.

"So what do you do when you aren't working or watching the Sox?" I asked Colton while lowering then pushing my upper body into cobra pose.

He arched his back alongside me, head lifted toward the ceiling while he planked on his palms. "Work on my fixer-upper. Go out with my buddies from Harper's Construction. How about you two?"

"We have—*had*—a group of friends we used to play cards with," I replied. "We used to play in other ways with them too." I didn't go into the fact we'd slowly pulled away from that group once Peter became a part of our lives, and we weren't open to sharing outside our throuple.

"Rummy? Hearts?" Colton asked.

I glanced at Hudson who'd pushed up onto his arms like we did, stretching with us since it was an easier pose. "We haven't pulled out any cards in months." Our gazes met.

"That's something we'll have to remedy," he murmured, that vulnerability in his eyes still present.

"I'm open to playing...cards," Colton tossed out, fishing for an invite he would definitely get before the day ended.

I smiled and sat, spinning my legs around in front of me to rest into corpse pose.

"Morbid," Hudson muttered over the name I told them but didn't complain about being totally relaxed.

Silence fell over the three of us for a few moments, and I soaked in the seconds ticking past in complete comfort as I lay on my back, eyes closed. We might not have meditated or focused inward—there had been too much giggling, snickering, and the guys connecting over their love of sports for that, but I felt calmer. Relaxed and ready for the rest of our day.

"So what did you think?" I asked, turning my head to face Hudson.

He grunted a noncommittal response, that grimace once more shifting his beard.

Laughing, I looked over at Colton. "And you?"

He reached across his mat to clasp my hand, his dark eyes twinkling. "I'd rather make a mess in the kitchen than contort my body to the point of falling on my ass."

Something he'd done—twice.

I heaved a heavy exhale, still smiling. So yoga would be my thing. I could live with that.

"Let's go get to work," I said, pushing up to my feet.

I retrieved us all glasses of ice water even though we hadn't broken into a sweat, and Hudson settled at the breakfast nook while Colton eyed the counter where everything was ready to roll. I'd even set out the butter and eggs to get to room temperature.

"What do you want me to do first?" Colton asked.

Kiss me all over.

Convince Hudson to lower his walls.

"Why don't you get the oven preheated, and I'll share my secret recipe that only exists in my brain," I said instead.

The sun shone outside the window and slider, matching my inner mood.

Nothing was going to ruin our day of getting to know Colton better.

I wouldn't allow it.

34

COLTON

I'd felt Hudson's gaze on me all through Madeline attempting to teach us yoga. My backside had tingled pretty much nonstop, and my dick attempted to twitch to life a few times. Something about that man just lit me the fuck up.

He'd worn a tight T-shirt, mesh shorts, and had gone barefoot. Hot as fuck. Turning from where I worked at the counter, I caught his stare once more on my backside. Heat resided in his eyes as he lifted his focus up to my face.

"Enjoying the view?" I asked with all the brat sass I could summon.

He narrowed his gaze but didn't reply.

He wasn't on the menu for the day, but I got a sense it was more than him not being in the mood to give me his dick. Even though his eyes said he wanted me, they held a reservation that reminded me of that first Friday night we'd spent together.

He'd been shut down that evening, and for whatever reason, it appeared he'd erected those walls firmly back in place.

Madeline had said I hadn't done anything wrong, but something had gotten Hudson's balls all twisted up.

He sipped his water while I went back to work, the creak of a chair at the breakfast nook letting me know he planned on watching for a little while. I had a million questions about Peter, wanted to discuss what had gone down the morning before, but withheld from bringing up an uncomfortable topic.

That whole situation was probably what had set Hudson on alert, understandably so. Not knowing me that well would ensure his insecurities would keep popping up until he learned to trust me.

At least, I hoped he'd give me that opportunity.

Since I had every intention of keeping shit in the right mood, I veered my thoughts toward an easier conversation like we'd been doing since my arrival.

"Hudson told me you aren't interested in opening a bakery, but you totally should," I said while cracking the first of a few eggs she'd set out.

She measured the dry ingredients on my right, using the back of a knife to level off a cup of flour. "I have no interest in the stress of running a real business. Mads's Sweet Treats is easily managed from my own kitchen with referrals bringing in more than enough work to keep me busy."

"Do you have a job outside the home too?"

"I like having Mads here," Hudson interjected from behind us.

"I like *being* here," Madeline added, glancing over her shoulder with a smile before turning toward me. "And since neither of us care about rolling in money, we're content to make enough to pay the bills and have a little leftover for a yearly trip to someplace sunny and warm in the middle of winter. Have you ever been to Aruba?"

"Nope." I cracked the second egg. "I've never been out of New England."

"No desire or no opportunity?" Hudson asked.

"I grew up in foster care so never had the chance as a kid. Now?" I shrugged, tossed the shells in the trash, and made my way to the sink to rinse my fingers off. "I saved my money to buy that house up on Groveland Street. It still needs a lot of rehab, but I've got big plans that mean more to me than traveling the country."

"What kind of plans?" Madeline asked.

"Flipping houses. Eventually having my own business. The house on Groveland is just the beginning—at least I'm hoping it'll be."

"If your work here at our home is any indication of your skills," Hudson said, "then I'd say you're going to do just fine."

His words of praise, whether meant to edify or not, warmed me right the fuck up, making me feel all squishy inside. Even my goddamn face heated. "There's still a lot to do. I remodeled the half-bath. Just have the kitchen to go, which will take me some time to save for."

"Have you looked into refinancing?" he asked. "We did that five years ago to upgrade this kitchen for Mads."

"I barely managed to get the construction loan on the house a couple of months ago, so I'm pretty much stuck where I am for a while," I answered.

"Well, I don't know how to hang cabinets, but if you want any help with the demolition, I'm good with a crowbar and tearing shit apart."

That warm squishiness inside me returned, bringing incredible happiness along with it.

I glanced over my shoulder at Hudson to find his focus on my face for a change. He was offering himself to me in a way I appreciated the fuck out of. Because it meant he was open to more than his dick in my holes. "When the time comes, I'll take you up on that."

"You do that," he said with a nod.

One command I would gladly obey. "What's next, Lin?" I asked, turning back around with a face-aching grin that wouldn't dissolve anytime soon.

She gave me a few tasks, and our conversation continued with all the usual get-to-know-you shit people shared on a first date.

But our time in the Youngs' kitchen didn't feel like a date. It was...a comfortable weekend day at home, full of easy discussion and eventually the sweet scent of cupcakes baking in the oven.

Hudson had a couple more estimates he hadn't finished up earlier that morning and left us for his office, suggesting some card playing later on.

Madeline and I washed up the dishes, her hands in suds while I dried the rinsed items she handed to me. I glanced at the oven's timer counting down, bummed that we didn't have many minutes left.

"So, frosting?" I asked, hoping like hell making that wouldn't eat up all our cupcake cooling time I was looking forward to since it meant I could keep my hands occupied with *her*.

"That recipe is also in my head and won't take very long to make." Madeline had her golden brown hair in a ponytail, and I ran my gaze over her neck, my dick stirring at the slight mark I'd left there the morning before.

"Nice hickey," I murmured, my voice dropping enough I gave my thoughts away.

"Mmm," she hummed her agreement, flicking a crooked

smirk at me. "A potential boyfriend was smooching on me yesterday."

I leaned my butt against the counter to better face her. "Potential boyfriend, huh?"

Pink flushed her face as she unplugged the drain.

"Tell me more."

"Are you needing an ego boost, Colton?"

I laughed, yanking her into my arms, wet hands and forearms be damned. She could cover me in suds, and I wouldn't complain. "All I need is to kiss you and I feel like a god."

She slapped at my chest, and I squeezed her tighter, angling my head to rub my nose along hers. "You're addictive," she whispered.

"So are you."

I licked over her lower lip, and she let me in, sighing as our tongues stroked. No rush of lust kicked me in the groin, but fuck did I love the hell out of the slow burn in the pit of my stomach. Same as when I'd kissed her in the entryway, she went all soft against me, pressing those lush breasts to my body, her wet hands winding around my neck and up into my hair.

Groaning, I palmed her ass in one hand and grasped her ponytail in the other.

Our mouths broke apart, our foreheads resting together as we shared breaths.

"Do I have any competition for this boyfriend position?" I had to ask, thankful as fuck no insecurity bled through my voice.

"You're the first since Peter, and I'm not interested in any other applicants."

"But there have been some?"

Madeline yanked on my hair so our gazes could meet.

"Are you always this hard up for affirmation?" She didn't sound wary or annoyed by my pushing, thank fuck.

I shrugged. "When you get tossed around from foster home to foster home as a kid, when you have no stability... yeah. It can make a grown-ass adult needy in lots of ways."

Her eyes filled with empathy as she smoothed her hand over my scalp, and I closed my eyes, soaking in her simple affection. "Did you ever have anyone you could call your own?"

"Got my heart crushed too often as a kid to try for more," I murmured, wanting to lose myself in her soothing touch.

"And now? With us?"

I studied her face, the cornflower blue irises, the sweet curve of her cheeks and mouth. "I'm nervous. Hopeful. Hell, I'm scared as fuck, but maybe I'll get lucky this time around."

Madeline's lips opened, but the timer went off before she could respond. "Hold that thought."

She grabbed pot holders and pulled out the muffin tins, the heat of the open oven door washing over us. Sweet, chocolatey steam filled my nose, and I groaned.

"Goddamn, those smell good."

"They'll taste even better once they're frosted —trust me."

"Oh, I do."

She turned off the oven while I took the cupcakes from the tins, setting them on cooling racks. "I love being here in the kitchen with you."

Our gazes met for a brief moment, the warmth of a bond I'd never experienced before settling deeply in my soul.

"I love having you here," she whispered, her smile soft and promising.

I wanted the words though. Longed to hear we would

continue moving forward toward a future together, that Hudson would eventually cave and give in to the energy that drew us together.

A door slammed, turning us both toward the noise. My hand paused long enough on a cupcake it burned.

"Fuck," I muttered, dropping it and quickly setting it upright since it didn't break apart.

Hudson hadn't worn shoes earlier, but his footfalls sounded loud as fuck heading our way.

He appeared in the doorway, cell phone clutched in his hand, his hair a wild mess, eyes hard as flint. "Leave."

I blinked, taking a second to process his command while realizing something had set him the fuck off.

"What?" Madeline asked, her tone sharp. "Why?"

Barely refrained fury etched over Hudson's face as he glared at me. Red stained his cheeks. "Get. Out."

I glanced at Madeline. Her face had paled while staring at her husband. She glanced at me. "Go," she whispered.

What the actual fuck?

I wanted to demand answers but knew when a man stood on an edge that promised shit would turn bad if pushed. Hoping that once Hudson calmed down from whatever had gotten him riled up, we could talk things over, I nodded.

This wanting more shit was about getting on my last nerve.

I walked out without another word, shut their front door behind me with a little more force than necessary, and definitely drove away from their house too fast.

Goddamn *fucking* roller coaster was messing with my head.

I didn't know how much longer I could hang on.

35

HUDSON

I'd been thinking too much about our morning which had gone really well instead of finishing up the final estimate of the day when my cell dinged with a text notification.

From Peter, the home screen preview had let me know.

All relaxation and hints of hope that had flicked to life inside disappeared in a blink.

Scowling, I'd swiped the phone open and clicked on messages.

Thought you might find this interesting, Peter's text had stated.

An image popped up before I'd finished reading his words, and I'd stared, my brain taking a while to make sense of what—*who*—I saw.

Fucking Ryan Foley grinning in a selfie.

With Colton hanging on him like a goddamn whore, licking his cheek and grasping his pec.

Heat had erupted in my guts, the same livid need to rage as that night I'd walked in to find Ryan balls deep in my boy.

"Goddamnit!" I'd seethed under my breath, my entire body vibrating as I yanked on my hair.

That fucking asshole...with my wife....in our house.

"Fuck." I'd shoved my chair back, slammed my office door behind me, and stomped toward the kitchen. I hadn't been able to process words past the red flames eating at my thoughts, the sense of betrayal that brought all of Peter's shit to the front of my mind.

"Leave," I'd snipped the only word outside of curses in my head as I'd rounded the corner and found them both looking my way.

I wanted him gone. From my house, from our lives.

Fucking *yesterday*.

Colton hadn't lingered with his inquisitive stare at my demand he leave, his dark brows furrowed as though baffled by my words and demeanor. A hint of hurt lay behind his silent question, but I hadn't given a flying fuck. If he knew the feelings that ripped my insides to shreds, he'd understand I held zero empathy. He'd done as told without argument, saving me from bruised knuckles and him from a goddamn bloody nose.

"What the hell, Hudson?" Madeline asked, her voice shaky as the front door shut loudly behind Colton.

Tears filled her eyes.

"He's a fucking liar!" I let loose, my voice rising with every word.

"What are you talking about?" Mads's escalated too.

"Full of shit playboy...fuck!" I spun out of the kitchen, too restless to stand still and argue.

She and I had one hell of a fight ahead of us because she was so far gone on him. Even if she'd caught him in the act, she would have difficulty believing he'd do any wrong.

"Hudson, you promised to communicate!" she called after me, hot on my heels.

I spun on her at the entrance to my office. "This isn't about my insecurities or fears," I shot back, my guts like granite. "This is cold, hard, fucking *facts!*" My hands shook as I swiped my cell to life and shoved it in her face.

Mads blinked, her mouth dropping open as she grasped my wrist to hold the screen steady since I trembled from the adrenaline rushing through my bloodstream. The angry flush on her cheeks faded to white, and her hand slipped from me. "I-I can't..." She shook her head. "There must be some mistake."

"Pictures don't lie," I stated through gritted teeth, dropping my arm since I couldn't stop it from trembling. "Colton did."

"In what way?" she asked, her gaze flitting over my face filled with confusion and doubt.

"I told him the name of the man Peter fucked, and he didn't say one single word about being *acquainted* with Ryan Foley." I barely managed to keep my tone restrained.

She processed for a few seconds before swallowing hard. "It just doesn't seem...he doesn't...there must be some other explanation than trying to hide his connection with Ryan," she reasoned, but she grasped at fucking straws. "Who sent this to you?"

"Peter."

A huff snorted through her nose. "Damn convenient he'd drop this through text after that confrontation yesterday morning. You need to give Colton a chance to explain," she stated firmly, her lips pressing tight.

"I don't need to give that lying piece of shit a goddamn thing!" I shoved the cell back in my pocket, ready to blow a fucking gasket. "He knows Ryan and should have made that fucking clear when I'd shared the shit that had started up after Peter's betrayal."

"Maybe it was just some random pic from happy hour? It looked like they were at a dance club or something."

I refused to listen. My mind was made up over that goddamn red flag, and I wouldn't budge.

"That man is no longer allowed to step foot in this house," I spat. "Do you hear me?"

Madeline visibly bristled, her nostrils flaring and chin rising. "If he shows up wanting to talk this through, you better believe I'll let him in!"

"This is my house—"

"It's mine too!" she cut me off. "And don't you *dare* try to tell me what I can and can't do, Hudson Young! This marriage isn't a dictatorship! We agreed to be equal partners in all things—both our businesses too, right from the start. We also decided on a polyamorous relationship, promised to work things out with clear communication and honesty. Just this morning you agreed to ask questions and discussion. And now you're judging him without giving him a chance to defend himself? Colton deserves a chance to at least explain!"

"He's not a part of this relationship, Mads," I stated through clenched teeth, leaning in toward her as my entire body shook. "He was a hookup we met through the app."

"And you said you were open to more because I was."

"Well, I have the right to revoke my decision!"

"Hudson—"

"Don't, Mads." I held up my hand, absolutely fucking done.

She clamped her lips closed, that fire I loved about her flaming in her eyes like cold ice.

A few tense minutes of silence reigned over our home,

the ticking of a clock somewhere like heavy gongs in my mind, a countdown that made breathing damn near impossible.

"I need some time," she finally said, her tone firm. Resolute.

I blinked, stunned by the quiet words and the coolness in her gaze. "What do you mean?"

"This isn't right," she stated, her hands finding her hips. "This *isn't* what we agreed on."

"He fucking lied!" I hollered, throwing my hands up. "If that isn't a stark fucking red flag waving in our faces, I don't know what is!"

"And he deserves the right to defend his lack of giving you personal information!"

"Goddamnit...fuck, Mads!"

We glared at each other in another tense, silent standoff, that damn clock ticking in my brain promising detonation.

"I'm headed back into the kitchen," she said, her voice barely restrained. "I'll finish up this order for the Webbers, then I'm leaving."

"You're what?" I gasped out, all desire to fight gone as though a bucket of ice water had upended over my head, taking my frozen heart to the fucking floor where it shattered into shards.

"I'm going to take some time away," she repeated. "Allow myself some space to get this figured out."

"For how long?" I barely managed to whisper, a sense of emptiness, of being completely and absolutely misplaced from reality settling over my entire being.

"I don't know, Hud." She glanced at the closed door, her shoulders sagging. "Just...take your anger back into the office. I can't handle you right now."

Heat rushed through me, and I grasped hold, desperate

to find footing as my world crumbled. "What happened to honest communication?" I spat out as my stomach twisted to the point of pain.

"This is me telling you how I feel as clearly as I can." She met my eyes and held my glare. "I. Need. Space. I would appreciate it if you would respect my wishes and give it to me."

Turning, she left me staring after her, my mouth working for words I couldn't find to make shit right.

How the fuck had we gone from enjoying life again to her...leaving me?

36

MADELINE

H udson's office door slammed shut, and the heavy quietness left me unsettled. Hurt. Angry. And a ton of other emotions roiled like sludge in my heart. Depression wanted to swoop in and steal my thoughts, but I clenched my jaw and focused on the job ahead of me.

A meltdown could wait.

The image on Hudson's cell screen haunted my mind though, and I struggled to make sense of its truth.

Maybe Colton hadn't heard Ryan's name when Hudson had supposedly told him it. Maybe Ryan was an ex that Colton had chosen to leave behind and wanted nothing to do with. Maybe he'd been drinking or forgot the night that picture had been taken. Perhaps it'd been nothing more than a quick hookup at the club showcased in the background, no names exchanged.

But how had Peter gotten the photo?

I shook my head, overwhelmed. Colton and Peter had faced off twice in front of me. There hadn't seemed to be any recognition between the two men and definitely no words of a past. I really doubted they'd met prior to those events.

If Peter had been the one behind the camera that night at the club, I had to believe they'd been drunk or high enough to not remember each other.

Nothing else made sense.

I iced the cupcakes and boxed them up for delivery while Hudson stayed put—and quiet, thank goodness.

Once finished, I cleaned up the kitchen and went upstairs, my body exhausted from too many emotions and heavy thoughts. But there was no way I could crawl into bed. I desperately longed for that space I'd asked my husband for. I needed clarity. Answers. And wallowing beneath blankets and pillows wouldn't give me either, leaving me depressed again.

I tossed some clothes and toiletries into a bag, my pulse thrumming from what I planned to do. Hudson and I had always talked things through. We never went to bed angry at one another. But in typical stubborn form, he'd become a brick wall and wouldn't listen to any reasoning.

And I wouldn't bend on my resolution to give Colton the chance to defend himself.

No sounds rose from the office as I went back downstairs. Hudson didn't come out as I gathered up the Webber's order, shut my cell phone down, and locked the front door behind me. His face didn't appear in the office window as I got in my car and backed out of the driveway.

Tears clogged my throat and stung my eyes.

I loved my husband wholeheartedly. He was my forever man, and that wouldn't change, but I wasn't about to ignore the questions that needed answers. Too many feelings had gotten involved with Colton in our short time together, a sense of belonging I felt sure had been real that I wasn't ready to give up without a fight.

I wouldn't accept excuses from Colton, but I would offer him a chance to explain.

Then I would go to my parents and process until I was ready for another confrontation with Hudson.

But I had cupcakes to deliver first.

Payment had already been made online, so I dropped the birthday treats for little Johnny Webber with his mother, and she stood at the door and chatted, her tone and smile bright. I struggled to even be polite and escaped the second I felt it wouldn't be rude to cut her short with my excuse of having some errands to run.

The only one being locating Colton.

We hadn't exchanged numbers, and Hudson had contacted him through the Missing Link app since that was the agreement we'd had going into the whole affair.

Colton had said he'd bought a house on Groveland Street, so I made my way across town, attempting to work through possible outcomes. My stomach churned, and my shoulders tensed as I clung to the steering wheel, but I couldn't keep my eyes from welling and occasionally spilling.

Relationships were hard work. Love sometimes sucked.

But both could be so rewarding and worth the pain.

Hoping for the best outcome even though I had no clue what that might look like, I flipped on my blinker and took a left onto Colton's street, fingers crossed he would be home and not out at some bar drinking his sorrow away.

If he was even truly upset by being tossed out on his ass without discussion.

He'd told us about his fixer-upper, but his truck with the Harper's Construction sign on the door revealed his location before the lumber and dumpster in front of the house caught my attention.

My heart raced as I pulled into the driveway behind his white pickup, and I braced myself for heartache while climbing from my car.

The heat of the afternoon hit me like a brick wall, suffocating and restrictive. It was like wading through split pea soup to make it to his front door. Eyes closed and inhaling deeply, I knocked, the keys in my free hand digging into my palm.

The door swung inward, and I tried for a smile that wobbled.

"Lin." Colton glanced toward my car as though looking for Hudson.

"Can I come in?" I asked, my tone shaky and reedy as hell.

He stepped back, rubbing a palm over his chest.

A quick glance around revealed his truth about fixing the house up. Construction tools lay scattered around, and two new windows leaned against the wall still wrapped in plastic. But a fleece throw was draped over the back of his couch and a pair of dirty socks lay beside the scarred-up coffee table, making the place appear at least lived-in.

"Have a seat." He motioned toward the couch, his focus on my face unnerving in its intensity.

I perched on the edge of one corner, trying not to wring my hands into tight knots.

He did the same on the opposite end as though unsure —as he well should be. God knew I felt the same.

"How do you know Ryan Foley?" I asked and held my breath.

"Who?"

"Ryan Foley," I repeated, searching Colton's face for any evidence he lied. He held my stare, didn't shift, and honestly appeared puzzled. "The man Peter cheated with," I explained. "Hudson told me he mentioned Ryan to you a while ago."

"I remember him telling me who the guy was but wouldn't have remembered his name to save my damn life until just now. Can you tell me what the hell went down? Why your husband looked ready to beat the shit out of me?"

"Peter texted him a picture of you and Ryan together at some club."

Colton stared at me, his gaze unwavering. "What the fuck? I have no idea who this Ryan dude is, and I never met Peter until that day on the library stairs."

A rush of relief swept through me, sagging me back into the couch. Unlike Hudson, I trusted easily, especially when no hint of shadiness and only puzzlement lined Colton's face. I'd spent three years living with a liar and had learned what bullshit looked like.

A little too late for that relationship, but tools hard-earned and appreciated in that moment.

"Is it possible the two of you hooked up without getting names?" I asked, at least needing to find another answer to how the image existed.

"Definitely not Peter." Colton shook his head, his tone firm. "But Ryan? I honestly don't know because I have a sexual history some might be ashamed of."

Considering my husband's and my polyamorous relationship, I didn't feel he ought to be. "I left my phone in the car, but if you want to look him up on social media..."

Colton hopped up. "Be right back."

His bare feet shuffled back the ranch's hallway, and I took a few cleansing breaths, hope renewed while taking note of the construction dust covering the coffee table and

TV stand in front of me. My fingers itched to straighten and clean, so I clasped them atop my lap again.

Colton hurried back, settling in a little closer and with a lot less reserve than when he'd first sat down. Dark eyebrows furrowed, he swiped and tapped. "There are over a dozen guys on here named Ryan Foley...what's he look like?"

I scooted closer until our thighs touched. Butterflies swarmed my stomach, but I focused on the screen in his hand. Nausea killed off the flutters. "Third one down," I said, easily recognizing the older man who'd desecrated our bed with Peter.

Colton clicked on Ryan's profile then the picture. He shook his head. "Never met him."

"You're sure? Maybe you were drunk one night—"

"I don't ever have more than two beers when I go out with the guys," he said. "I don't touch hard stuff or drugs either. That's what left me an orphan and made my childhood a living hell."

That motherly instinct that had gotten me in trouble with Peter rose to the surface. I wanted to wrap Colton in my arms and give him all the words of affirmation he must have not received when he was a little boy. The possibility of that truth hurt my heart.

I longed to ease both of our pain. "Come here," I murmured, winding an arm around his shoulders and opening the other in invitation.

He moved closer without hesitation, angling in an awkward bend to put his head on my chest. A shuddered exhale left him sagged against me, and I closed my eyes, resting my cheek on his silken hair. The sense of rightness I'd always felt with him settled into place.

Hudson would get back on board once he allowed Colton a chance to speak.

But that confrontation would have to wait because I had no more energy to even think beyond the feel of Colton winding his arms around my waist and holding me tight.

37

COLTON

I clung to Madeline, and some of the upheaved pieces inside me clicked back into place. Hudson had flipped the fuck out, and I knew from experience when to give a man space without question. But leaving without understanding what had happened for him to turn on me like that drove me fucking insane.

A couple of days would give him time to calm down, and I'd planned to reach out to him through the app to find out what I'd done wrong.

Because he'd obviously thought I had.

And Madeline's explanation provided the answer even though the reason only raised more questions.

I had no fucking clue who the hell Ryan was outside the knowledge he was the guy Peter had cheated with. He didn't look familiar at all—and I'd have remembered the guy's baby blues and the lines around them from his wide grin. Another silver fox like Hudson but clean-shaven, if he'd given me a hint of interest before I'd met the Youngs, I'd have been all over his ass.

Madeline ran her fingers through my hair, and I sighed

against her soft breasts, loving how her heart beat beneath my cheek in a soothing rhythm.

Almost perfection.

"We need to go talk to Hudson," I said, not shifting from her even though the weird way I twisted my core to hug her was far from comfortable. Almost as bad as that yoga shit she'd insisted on.

"I can't right now. Too exhausted."

I pulled away at her tired, resolute tone. "Are you okay?"

She smiled even though her eyes held hints of moisture. "Hudson can be stubborn."

I huffed a snort of agreement.

"And when he feels wronged," she continued, "he won't listen to explanations."

"He sees them as excuses," I tacked on, having firsthand knowledge of such a man from my last foster family's figurehead. Unease from having been in similar situations triggered all the negative feels in my chest, dropping my shoulders even farther.

I doubted I would ever be given a chance to prove myself.

"He does," Madeline said, "and if we went over there now, it would turn into another screaming match."

"How bad was it?" I asked, grasping her hand. A bit of comfort bled through the light touch but didn't ease the ache in my chest.

"Bad." She wound her fingers through mine, studying how our palms fit snugly together. "Peter is a liar and manipulator, and considering how he hurt Hudson, it'll definitely be a while before he's ready to discuss this and try to figure out what's going on."

I exhaled a heavy, concerned sigh while sagging back against the couch. Cheek against the back cushion, I studied

Madeline's sad eyes and the lines at the corners and around her downturned mouth. She didn't shy away when I tucked some of her silken tresses behind her ear that had escaped her messy ponytail. Leaning into my palm, she closed her eyes.

"I'm not willing to give this up without a fight," she murmured.

My heart skipped, and I rubbed my thumb over her chin. "This?"

Her eyelids opened, allowing me to see all the hurt and hope inside her heart. "You feel the connection between us, don't you?"

"As tangible as the smooth skin beneath my fingers," I stated without hesitation.

Smile wobbling, she clasped her palm over the back of my hand, holding me in place. "It's going to be tough, but I'm more than willing to endure whatever is necessary so we can see where this goes. But not today. I'll head to my parent's tonight and will go home to talk to Hudson once I'm rested."

"Stay here," I tossed out, far from ready for her to leave me. "But not...no messing around. I know Hudson gave you his consent in the past, but it would definitely be crossing a line at this point in time."

Her smile steadied as appreciation flooded her face. "Agreed."

Our hands dropped from her cheek and wound together again atop her thigh.

"He's being an asshole right now, but I won't disrespect him," I told her, unwavering in my determination to keep from touching her in intimacy.

"Once things have settled, he'll appreciate that choice

even though I could really use a good fuck into a mattress until I pass out."

Blood seeped into my groin at the image she'd created in my head, but I pushed the erotic thoughts away, needing to give comfort in a way that wouldn't be cheating. "How about I just hold you instead—with clothes on."

She sighed and slumped. "That sounds heavenly."

"Are you hungry?" I asked. "I already ate a little earlier, but I can get you something."

"No. I'm good. Too many emotions on high alert to handle food."

It wasn't yet dark outside the living room windows I needed to replace, but Madeline looked like she needed to lay down and pass the fuck out.

"Come on." I stood, tugging her to her feet. She already wore another pair of leggings and a long T-shirt, so I didn't offer to get her something more comfortable to sleep in. "Bedroom's back here. We can snuggle and chat until you're ready to sleep."

"Let me go grab my bag and those extra cupcakes for your co-workers first."

I followed on her heels to her car parked behind my truck but shoved my hands in my pockets to keep from touching her. "So you got the cupcakes finished," I said while she pulled an oblong box from her passenger seat.

"Frosted and delivered," she said. "I dropped them off on the way here, but these are the extras."

I took the offered box with heartfelt thanks. "So how did you find me?"

She retrieved her duffle from the backseat. "You said you lived on Groveland Street, so I decided I would drive down its length and keep my fingers crossed you were home and didn't park in a garage."

Once back inside, she called her parents, telling them she and Hudson had gotten into it and that she was spending the night with a friend. If she hadn't, she explained while I led her to my bedroom, Hudson would cause an even bigger ruckus when he got in touch with them—which he would eventually do—and her parents would worry.

I left the cupcakes on my small table and motioned Madeline into my bedroom, which didn't consist of more than a queen-sized bed, a chest of drawers, and one bedside table.

She eyed my mussed bedding while doing that female magic thing of taking off the bra beneath her shirt.

I set her bag on the floor at the same time her bra landed there as well.

"Sorry about the mess," I muttered while attempting to straighten the top sheet and comforter atop my bed.

"Don't worry about it." She climbed onto my mattress, curled into a fetal position, and rubbed her face on my pillow. "Smells like you."

"Hope that's a good thing," I replied with a snort, trying to remember when I'd washed my sheets last.

"The best thing."

Well, pump my ego and make me grin.

I kept my back to her while stripping off my sweats in exchange for boxer briefs. The T-shirt I'd put on at hearing her knock stayed stretched over my shoulder.

Just seeing Madeline in my bed chubbed my dick up, so I kept my groin away from her lush ass when I wrapped around her in big spoon style. "Okay?" I whispered against the top of her head, stray hairs from her loosened ponytail tickling my nose and chin.

"Yeah." She snuggled back a bit, and I gritted my teeth as we connected fully from chest to thighs.

"Sorry." My voice was rasp and sex. Couldn't fucking help it.

"I don't mean to tease, but knowing I'm desired..."

"Now who's being needy?" I asked with a grin, winding my arm tighter around her belly.

"I'm not going to apologize."

"I don't want you to." I kissed her head and closed my eyes, deciding to keep quiet and allow her to rest unless she chose differently.

Madeline's silence lasted all of three minutes. "Talk to me so I don't think about sex."

I huffed a laugh. "What about?"

"Anything. You," she hastened to correct herself. "Tell me about the childhood that created the man I still see as my future boyfriend."

A swell of hope rose inside my chest even though the idea of reliving my past would hurt like a bitch slap. I gave Madeline what she wanted, starting with my earliest memories of sharing a bedroom with three other boys, two of us sleeping on the full-sized lower bunk bed. We'd been crammed in like sardines, ate box mac and cheese along with cardboard-like chicken nuggets for lunches and dinners. I remembered cornflakes and oatmeal without nearly enough sugar.

I'd lost track of the homes I'd found myself in after that first one. By the time I hit thirteen and finally settled into what appeared to be a possible forever home, I had chips on my shoulders, didn't trust a soul, and hated authority.

My foster family from that time and I had gotten along well enough in the beginning because their large, spacious house didn't smell like stale cigarettes and booze, and it seemed like heaven. They didn't take in kids for the government handouts. They had money of their own and bought brand cereal full of sugar and cavities. The mom also stayed home, and we sat down as a family of three to dinner at least five out of seven nights a week.

"But then I got into a fistfight at school, and they thought they could discipline me atop the suspension," I said. "It didn't matter the asshole bully had called me names and made school a living hell for close to three months. I lost my shit a second time when the couple I'd hoped to have adopt me thought a double punishment was called for."

"What did you do?" Madeline asked.

"Knocked over a bookshelf. Smashed a lamp. Kicked my foot through the drywall. I knew they hadn't really loved me, so the whole 'This isn't going to work out' didn't come as a big surprise. My caseworker had my ass in the back of her car within a few hours."

Madeline laced her fingers through mine atop her belly.

I went on to tell her about the next two families that put up with a lot of bullshit—because I'd been full of it for close to a year before calming and *hoping* again.

Then high school hit. A whole new world. Girls, boys, sex...

Another well-to-do family had brought me into their fold, making me a middle child of sorts between their two beautiful daughters. I had affection from the mom without hesitation. Words of affirmation from the dad.

And a boner for both girls.

Like a typical teenage perv, I'd watched them—a true Peeping Tom—the same as I'd done that day with Madeline and Hudson while he'd fucked her in their kitchen. But unlike that day, the girls hadn't been aware someone stole around on silent feet, attempting to get a peek of flesh whenever possible.

The dad had caught me jerking off while pressing my eye to the crack I'd silently created in the bathroom door while his younger daughter showered.

He'd grabbed me by the hair and tossed me down the stairs, my dick hanging out and everything.

That had ended the second promised home and forever family.

"Did you wind up on the streets?"

"A group home until I turned eighteen," I answered. "By then, I was already working for Blake's dad, and he helped set me up with an apartment and gave me an old beat-up truck. That man kept me out of trouble, and I stayed on to work with Blake once his dad retired and moved to Florida."

"You finally had a little bit of luck in your corner."

"I did," I agreed wholeheartedly. "There are thousands of kids in foster care, desperate for love. A family. A place to belong."

Madeline didn't speak for a while, and I allowed myself to sink into deeper rest. Talking about the shit of my past hadn't stirred up the type of bitterness it usually did.

Instead, I felt that sense of all I'd been looking for in life as a kid right there in her arms. I even found the courage to hope for more though we had one hell of a stubborn mountain to climb ahead of us.

38

HUDSON

I'd smashed the fucking clock with my fist after countless hours of its ticking down mocking me from my desk long after Madeline had left. Silence hovered over the house like a death shroud while I'd nursed my bruised hand and didn't move from my office chair again until darkness took over the window.

My full bladder eventually enticed my aching bones into action, and I fought the constant replay of our argument through my head.

My sweet, loving Mads had actually walked out without letting me know where she headed or for how long. Honoring her desire for space left me desolate, my shoulders sagging and head pounding. More than anything, I'd disappointed my wife in how I'd handled the entire situation, but I wouldn't bend on my stance.

Colton had basically fucked me without lube, and I refused to hear any bullshit excuses as to why. Once with Peter had been bad enough. A second time even though it wasn't our ex? Infuriating and finishing all the same. There would be no more playing. No more sharing of my wife.

And sure as fuck no more lowering my walls to the possibility of hurt.

Peter had ripped my heart out.

Colton? We didn't have much history, and I'd been wary even while messing around, but I still felt the edges of the jagged knife stabbing into my chest, severing the connection we'd begun to build.

Once finished in the bathroom, I made my way to the kitchen, wishing for numbness and quiet thoughts.

The place sat spotless, all trace of cupcake making gone —including the scent of baking I sought a whiff of. Mads also hadn't left any of the extra treats behind like she normally did when filling an order.

That pain in my chest intensified until I struggled to breathe.

I stood at the kitchen window, still able to see the outline of the deck in the darkness through the wetness hazing my eyes. Memories of watching it being built swelled inside my mind.

Images flashed through my consciousness, every goddamn one of them featuring Colton front and center. Sweaty. Shirtless. Bent over the couch taking my dick. Naked in bed wrapped around my wife, his muscular backside pressed against my front.

Hanging on Ryan Foley and licking his cheek like that fucker was the sweetest treat on the planet.

My jaw ached from clenching even though my throat swelled to the point I struggled to draw breath.

There would be no coming back from his betrayal, same as with Peter.

What mattered to me was keeping my wife safe even if it hurt like fuck to give her that space she'd requested.

I fished my cell from my pocket and called her mom,

needing to at least know she'd gotten there without issue so I could put some part of my brain to rest.

But she hadn't gone there.

"She's staying with a friend" was the explanation I got from her mom.

Knowing Mads, that was all she gave her parents to ensure I honored her desire for me to leave her alone.

"Fuck." I rubbed weary hands over my face, remembering the woman she'd met at her support group. Tara. I didn't know her last name or her address, but Mads had told me she walked to the library on Wednesday nights for their weekly meetings.

As bullheaded as Mads and I both tended to be, I expected it would be a few days before we would be able to get back on track, but I needed to at least find out where she was.

Three years earlier, I'd have bet money she'd be with one of our friends from the poly group we used to hang with. Getting together with Peter had steered us in a different path, and we'd definitely lacked companionship outside each other ever since he'd betrayed us. Tara was the logical choice since they'd done lunch and coffee quite a few times after becoming friends..

I climbed into my truck and made my way toward the center of town, my radio silent and windows down. For the first time in days, a cool breeze had conquered the night air, allowing me to finally fill my lungs.

Taking the second right off the rotary toward the library, I slowed, my head swiveling side to side while checking out the houses. A thorough search of every side street and alley within the neighborhood didn't allow me sight of Mads's car.

Sitting at a stop sign, I pondered where else she might go, and the second option tightened my jaw once more.

Should have thought of him first.

Mads was thoroughly disappointed in my refusal to allow that cheating whore a chance to explain himself, but I knew she would sit and listen until Colton convinced her of his innocence.

I stomped on the gas, heading north toward Groveland Street, my stomach twisting tight.

For the first time since our fight, worry dug its slithering tentacles through my thoughts. In all the times we'd invited a man into our bed, I'd never felt a hint of insecurity about her leaving me—but Colton wasn't like our usual. He was somehow...more. A force I hadn't been able to deny. A delicious temptation who knew how to please my wife as though he'd spent years mapping out her body and mind, thus satisfying *me*. A connection that had dug its nails into us even though I hadn't wanted it.

Faced with him alone and hurting, would Mads cross lines we'd set in stone years earlier? If he convinced her he'd done nothing wrong, that he'd never caught the name of the guy he'd smothered like cling wrap, would she allow him to love on her without my consent?

Had my inability to listen to excuses caused a breakdown of our marriage I'd thought indestructible?

Nausea stirred regardless of the lack of food in my stomach. I clenched the steering wheel to keep my hands from trembling as I worried my lower lip between my teeth. The fucking waiting to find out the truth damn near stopped my heart.

I couldn't fathom losing the only good thing in my life, refused to imagine it.

Colton's fixer-upper sat a few houses down on the left...

My breath ripped from my lungs at seeing Mads car parked behind his truck in the driveway.

Relief at having found her did nothing to lessen the toxic swirl of emotions eating at my guts.

Doing a slow drive-by, I craned my neck to check the place out as best I could in the darkness. A lone light shone down onto the stoop, but no others appeared in the windows. Making a U-turn at the next intersection, I considered the assumption that slammed into my head like a goddamn axe.

It was well past eleven, and all the lights in the house were off.

She was in his bed.

Rage should have lit like a short fuse, promising an explosion, but my goddamn mood crumpled under the weight of her decision.

She'd gone to Colton, and whatever bullshit excuse he'd given, she *had* accepted it.

I'd fucked up even if my sense of self-preservation screamed I'd done right by both of us.

Slowly passing Colton's house once more, I double-checked the visible windows, holding my breath. Hoping. Actually fucking praying for a hint they still stayed up and chatted before she left to either go home or head to Tara's.

Not one goddamn light glowed from within.

Knocking on the door would only lead to a shirtless Colton answering the door smelling like my wife, pussy, and cum. I growled, hating that my dick twitched with life when it should have been hiding like a fucking turtle, hissing and pissed off.

She'd chosen Colton for the night, but I wasn't going down without a confrontation for the fucking ages. Mads and I had too many years, too much of our past lives intertwined to split apart into two separate entities again.

Knowing an argument in that moment would lead to broken knuckles, bleeding faces, flashing lights, and sirens, I tore my focus off Colton's house and headed south. Every block put between us caused the fissures inside my soul to split further, and I focused on the heat of anger rather than the heartache her choice had caused.

I might have been the catalyst, but she'd still made a conscious decision to step outside the bounds of our marriage.

Sleeping would hopefully dissolve some of my displeasure, and I would give Mads another full day before setting shit right between her and I. If that meant hearing Colton's bullshit reasons for hiding the fact he knew who Ryan was, then so be it.

I would listen, but that didn't mean I had to believe him.

Because I'd been bitten once before, and there was nothing he could say that would be reason enough to justify deception.

39

MADELINE

I woke up pressed against Colton's back, my arm wrapped around his muscular core in a protective hold. We shared a pillow. The other, he clutched to his front, its softness against my forearm.

Had we been in our bed, it would have been Hudson rather than the feather-stuffed material cradling Colton between us.

I couldn't help but wonder if Colton had sought out something to hold during his sleep, unconscious in his desire for my husband. The thought tightened my throat as the reality of our situation swamped back into my mind, stealing those first few seconds of peaceful waking before my mind began to race.

The moment had passed much too quickly, but I closed my eyes, trying to grasp that sense of contentment for just a little while longer. I breathed in the scent of Colton's soap, staying still instead of rubbing my face over his neck to feel his soft skin on my cheeks.

Heat radiated off his hard body like a furnace, and I

wanted to burrow in closer, wiggle around until he woke, turned, and gave me a sleepy-eyed smile.

My heartbeat picked up pace at the fantasy of even more, and I parted my lips as my lungs demanded more oxygen.

How easily he turned me on when I thought I'd been broken, barely on the mend. Like a double shot of espresso, he'd woken my libido back to what it had been before, my desire to feel—to enjoy everyday things.

But not without Hudson.

I slowly pulled away, hating the coolness over my front, the emptiness of my arms.

Colton didn't stir, and I slid from his bed. I crept around the room, retrieving my bag before exiting his bedroom on near-silent feet.

Setting my duffle on the kitchen table, I took a look around, noting the coffeepot, a toaster, and a drainer full of clean dishes.

A slight smile curved my lips to find he'd washed up his dinner things rather than letting them sit in the sink like Hudson would have done.

"Such a good boy," I murmured to myself, happy even though heaviness and licks of depression still weighed, wanting to own my heart and thoughts.

I found the coffee tin and filters in the cabinet above the pot but didn't head to the fridge immediately after getting the brew.

Lips in a thin line, I dug my cell from my bag and powered it on even though I hadn't downed a sip of coffee to further wake my brain.

Two texts waited for me from the night before, one from my mom, the other from my husband.

Mom had just let me know that Hudson had contacted her and that she told him I was staying with a friend.

Hudson: **I hope your night with him was worth it. This is far from over.**

Brow furrowed, I fought to read between the lines, my chest tight as my heart raced. Did he think I'd left him for Colton? Did he honestly believe I would betray him the way Peter had done? And were his words meant as a threat or a promise of reconciliation? They sounded like the former, but I couldn't tell.

All I knew for certain was a pile of bullshit drama awaited me. I was over Hudson's stubbornness, and he was *going* to listen. We would get to the bottom of the shit Peter had stirred up to hurt us.

The little brat had been a master manipulator, and I'd learned a few things in hindsight. While staring at the brewing coffee, a plan began to form in my brain. One that included lying, which I normally wouldn't condone, but desperate times and all that.

Soft footfalls sounded behind me, and I glanced over my shoulder, my heart stuttering at the sight of Colton with mussed hair, those bedroom eyes half-lidded and still sleepy.

"Morning." His voice held a sexy rasp as he wrapped his arms around me. Face in my neck—what was it with his and Hudson's addiction to my neck—he breathed me in while his morning wood poked at my belly.

I hugged him tight, releasing a sigh at how easily he settled peace over my mind.

"Did you get any rest?" he asked, easing away from me.

"I slept through the night."

A crooked smirk quirked his lips. "Me too. Second best night I've had in my life."

"And when was the first?" I couldn't help but ask.

"When it was a Young/Colton sandwich in a bed I really hope I get to lounge in again." His gaze lingered on my lips, and I knew we both wanted the same thing.

"Last night's pillow couldn't replace Hudson, hmm?"

"Not even close."

We stepped away from each other as though of the same mind. "I'm going to make us breakfast," I stated, moving toward the refrigerator, "then I'm going to head home—but after a pit stop."

"Where?" he asked as I scanned the shelves.

"Peter's."

I turned with a carton of eggs and OJ in my hands.

Colton's brow furrowed, but his smirk grew wider. "What do you have up your sleeve?"

"Bread?"

He motioned toward a basket atop the counter.

"Frying pan?"

He pointed at a drawer.

I set about making us some food and laid out my thoughts. He held his peace until I finished.

"While I like your plan, you aren't going over there alone," he stated firmly, staring at me over the kitchen table as we went to dive into our breakfast.

"Don't you have to work?"

"I'll call Blake and let him know I'm taking a personal day. I want this situation resolved and over with for good. I wouldn't be worth a shit on the jobsite if I didn't take care of this."

"And you really want those cupcakes all to yourself," I tacked on with a smile.

He shrugged, the slightest bit sheepish. "Maybe."

"I'm more than happy to have you by my side."

With his input, we adjusted what I'd put together in my head then readied for two confrontations both of which I hoped could go well.

But would probably blow up in our faces.

———

Peter had friends from before his time with us, and with how he'd hinted at needing safety again, I expected he'd gone back to live with them.

Sure enough, his Camry sat in front of the dilapidated house a couple of towns over, which was well-known for drugs and crime.

I clutched at Colton's hand for support and appearances. We represented a united front, and if Peter could see that from the onset, we might stand a chance of swaying him into giving us answers.

Colton set his phone to record in his free hand, keeping it pointed at the ground to not raise suspicion. "Ready for this?" he whispered near my ear as we climbed crumbling block stairs to the front door.

"No—but here we go," I muttered under my breath while smiling in case Peter glanced out one of the house's filthy windows.

Some greasy-haired, too-thin guy answered to our knock, the open door releasing a waft of weed skunk and burnt toast past my nose. Track marks littered his arm that he used to scratch his balls through boxers—his only item of clothing. "If you're here to tell me Jesus died for my sins, you can go fuck yourselves."

Colton chuckled.

"Actually, we're here to see Peter," I said with a kind smile.

He took his time checking us both out head to toe. "The fuck are you to him?"

"Hopefully, his soon-to-be lovers," Colton supplied while I scrambled for an answer.

"Kinky fuckers," the guy muttered. "He expecting you?"

"No," I answered, "but if you let him know Madeline is here, I'm sure he'll tell you to let us in."

Shrugging, the guy stepped back and motioned us toward the dim stairwell. "He's up in his room. Second door on the left. Pretty sure his hookup from last night took off earlier this morning, but knock before barging in unless you want an eyeful of twink dick and tits."

The scent of mildew lingered beneath the visible haze of pot inside the house, and I refused to look at the carpet beneath my flip-flops...until concern I might step on a used needle had me scanning for hazards before putting each foot down in front of the other.

Every tread groaned beneath us as we climbed the stairwell, and I kept my breaths shallow, grimacing at the overwhelming smell of dirty laundry.

One of the roommates had a cat that went flying down the stairs, hissing at us as he went. We encountered his fresh mess in the middle of the hallway, its stench gagging me.

"Fuck, this place is awful," Colton muttered.

I hummed an agreement and came to a stop before Peter's door. Adrenaline had me on edge, and I squeezed Colton's hand.

"Okay?" he asked.

"Yeah," I whispered. "Let's get this over with." I knocked, having zero wish to walk into a bedroom and see someone owning Peter's ass. Not that it would upset me, but the memories sure as hell would.

"What?" Peter hollered from inside, his tone annoyed.

"It's Madeline," I called through the door.

With a couple of hard thumps, the door flew inward. Pink fused Peter's cheeks while the remainder of his face appeared sickly pale, his pupils pinned. "Mads! I—"

His voice cut off as his gaze moved to Colton.

I waited, giving him a moment to glance at our entwined hands.

"Can we come in, baby?" I murmured, using the sweet tone he always used to melt for before he flipped out and slammed the door in our faces.

Peter blinked, his hitching shoulders falling back down as the rest of his body twitched. "Wh-what's going on?" he whispered, appearing so damn lost I'd have been sucked right back into caring for him if he hadn't hurt me so badly with his stupid choices.

"I finally got smart, left Hudson, and I'm missing my precious boy."

Peter eyed Colton again before giving me his attention, shifting restlessly on his feet. "You're...with this guy now?"

"Yes, and we've talked things over. I explained what had happened with Ryan, that you were only trying to show us how you were feeling. Can we come in and talk? Please?" I used my begging tone he'd only heard in bed, and he swallowed hard, nodding.

"Yeah." He rubbed a forearm beneath his nose and stepped back.

The room was a disaster and smelled heavily of cloying incense. Dingy curtains framed a disgusting window, so badly smudged that hardly any sunlight filtered through. Soiled sheets clung to two corners of the double mattress dumped against the far wall. Empty booze bottles scattered around mounds of clothing.

I picked my way toward the room's center, taking a quick

scan of the only piece of furniture. An old, low bureau. Coins, deodorant, the burning incense stick, and a few other toiletries lay atop it—along with a square of glass littered with white powder, stark cut lines through the substance revealing its identity.

Turning toward Peter once more, I gave him puppy dog eyes, hating how my heart ached for the depravity he'd fallen into. "It looks like you *do* need me," I told him, releasing my hold on Colton to open my arms.

I'd warned myself I might have to hug Peter. Readied my mind, but my stomach still heaved as Peter threw himself at me, big fat tears rolling down his gaunt cheeks. Sobs wracked his body, and I glanced at Colton, nodding at the bureau, my heart no less softened toward the young man clinging to me like a life raft.

Colton lifted his cell.

"Shh," I murmured to Peter while I'd have preferred to toss him into the deep end of a pool. "It's going to be okay, baby, I promise. Just let it out—tell me everything like you used to do when you got overwhelmed, and I'll keep you safe you through it all."

"I messed up," he started, and I bit back the snort wanting to escape me. "After I fucked Ryan...I came back here, and it's been one big backslide to where I was before you and Hudson saved me."

He'd messed with drugs a little before my husband and I had invited him into our lives, but things had gotten worse, I realized as he continued to spill his poor life choices. Drugs, sex, and alcohol. Refusing to cringe away from him, I kept my arms locked as he soaked my T-shirt with his tears.

"There's nothing wrong with a little recreational use," Colton interjected the second Peter stopped spilling, and I shot him a glare.

He winked. *Trust me*, he mouthed while slipping his cell phone into his front pocket.

I nodded.

"Coke keeps me going all night long," Colton continued, and had I not known his expressive eyes, I'd have thought he told the truth.

Peter lifted his head off my chest and sniffling, turned a wary gaze his way.

"My ass is dragging from working the night shift." Colton nodded toward the bureau. "Mind if I have a hit?"

"There's not much left, but go ahead."

Colton turned his back on us, a slight scraping noise reaching my ears. "There's plenty here for two—and I'll reimburse you. Promise." He bent his head and inhaled noisily.

What. The. Fuck.

40

COLTON

I straightened, not sure what else to do to make it look like I'd just filled my nose with cocaine. Having no clue, I stayed put with my body between the drugs and the two people behind me. "That's some good shit," I said, using an old, rusted razor blade to scrape what remained on the glass from his prior uses into a thin line. "Gotta get me more of this."

Turning, I found both Peter and Madeline eyeing me. He craned to peer around me to see how much I'd left him.

She frowned at me, her eyes troubled.

I winked again, shaking my head the slightest bit.

She visibly relaxed.

"Get your sweet backside over here," I told Peter, holding out the cut piece of straw he must've used to snort with. The thing hadn't come anywhere near my nose, but he would never know that. "Finish this bit off, then hook me up with your supplier, yeah? I see a lot of fun in our future, boy. Oh, and I'm sorry about all that shit I gave you at their house— had to make myself look good for Hudson. Didn't mean a goddamn word of it. Felt guilty as hell after you took off like you were afraid I was gonna kick your ass or something. Fuck knows it's too damn cute for me to hurt—unless you'd want me to."

"Not into that shit," Peter muttered and stumbled from Madeline's arms, his hazed-over gaze a little wary of me.

"Then I won't touch you with anything but gentleness while making you come." The idea of doing anything with the little shit churned my guts, but the words had the desired effect.

He approached me, and I stepped back from the bureau to give him room while sliding my cell from my front pocket.

Peter lowered his head, and I turned my camera his way, catching him snorting the entire line. The second he stood, I let the camera hang limp in my hand, pointed toward the floor.

"You gonna be a sweetheart and hook me up?" I asked, moving in close and placing my hand on his hip.

He was so damn bony...the kid was a goddamn mess.

Peter peered up at me with big blue eyes and pinned pupils. He sniffed, studying my face. "Are you serious about wanting me with the two of you?"

"Let's face it—Hudson is one sexy silver fox, but you're the kind of boy I want to spoil rotten," I lied. "I wanna hold you all night long and lose my voice telling you how beautiful you are. Pet every inch of your body..." I feigned lust while glancing down over his slight form and leaning forward to whisper, "Want to hear you whimper my name while I fill you with my dick."

A shiver pebbled his skin.

Madeline wrapped her arms around me from behind, pressing her cheek against my bicep to better see Peter. "Say you'll be ours. Let's find that heaven we had once before but with a man who isn't as stubborn and strict as

Hudson. Someone who won't flip out because of one bad decision."

Peter's eyes welled again. "O-Okay."

She reached around me to cup his cheek, and he leaned into her touch as though starved for affection.

I knew that feeling well.

But not one lick of empathy lit inside me for the idiot.

"That picture you sent Hudson is what broke us apart," Madeline whispered. "I can't thank you enough for opening my eyes to how unforgiving he is, Peter."

"Yeah?"

"Yes. I don't know where you got that image—or *how* since Colton hasn't ever met Ryan, but—"

"I swapped his face out." Peter shrugged, his grin almost feral when he'd been teary-eyed seconds before. "Easy as shit."

"You're so smart," Madeline murmured, and fuck, I admired how the lies slid from her tongue without hesitation or a hint of bullshit. "Now, Colton and I have to go to the house and tell Hudson that our relationship with him is over for good, but we'll come back to pick you up. You have to be patient this time though, okay? Can we trust you to stay put and wait for us?"

"Yes."

"Who do I need to see to get a baggie of that shit?" I asked, nodding toward the empty glass and straw because I needed more info to set this place on fucking fire.

"Kevin. He lives here too."

"Dark hair? Thin as fuck with pitch-black eyes?"

Peter nodded. "He's the only one allowed to answer the door, so yeah."

I leaned down and kissed Peter's forehead, forcing my lips to linger when I'd rather have broken his nose. "I can't wait to see what our futures hold," I said, pulling away and smiling. "Pack up your stuff, Peter."

He blinked up at me with a hesitant smile. "I'll be a good boy for you. Promise."

"I'm sure you will." Ruffling his hair, I slid my cell into my pocket and grabbed Madeline's hand.

She didn't say a word as I led her out of the bedroom and down the creaking stairs. Luckily, Kevin wasn't in the entryway, and we unlocked the chain and stepped out into fresh air and sunlight. It felt like dead skin shed with every step we took down the walkway away from that filthy-as-fuck house.

One bad decision had taken Peter from the Youngs' home to that shithole.

I'd had similar things happen to me, my life turned on a dime from poor choices, but I still didn't feel sorry for the little shit. He'd made his fucking bed by intentionally hurting two people I...cared about.

Could definitely fall for.

Maybe one day love—if I ever figured out what that felt like.

I opened the passenger door for Madeline before rounding the truck to climb in.

Neither of us spoke as the AC kicked on, and I pulled away from the curb.

Madeline released a slow exhale and once out of sight from the house reached over for my hand. "That was almost too easy."

"I didn't expect to just walk in, hear what we wanted, and get the hell out without issue. That kid is high as a fucking kite and desperate though. Fuck, what a mess."

Madeline hummed an agreement and squeezed my hand. "Just checking, but you didn't actually..."

"Nope. Never have, never will."

I pulled into a strip mall and parked.

"You recorded everything?" she asked, rubbing her hands over her stretch pants as I retrieved my phone.

"Yep." I clicked on the edit button and set to work. "Just gonna cut this shit up a bit and send it on to Reid's uncle."

I'd gotten Chief of Police Sullivan's number before we'd set out, and even though he could easily track where the texts came from, I asked him to take the info I sent along as an anonymous tip to the proper authorities of Peter's city. I hit send on a few clips along with the house's address.

Maybe it would be enough for a warrant to search the place, maybe not, but at least we tried to get Peter in trouble so he hopefully wouldn't bother us for a while.

"Ready?" I asked, one hand on the steering wheel, the other grabbing hold of Mads's again.

"This is by far going to be the worse of the two."

I expected she spoke the truth, but I just hoped Hudson would give me enough time to play back Peter's confession about that goddamn picture before slamming a fist into my nose for holding his wife all night long.

———

Being a Monday morning, we weren't sure if Hudson would be home. But his truck sat in the driveway, and had I been in his shoes, I would have taken the day off too.

Madeline and I didn't hold hands while walking up to the front door. We didn't so much as touch as she unlocked, went inside, and I followed.

I shut the door behind us, my heart pounding as adrenaline coursed through my system, ten times more intense than with getting ready to face Peter. My goddamn hands shook, so I shoved them into my pockets. The eggs and toast breakfast Madeline had made for us settled like a rock in my stomach.

Footsteps sounded from the office, ramping up my jitters, and seconds later, Hudson appeared, haggard and unkempt like he hadn't slept since Madeline had left. He studied his wife's face first, a tenderness in his gaze, before turning toward me.

Cold solidified in my bones at his hardened eyes, but he didn't light into me like I'd expected.

He once more gave his attention to Madeline, staying silent, as though waiting on her. I'd never seen him take a back seat and definitely hadn't imagined he would hold his tongue.

"We need to talk," Madeline stated quietly, her voice shaky.

"I've got nothing to say."

"Good," Madeline shot back. "Then you can just sit your ass down and listen."

Without argument, Hudson headed toward the living room and settled in a recliner, leaving the couch for me and Madeline. Definitely not what I had expected. She and I both sat, keeping a good two feet between us.

"Let's hear it." One barked command from Hudson at his wife—not me—and Madeline glanced my way.

Rather than opening my mouth, I pulled out my cell and clicked into my videos. Having made a copy to splice apart for the Chief of Police, I chose the original full-length and hit play.

Our voices sounded muffled, but I turned the volume all the way up and set my cell on the coffee table between us so my shaking hands wouldn't betray my nerves.

Hudson didn't stare us down. He watched my phone as

though it might rise up and strike like a cobra. Wary. Unsure. Even a little bit pale as he heard us ask Kevin if Peter was there. "You went to see Peter?" he muttered, thunder in his eyes as he glared at Madeline.

"Just listen," she snipped, sounding a lot more put together than I felt.

At Madeline telling the little shit she missed her boy, Hudson growled. When she admitted to being with me instead of Hudson, his brow furrowed, and he settled back in his chair. Those intense eyes of his lifted once more to flit between us, and the second recognition of what we'd done hit him, he rubbed a hand over his beard.

Again with the pursed lips...a few raised eyebrows while eyeing us as the video played.

"Sneaky little fucker..." he mumbled, his focus on me when I'd feigned taking a hit of cocaine.

When Peter admitted to swapping out faces on that texted picture, Hudson tipped his head back against the chair, staring at the ceiling and listening until the video played out. "Fucking cunt," he whispered harshly before his head shot back down, and he captured my gaze.

I swallowed hard at the regret in his eyes, noting the rasp in his tone rather than admonishment.

"Tell me you didn't really snort that shit," he demanded, his face twisted as though concerned for my wellbeing.

Some of the tension slid off my shoulders, and I breathed a little bit easier. "I faked it so I could get Peter to give us what we needed."

Relief flooded Hudson's face, but his complexion remained pale. "I'm so fucking sorry," he said, gripping the arms of the chair.

I leaned forward, elbows on my knees, my focus on his

face. "I understand why you reacted the way you did to his text."

"There's no fucking excuse for how I just turned my back on you, treating you like garbage."

Exactly what I'd told Peter he had done to him and Madeline—and Hudson had overheard. My throat tightened over how Hudson had realized the level of hurt he'd caused.

"But I get it, Hudson," I insisted, determined to ease the guilt he had to be warring with. "I forgive you. End of. I would have flipped the fuck out too if that image had popped up on my cell's screen."

Hudson released a slow, steady exhale and nodded. "So next order of business—how the fuck did Peter get a picture of you to swap out your face?"

"Can I see the image he sent?" I asked.

Hudson got up and left us for a few seconds, and I grabbed Madeline's hand, squeezing and grinning like a goddamn dork.

"It's going to be okay," I said, my sense of relief palatable.

Pink had flushed her face, her eyes sparkling and so goddamn content my heart got all tingly and shit.

I kissed her fingers but dropped her hand when Hudson came back into the living room.

He handed me his cell with the texted picture already on screen.

I definitely didn't recognize the guy with me. The image itself, however, looked familiar. Hanging on the guy like a goofball rather than lover, my front leg lifted around his thighs as I faced him—licking his cheek...

Something scratched at the back of my memory, but I couldn't place it.

Zooming in, I noted it was definitely me. My profile

didn't appear fake. Sliding over to Ryan, I realized his face wasn't quite in proportion to his neck—a tattoo I recognized peeked from beneath the tight T-shirt of the arm grasping hold of my thigh.

"That's Blake, my boss and one of my best friends," I stated with a snort before chuckling as I remembered where that picture had originated and how. "Here." I handed Hudson back his phone and swiped mine to life. I rarely went on social media, so it didn't take me long to scroll back through time and find a picture Reid had taken three years earlier—of me hanging on Blake like a slobbering dork. The whole fake text fiasco settled in my head, I handed my cell over to Hudson.

Lips pursed, he shook his head, his eyes glinting with that hardness I hated to have focused at me. "That lying little piece of shit."

"Let me see." Madeline fluttered her fingers his way, and he gave her my cell.

"Did you fuck him?" she asked, making me blink and rethink her question.

"Blake?" I asked with a laugh even though I fucking *adored* the hint of jealousy in her tone. "Fuck no! He's all about the ladies and wouldn't let me on his dick even if I begged for it—which I've never done. The dude is hot but not my type. We were just giving him shit is all. Zoom in and you'll see he's rolling his eyes, and that hand on my thigh? He was pushing me away, not tugging me in tighter."

Madeline looked closer, and seemingly satisfied, handed my cell back to me.

I glanced up at Hudson who still stood beside me, my heart rate once more kicking back up. He'd apologized, and we'd gotten to the bottom of Peter's deception, but was he willing to lower his walls again? "So what happens now?"

41

HUDSON

I wasn't sure how to answer.

While I wanted to wholeheartedly believe every-thing I'd seen and heard, I needed all the thoughts in my head put to rest before making a decision to move forward and put the shit behind us.

"How did Peter know who you are to even find that picture of you on social media?" Mads asked the second glaring question in my brain before I got a chance to spew the first.

"I'm wondering about that too," Colton replied, his head tipped back to hold my gaze rather than addressing my wife. There was no hint of lies or manipulation in his dark eyes as he peered up at me, simply a longing. For understanding or me, I wasn't sure, but fuck how I wanted to fully relent and just fucking trust him.

"Blake posts to Harper's Construction social media and will sometimes tag the employees," he continued. "Seeing as how I have that magnetic sign on my truck indicating where I worked..." He shrugged. "It wouldn't take a detective to find my name. My profiles are public, so it's even easier to save an image and put Ryan's face atop Blake's. If you want, scroll through the posts. You'll see I was recently tagged in a couple from that project we have going on up north along the Merrimac River."

His words made perfect sense, and knowing how attached Peter had been to his cell and all those social sites he constantly scrolled through, I expected Colton had hit the nail on the head.

I inhaled fully, steeling myself for what I needed to have answered next.

"And what about last night?" I asked the number one question on my mind that had kept me awake until almost dawn.

I wasn't sure I could forgive intimacy when I hadn't given my consent. Their fucking wouldn't have been any different than Peter's betrayal, although the idea of them together didn't sicken me in the same way his had.

"What about it?" Mads asked.

I gave her my attention, easily reading her open expression. Not one ounce of guilt lay in her eyes she kept locked on mine. Her body also didn't bristle with aggravation at what she had to know I questioned.

"You stayed at his house," I stated quietly rather than throwing the words out as an accusation.

"She slept in my bed with me," Colton stated, pulling my focus off Mads, clearly taking full responsibility and hoping to shield her from whatever he would say next.

I feared the worst at his doing so and held my breath, waiting for an explanation.

Like Mads, his eyes didn't show any evidence of wrongdoing.

"We were fully clothed and didn't touch," he said. "I didn't even kiss her, Hudson—I would never do that to you."

He'd had the perfect opportunity. An upset wife he definitely had a thing for, and Mads was addictive as hell.

Swallowing hard and insides settling, I nodded in acceptance of his explanation. "Thank you," I rasped, believing every word he spoke.

I'd known from day one he was nothing like our ex, and both his and Mads's honesty in their eyes and on their faces released the rest of the tension riding my shoulders.

"So what happens now?" Colton repeated his question, his expression hopeful—and guarded.

He wanted us with clear desperation, and I recognized his need for acceptance and love. Mads had given it to me, and I was ready to open up to the possibility of doing the same for him since he'd more than proven I could trust him.

"It's not always going to be easy," I muttered before looking over at my wife. Desire shone in her eyes, and her quirked smile brought butterflies of all fucking things to life in my stomach. "I'm sorry," I told her.

"And I'm sorry if I said anything mean that might have upset you," she said, standing to come to me.

I opened my arms, and she settled in where she belonged, her cheek on my chest, her arms around my back. Relief flooded through me at the sense of rightness between us—but there was something missing. Clasping the back of my wife's head, I held out my other hand to Colton.

Wetness hazed his eyes. "You sure?"

Loaded fucking question.

I wanted him. That was the damned truth, and the only way we were going to move forward would be by squashing my suspicions and fears caused by past hurts. Some steps would be easier, some would be hard as fuck, I expected, but that brief taste of Colton had been more rewarding than any other time we'd invited a man into our bed.

And having him share in something as ridiculous as yoga then baking on a Sunday afternoon as though we were one happy family?

I sure as hell wanted more of that and was willing to make the effort. Especially if it meant finding a new foundation to build something beautifully fulfilling like Mads and I had always dreamed about.

"Get your ass over here." I growled the words.

He hopped up and slammed into my side, grabbing hold of both me and Mads with his strong arms. Snuggling in close, he nosed over my neck before nipping lightly.

"You need a shower, old man," he muttered.

I swatted his ass and grabbed a handful of his meaty backside when he groaned from the impact.

"So you really didn't give in to the temptation of this fine woman last night?" I pushed Colton for a second confirmation. Fuck knew I wouldn't be able to keep my hands off either of them if we lounged in a bed sharing breaths and pillows.

"If I said I might have licked her sweet pussy, would you call me a bad boy and spank my ass?" Colton asked, pulling back enough to smirk.

The fucker played with me.

"Brat," I muttered even as my dick swelled, thoroughly on board with his suggestion.

"He *didn't* touch me inappropriately," Madeline muttered, poking at my side.

"Morning wood?" I asked, *looking* for a reason to redden Colton's backside.

Both snickered.

"Fuck off," I muttered even though I didn't really care that they read my mind. "You know you both want it."

"Lin slipped out of bed before I woke up, but I was hard as fucking nails and dreaming about her mouth on me when I opened my eyes," Colton admitted, pressing his thickening cock against my hip. "I probably crossed a line or two while sleeping though, rubbing all over her curves with my hard dick."

"Mmm," I rumbled in appreciation for his honesty but more for his offering me what we all were thinking about. "That a fact?"

He shrugged, his dimple popping. "Maybe."

Good enough. "On the chair, Mads."

She moved away from us without question, her face flushed and eyes bright.

Peter had hated pain. Not even pinched nipples or hickeys.

Mads and I had both been a little disappointed with those limits of his—

I pushed the thought aside and focused on the *now*, the man who stood before us waiting and willing to fulfill our desires.

I settled in Madeline's spot on the couch and eyed Colton. "Are you sure this is what *you* want?"

The smirk died on his lips. He knew I asked about more than a couple of red handprints on his backside.

A married couple.

An old man who wouldn't be able to keep up with his youth.

"I've dreamed about this since the first day I met you," he told me. "Fantasized about every damn sex position three people can engage in. You've been the best spank bank imaginable, Hudson, but there's more to this—*us*—

than just the physical. I already feel it with Lin, and I think there's serious potential for the same with you and me. I've enjoyed every second I've been with you. Sharing lunch breaks. Bullshitting. Even the yoga I'm not sure I'll attempt ever again." He shrugged. "I just like hanging with you, Hudson."

His declaration increased the blood traveling to my groin and settled a sense of rightness in my head and heart.

I patted my lap, ready to give our good boy what he wanted. "Facedown. But bare your sweet ass for me first, Colton. And hurry it up."

"Jesus fuck, yes," Colton muttered, all but ripping his jeans down to his knees and throwing himself over my thighs. He shuddered against me, his dick hard on my leg.

I smoothed a hand over his pale cheeks, squeezing, spreading them enough for a peek at his hole. My cock stiffened to full mast, and I hummed approval at his complete submission. "Gonna paint this skin red with my hand, Colton," I warned him, reaching between his thighs to pull his cock straight down so he couldn't hump my leg. "You okay with that?"

"Shit yeah," he half-moaned as I stroked along his length.

"He's going to smear pre-cum all over the couch," I told Mads as the head of him brushed over the cushion and dragged a groan from his lips.

"Don't care," she whispered, the lust in her tone making me grin.

I glanced up to find her lips parted and pupils blown— and her gaze glued to my hand on Colton's dick. We'd fantasized about a fun spanking but hadn't ever gotten to enjoy one.

"Are you ready, love?" I asked her.

She licked her lower lip and shifted on the chair. "Mmm hmm."

"Wet already, huh?" I asked with a chuckle, tugging on Colton's balls.

"Soaked."

"Ah, shit," Colton whimpered.

"Be a good boy and take it without complaint," I told him and let my hand fly, the crack of skin against skin sudden—and fucking loud.

"Christ," Colton bit the curse out, trying to grind on me.

I swatted again. "Keep those hips still, boy."

"Fuck—I'll try. Shit, that felt so fucking good." He groaned the final word but didn't move. "Do it again.'"

Bossy brat. I should have denied him, but I realized I was done doing so.

Two more handprints rose to the surface on his backside from my swats, and his curses mellowed into moans. By the fifth, his hips lifted as though seeking out more, and my wife's breaths heightened along with ours.

"Hudson," he pleaded.

I gave him what he wanted, smacking the tops of his thighs, getting dangerously close to his swollen cock and balls. Wrapping a hand around the latter, I rolled their softness between my fingers.

"Mmft," he grumbled, his backside twitching as though he fought to hold still.

"So goddamn needy," I muttered, smoothing my hands over his cheeks, spreading them for a groin-throbbing view of his hole again. I spat on the puckered skin and used my thumb to smear it around, tapping a few times.

"My God, you two are so damn hot." Mads moaned the sentence, amping my own arousal.

He shifted, but I continued with my teasing, rimming and pressing just enough to make him squirm.

"Hudson, goddamnit, man, give me—"

I sank my thumb into his ass and swatted him with my other hand.

A deep, rumbling groan left his mouth as he scratched at the couch cushion as though needing something to hold onto.

Rubbing the pad of my finger along his silken walls, I smacked him again. A third time—and found his prostate.

He jolted beneath me, and I pushed my hand against his lower back, keeping him in place.

I glanced over at Mads while slowly nudging gentle pulses against that spot deep inside him.

Tensed up tight, she had her hand down her stretch pants, finger fucking her pussy.

The sounds of her sopping core bucked my dick inside my jeans.

"You love when I play with his ass, don't you, love?"

"I'm so damn wet. The two of you...I can't even..." She bit her lip, her focus riveted on where I worked in a second finger and began to slowly fuck Colton's ass.

"No coming, Mads," I stated firmly.

An annoyed huff flared her nostrils, and I chuckled. "I'll make it worth the wait. Promise."

Sighing, she eased back in the chair, the movement beneath her pants slowing.

"That's it," I told her. "Edge yourself for us." Turning my focus to Colton, I pulled from his hole and rained down three harsh swats in quick succession.

A soft curse left his lips, but he remained steady like a goddamn champ, taking it like I'd told him to.

I could have gone on, dragged out his pain/pleasure

until he came untouched—he'd done so once before—but I wanted more.

I nudged his hip. "Upstairs. Now."

He stood on shaky legs, but the sight of his leaking dick had me reaching for his hip before he turned away. I tugged him closer, both hands on his thighs to keep him still—and swallowed his cock down.

"Fucking hell," he dragged the word out, his hands grabbing hold of my beard as I backed off. "Hudson—fuck."

I grabbed his tightening sack and tugged hard, pulling another curse from him as I took him deep into my throat again.

"Jesus...so fucking good."

Swirling my tongue, I eased away, tonguing at his slit for more of his salty flavor.

His dick jerked, and a hiss escaped his lips.

"Upstairs," I repeated, backing off fully because I had plans for his cum that didn't involve shooting deep into my throat.

Pupils blown and eyes hazed as though floating, he stared down at me. Pink flushed his face—he was so fucking gorgeous. How had I ever managed to deny him? The want, the longing in his eyes for more than just my dick...Christ, the man wrecked me in the best way possible.

I reached around his backside and grabbed a handful of his abused flesh, squeezing hard.

He swore under his breath but didn't pull away.

"I wish I could etch these prints I left behind permanently into your skin."

A low groan rose from his chest.

"Are you going to be my good boy and listen?" I asked well aware of my wording.

"Fuck yes," he choked out his agreement.

"Then upstairs." I patted his backside. "Now."

He kicked off his sneakers and jeans and ripped his shirt off overhead.

Mads didn't say a word, just got up to follow him toward the stairs, leaving his stuff behind on the floor. For her to do such a thing meant she was desperate for her release too.

And I planned to give her one she wouldn't ever forget.

42

MADELINE

Hudson dimmed the lights and told Colton to lay facedown on the bed, and the second he pulled the massage oil from my bedside table, my pussy pulsed at emptiness.

I sat on the chair he usually perched on to watch, my lower lip between my teeth.

It had been years since I'd gotten to enjoy Hudson oiling a masculine body from neck to toe, turning them into a human slip and slide. Peter had hated the mess, but for me, nothing got me hotter than seeing his forearms flex, those thick fingers of his digging into muscle, and the resulting groans of the men he worked over.

Coiled tight, I attempted to slow my breathing.

Hudson never disappointed, and with how needy Colton was for his touch, I expected *not* coming while drooling over them together would be a fight.

I whimpered as Hudson peeled his clothes off.

Colton had been full of shit, looking for a reason to rile my husband up with his comment about Hudson stinking. I'd had my face against his chest, and he smelled like soap and dryer sheets, same as always after he'd showered even if he'd appeared like death warmed over when we'd first arrived.

I loved the width of his shoulders, his trim waist, and his thick thighs appearing with every piece of clothing dropped to the floor. The ripple of muscle flexing as he climbed on the bed and straddled Colton's ass sent another pulse of desire through me.

Rubbing over my pants with just enough pressure to tease my clit, I sat back to enjoy the show.

Hudson snapped open the bottle's cap and drizzled oil down along Colton's spine. No soothing instrumental music sounded in the background like with similar porn videos, so I was able to hear every slick, wet noise as Hudson spread the oil across Colton's broad shoulders and back.

His focus stayed on Colton's upper body, and the anticipation of what was to come soaked my panties through.

Shoulders. Neck. Traps. Hudson didn't ignore one single inch, kneading and pressing as Colton went lax beneath him, the same as I always did whenever I got the full body treatment.

Neither man spoke, but the occasional moan rose from Colton's mouth as Hudson used his forearms and elbows to press into his muscles. He worked his thumbs along Colton's spine, painfully slow until he reached his lower back. He slid off his perch on Colton's ass to his thighs before retrieving more oil.

Yes...

I swallowed a whimper as the cap once more snapped, and oil drizzled all over Colton's backside. My gaze glued to my husband's palms as they slickened up Colton's ass, tugging and pulling his cheeks apart.

"Mmm," Colton murmured his approval, shifting his

hips slightly with every tease of fingers ghosting along his crack.

Crossing my legs, I tried not to wiggle as my core pulsed.

Hudson rearranged himself between Colton's legs, pressing his thighs wide enough to make room. Kneeling, he focused on Colton's hamstrings and calves, adding more oil as needed.

Such a delicious, teasing mess.

Since Hudson enjoyed giving me the same treatment, I'd learned to keep waterproof mattress pads beneath our sheets. There would be a definite need of doing laundry the following day, but the extra chore would be so worth it.

Finally—*finally*, Hudson returned his focus up over Colton's ass again.

Heavy breathing rose from all three of us, and I tensed with every pass of Hudson's forearms and palms over his ass. He smoothed through Colton's crack with the sides of his hands, swiping downward but ignoring his hole.

Unlike some of our favorite massage videos, I only had the one view...

Lower lip between my teeth again, I squirmed, desperate to strip down and sit closer.

My shifting broke the bubble around the two men, and Hudson glanced over at me, not losing rhythm in making Colton moan. Lust filled his eyes, and lips parted, he glanced over my antsy body. "Anxious to come, love?"

"Dying," I whimpered the word.

"Take off your clothes and move to get whatever view you want, dirty girl."

He didn't have to tell me twice.

Colton's eyes opened, and he drank me in while I stripped down to my tingling skin. "So damn beautiful," he murmured and immediately groaned as Hudson dug an elbow into his lower back. "Fuck, that feels good, old man."

Growling, Hudson planked over Colton's back and nipped at his neck. He lowered his hips and slid upward, gliding his hard cock through Colton's crack.

Fingertips ghosting over my pubis, I moved in closer and sat on the end of the bed near their feet, getting a delicious view of Colton's balls and hard cock pressed downward along the mattress. Oil coated both.

Staying planked, arms flexing, Hudson slid down Colton's body and pulled up, using his knees to press alongside Colton's spine.

"Aw, fuck," Colton groaned, and Hudson slid back, legs widening to rub his inner thighs along the outsides of Colton's.

He repeated the seesaw motion, pressing Colton into the mattress with his knees up his ass cheeks and into his back.

The next pass, Hudson lowered his entire body and rocked over Colton's slick skin. Backing down angled his dick toward Colton's balls, and the drag forward sent his thick head upward through Colton's crack.

Colton lifted his hips, chasing...

Hudson denied him and continued the forward and backward motion, occasionally lifting to use his knees over Colton's back and his thick glutes.

The wet schlicking noises pulsed need through my pussy, and I couldn't sit still any longer. I reached between my thighs. Warm wetness coated my lower lips.

Colton spread his legs wider, and on the next backward glide, Hudson slowed until the head of his cock nestled against Colton's hole.

"Fuck—please, oh fucking hell, please," Colton whispered, trying to shift enough to make Hudson impale him.

I moaned while gently smearing my slick cream over my clit, but Hudson continued his descent over Colton's back.

He rocked forward, slightly notching and stilling, and I held my breath same as Colton.

Hudson retreated once more without breaching his tight ring.

"Fuck."

Swallowing hard in agreement with Colton, I stared between their legs, half-tempted to grab Hudson's dick and just shove him into Colton's hole that had to be aching with need.

Onto his knees he went, digging into Colton's muscles, lingering on his glutes, rolling then gliding back down.

The continued teasing left me hot and achy, and I kept my own touch light over my pussy, dipping in just enough that Hudson would be proud of how I edged myself.

He finally lowered his body completely, still grinding his dick over Colton's slick crack.

I rimmed my opening, gaze riveted on Hudson's drawn up balls.

The control of that man...

His ass cheeks flexed as he lifted his backside and notched once more, Colton's hole giving way to the tip of Hudson's dick. He stilled, a pause that seemed to go on forever and starved my lungs of oxygen.

Colton raised his hips, and I pressed two fingers deep inside my core as he filled himself with my husband's dick.

My breath left in a rush, my pulse singing.

Hudson hissed, allowing Colton to fuck himself a few lazy strokes as my wrist moved in time with his hips.

"Mmm," Hudson's chest rumbled, but he slid out and began his oiled glide up over Colton's body again.

Colton cursed him to high heaven, no longer able to lay still beneath the weight of my husband.

I couldn't handle it anymore either. I'd reached my breaking point. "Hudson," I whimpered, removing my hand from between my thighs before I came with a gush.

He looked over his shoulder while continuing to grind his dick and balls all over Colton's crack.

"I want you in the middle," I told him, my tone firm even though butterflies rushed through my chest.

Hudson paused his teasing movements as though frozen by my request.

I seriously pushed his boundaries, asking him to lower his walls completely by giving himself to Colton.

"Let him in," I whispered, so damn desperate for it my entire body ached.

Heightened pants filled my ears as I waited, an unbearable near-silence that raced my heart.

"Trust us to take care of you." I pushed but without the manipulative pleading I knew would get me whatever I wanted.

This had to be Hudson's choice. His decision rather than beginning coerced.

I found myself once more holding my breath.

Hudson sagged as his lungs fully emptied with a heavy exhale. "Okay, love."

43

COLTON

M y dick ached to the point of pain—luscious, brain-fogging pleasure. Hudson had soothed the stinging in my ass with his hands, elbows, and knees. I'd never had my body worshiped before. Never had a full massage that allowed me to appreciate the meaning of slick skin rubbing all the fuck over mine.

And his cock teasing the hell out of my asshole?

Yes fucking please, give me more of that shit.

I'd been edged before but not like that.

I couldn't lay still and bit my tongue to keep from begging for him to stuff me full like a greedy little slut—which I totally was for Hudson's dick.

When Madeline said she wanted Hudson in the middle, I thought she wanted to peg his ass while he had mine, and he agreed...backing off me fully, leaving my heated skin cool.

Madeline lay beside me.

Our gazes met and held as Hudson rustled with something on the bedside table. Pupils swelled and her face flushed, she'd never looked more beautiful.

I stared at her, drinking in the sight of arousal. My dick leaked a fucking mess between my spread thighs, and need pulsed through my hole to be filled.

"Go easy on him," she whispered. "It's been a while."

What she'd asked for slammed into my brain, and I pushed up to my knees, glancing over to find him using wipes to clean his jutting dick.

Mine bucked between my thighs.

He turned, capturing my eyes with his. Vulnerability lay in their depths, so damn raw and open that my throat tightened. I regarded the man who I'd thought would never relinquish control to me after having done so with that one man he regretted—I expected Peter—but the steadiness of his gaze offered me the reins.

The level of trust he gave hit my chest like a fist, stealing my breath.

"I'll take good care of you," I murmured, my pulse pounding in my ears. "Promise I won't ever hurt you."

"I don't mind a little pain," he stated gruffly and broke our eye contact to climb back on the bed.

Madeline spread her thighs and held out her arms in welcome to the man who still attempted to hide his feelings from me with his offhanded tone. The man fought vulnerability outwardly even though he would allow me access to the most intimate parts of him.

I smirked, a level of happiness I'd never felt before swelling up inside me.

Grumpy Hudson, it seemed, was my favorite Hudson.

He sank into her body with one slow thrust that melted him over her like warm butter. "Ah, fuck, love," he moaned and sought out her lips as she wrapped her arms around him.

Pre-cum oozed from my dick as their mouths met, and he gave a few, unhurried strokes into her pussy.

The scent of sex rose along with the slightly sweet herbs from the massage oil, filling my lungs as deeply as the sight of them loving on one another did for my eyes. Her hands slid down his spine to where her ankles hooked over his lower back.

I eyed his furry ass and squeezed the base of my dick to ease the tightening of my balls. Captivated, I stared at his flexing backside. He might like a little pain while being stretched open by a thick cock, but I wasn't about to shove in without plenty of prep—of the teasing sort since I owed him.

I palmed his ass, and he stilled inside Madeline's body, moving his knees wider to give me access to his hole. There had been no hesitation in his action but simple submission to his wife's request for him to offer himself to me.

But did *he* want me, I suddenly wondered. Or was he only appeasing Madeline's desire?

That bubble of joy inside me leaked air, flattening out slightly, but I refused to let the insecurities those thoughts brought to mind ruin the moment.

There was only one way to find out the truth.

Running a finger down his crack, I grazed over his back-door, the softness of his skin making my lips tingle and mouth drool.

"Fuck," he muttered, a shiver pebbling the skin over his back.

So not completely turned off by the thought of me taking him there...

The pucker clenched at my feathering touch, causing my dick to throb, but Hudson sighed and relaxed after a few strokes meant to entice him into that state.

The temptation to call him a good boy had the words on the tip of my tongue, but I swallowed them since releasing the thought would only tense him again.

Planked on his elbows, he returned to kissing his wife, slowly fucking into her wetness. I trailed my fingers over his taint to his warm, heavy balls.

Hudson moaned against Madeline's lips, stilling once more to let me fondle him. Tease him. Hopefully, drive him so out of his goddamn mind that he would be ramped up enough to take my dick without difficulty.

"Stick your fingers in me already, boy," he grunted, and I chuckled.

Grasping his ass cheeks, I spread them apart and squeezed hard. "I'll offer up my ass to you any day of the week," I told him, "but you're delusional if you think this good boy is going to let you top him from the bottom."

I'd had every plan of stretching him until he begged, but his attempts to gain control changed my mind. If he didn't allow access to his asshole too often, I would take my damn time and enjoy every second of having him at my mercy in the event he never let me have him again.

Whorls of dark hair lay around his furled hole, and I nosed up through his crack, sniffing his musk deep into my lungs.

"Fuck, you smell good."

I repeated the motion, half growling at the scent of him combined with the arousal of his wife mere inches below. Settling onto my belly, I took a moment to enjoy the pornographic close-up of glistening pink pussy lips stretched around his girth.

I nuzzled his warm sack, up his taint, and flicked my tongue over his hole.

"Shit," he whispered.

Repeating the motion earned me a husky curse along with his pucker twitching beneath my tongue.

Fuck yeah.

"More," Hudson grunted, and that command I willingly obeyed.

I spread his cheeks wide and toyed with his hole, lapping and sucking. Licking and poking. Teasing like he'd done to me until he writhed against my hold, steadily sinking into Madeline over and over again. The second I pushed the tip of my tongue with intent to breach, he bore down.

Pre-cum leaked from my throbbing dick, and I ground my hips against the mattress, growing desperate with every growl and muttered curse from Hudson's lips.

I lapped lower, licking at Madeline's cream around his dick, and he pulled back, giving me access to his full length. Grasping his base, I angled his cock downward to engulf as much of him as I could in my mouth.

He grunted as I suckled hard. "Jesus—fuck!"

Humming, I took him as deep, smooshing my nose up against his balls.

Madeline whimpered, gliding her heel down over my back. "I can't even see, but you two are driving me insane," she whispered, her voice ragged with need.

Releasing Hudson's dick from my mouth, I shifted onto my knees, guiding him back into her wet pussy. He sank in with a groan, ass flexing, thighs shaking.

Lifting my gaze, I watched them kiss lazily, her sighs and the low, rumbled noises from his chest filling mine the fuck up. They were beautiful together, exactly as love should be. Accepting and open, willing to admit wrong and offer forgiveness.

I wanted in on that shit.

Bad.

Grabbing the oil, I set my jaw against the need to rut and thrust until I unloaded inside Hudson for the first time. We would get there, but the man had a ways to go before I could breach him.

I drizzled oil over his ass, the liquid running down his crack and onto his sack.

His entire body tensed, but I soothed a hand up his spine, petting him while setting the oil aside. I went to work, slickening up his balls, taint, and hole until he released a heavy exhale and relaxed. He rocked his hips against his wife in time with my massaging thumbs, every slick glide of my pads over his pucker all but begging for me to push in.

"Just do it," he muttered, burying his face in Madeline's neck.

She watched me with blown pupils. Trust lay in her gaze, a heady fucking thing that sent a strange as fuck feeling through my chest.

Love...or perhaps the beginnings of it.

"Let me in," I murmured—for Hudson's body. For access to both their hearts.

Hudson bore down on the tip of my finger. Exquisite heat enveloped me to the first knuckle as the air left Hudson's lungs.

"Goddamn," I groaned, swirling around inside his silken hole. "So tight and smooth in here. It's no wonder you like to plug up my ass and stay there for hours." A shot of need tingled through my groin at the idea, but his canted ass invited me to delve deeper.

I moved in and out, slowly pushing until my knuckles brushed against his cheeks.

So fucking tight—my dick wouldn't last three seconds once buried inside his heat.

He hissed when I worked in a second finger, but his hips lifted as though seeking out more. "Shit, boy...that feels so goddamn incredible. Fuck."

A rush of warmth flooded me, elation at hearing how he enjoyed me playing with his body.

Holding Madeline's heated stare, I continued pumping into him, loving how she shifted beneath him, gently lifting her hips to keep his mind off how I worked his ass open.

Our heavy breaths sounded loud in the bedroom's stillness only broken by the wet schlicking noise of my slow thrusts into his tight hole. A little more oil, and he took a third finger like a goddamn champ. Not one utterance of discomfort, no curse or demand for me to hurry up left his lips.

But fuck, how he shivered. Shifted toward me with needy groans. Nuzzled his wife's neck, lips parted and eyes clenched shut.

"Want you inside me, Colton." His ring clenched around my fingers as a shudder ripped through him, tensing the muscles over his back. "Please—right now."

A sweet ache slammed into my chest at the desperation in his voice, the broken begging...for *me*.

Not just a fulfillment of his wife's request.

Hudson Young arched his back with clear invitation, offering me everything.

Suddenly shaking, I removed my fingers and quickly wiped them on the sheet beside me. My heart pounded, and I swallowed hard, determined to keep my shit together and take all three of us where we needed to go to find satiated fulfillment.

Another squirt of oil lubed my dick to the point of dripping, but better too much and ruin the sheets further than cause him any discomfort.

Dilated, black pupils blowing up Madeline's blue eyes held mine as I moved in close, sliding the back of my dick up through Hudson's crack. I didn't give him the whole body rubbing but teased him all the same, gliding the spongy head of my cock over his pucker time and again. Nuzzling and nudging just enough his hole gave way slightly in a hot kiss to my tip.

He'd shown unbelievable control, and I fought to do the same, wanting to make it good for him.

"Goddamn it, boy, don't make me say it again!" Hudson snapped.

Madeline smirked up at me, one eyebrow raised. "Better give the man what he wants." Her voice sounded like pure sex—sensual and siren-like, reeling me in even deeper to the swell of emotion settling over us.

My pulse rushed with such force I could feel the throb in my dick. Hard enough to pound nails, I didn't need to hold my base while getting ready to notch into his body. Hands on the bed beside him, I leaned down and kissed between his shoulder blades. Damp from sweat, he tasted salty on my tongue, so goddamn delicious I wanted to swallow him whole.

Eyelashes fluttering closed, I inhaled the scent of him and Madeline's sweet panted exhales.

Musk and cotton candy—the perfect combination that could sustain me for life.

"Let me in, Hudson," I rasped against his skin, wanting so goddamn much my chest threatened to crack open. Affection and need alike pushed me forward.

He bore down, and the head of my cock sank inside his body.

We both groaned.

Teeth gritted against the tightness, I struggled to hold still, allowing him a moment to adjust to my girth.

Madeline rubbed over his back, kissing the side of his head as a tremor shook him between us. "Relax, baby," she murmured. "You know you want him."

The second he exhaled fully at her words, she nodded at me.

I flexed my ass, gaining another inch into his heat.

Hudson shifted, pushing into her body—and pulled back, filling himself a little more with my dick.

I fought the instinct to thrust and fuck into him like a goddamn animal. Hovering and letting him take his time fucking himself onto my dick and into his wife in opposing strokes drew my balls up against my body. No fucking way was I going to last.

But I wanted the moment to stretch into eternity. A burning desire swelled inside my body, making my damn eyes sting.

I needed to focus on the physical or I would end up fucking him with tears rolling down my cheeks.

Pulling out fully, I massaged his ass and tugged down on my nuts, staring at his wet hole. So fucking tight and silken...needed back in there so bad...

"Fuck." I crowded close and pressed in, seating myself fully in his ass with one steady thrust that pushed him deep into Madeline's core. "Goddamn—I'm *inside* you, Hudson."

Both of them moaned in response, the most gorgeous harmony in my ears.

Shit, it felt *delicious* shoving through all of Hudson's walls. Being invited to invade and take what the man didn't offer to just anyone. Pulse thrumming, I swallowed hard and slowly backed out until his ring clung to my glans. "Love this so fucking much," I told him, pressing in deep once more and never wanting the head of my dick to see the light of day again. "Thank you—Jesus fucking Christ, you're so hot."

He'd squeezed around my girth with a deep rumbled groan, and I sank back onto my haunches to dig my fingers into his canted hips.

"Do that again, and I'm going to empty in your ass before either of you come," I warned, my body taking over my brain.

Hudson growled and bucked against me, creating space between him and his wife. "Touch yourself, love," he told her, his voice every bit as wrecked as I felt.

He kissed her as she reached between their bodies, but her eyes stayed open and on mine.

Hudson shifted, nudging into her, every flex of his ass strangling my dick.

"You gotta come, Lin," I told her through my clenched jaw, barely managing to gyrate with him and stay buried in his hot hole while he fucked into her, since one full stroke in and out of his ass would take me past the point of no return. "Cream all over his dick, baby."

She gasped and arched, tearing her mouth from his. A guttural cry left her lips as he latched onto her neck.

A low groan, a steady, harsh clamp of his ring around my girth—and that was all she fucking wrote.

"Shit yeah—just like that." I snapped, fucking in and out of his ass with steady thrusts. Panting, I felt myself cresting, my hips stuttering with erratic jolts forward as he grunted his release beneath me. "So good...gonna come inside you— I'm gonna—"

"Give it to me, Colton," Hudson gasped.

My spine stiffed as cum shot up through my length, ripping cries from both of us.

"God—fucking—" I gasped between spurts, shuddering and shoving into him over and over. Ears ringing, I struggled to breathe. Limbs tingling, I twitched, my mind soaring.

And Hudson squeezed around me the whole time as though wanting me deeper, lusting for every drop of cum I had inside his body.

I gave it to him—all I had. My vulnerability. My heart.

Drained, I sagged atop them, hair damp from sweat sticking to my forehead as I fought to steady my breathing.

Still buried deep, I leaned forward and licked up his spine, tasting his salty skin until my mouth reached his wife's.

I gave her my tongue while attempting to nudge deeper into him with my spent dick.

Hudson lay like a dead man between us as Madeline and I kissed ourselves down from the high of a lifetime. Gasped breaths and shuddered sighs eased us back to reality.

"Thank you," I whispered over her lips before turning my face to nuzzle along Hudson's whiskers.

Groaning, he pulled away from her neck and gave me his mouth.

It was an awkward as fuck angle, but I wasn't about to turn down his offer. Soft kisses between still-heavy breaths, tongues in no hurry...we shared one lazy-as-fuck saliva swap.

His mouth was just as perfect as the rest of him. Firm yet soft. Hungry yet satisfying. I wanted the taste of both of them on my tongue, lingering long after old age left me white-haired and breathing my last.

"Goddamn, Hudson, you're gonna have to let me do that

again," I muttered, knowing that I needed to tear myself away since Madeline had to be squished beneath him.

Hudson didn't say yes—but he didn't say no either.

With reluctance, I shifted back to my haunches while slowly dragging my dick from Hudson's body.

He groaned when I slid free, and I rimmed his leaking hole with a fingertip, gently pressing in a few times and massaging until it fully shut.

"Okay?" I asked, and he moaned an affirmative. I leaned in and nipped at his ass cheek. "You have one sweet hole, old man."

"Brat," he muttered.

I swatted where I'd bitten because why the fuck not? "And you love it."

44

HUDSON

F uck yeah, I did.

So goddamn much it scared the hell out of me. I'd given in—to Mads's wants and the young man who fit with her and I better than Peter ever had. Colton fulfilled parts of me I hadn't realized sat empty. I'd bottomed for our ex a few times, but he'd never instilled a bone-deep craving for more.

Colton had eased into my body with gentle tenderness, unselfish in his desire to please my wife.

Please me.

He'd weaseled his way into my soul, finding the parts I'd kept hidden from everyone but Mads.

And I let him in. Welcomed him with open arms, knowing both my lovers would help me during the times I wanted to cower behind my walls again.

Mads stood between us in the shower, and I lost my heart to how Colton caressed her neck, studying her face, her mouth, with such sweet affection and stirrings of heat that my chest ached. She submitted to him fully, sagging against my body, head tipping back to my shoulder as he continued to touch her, mapping out the ridges of her cheekbones, the soft pillow of her lips.

He turned his dark eyes on me, the heat in those orbs tempting arousal to slide back into my blood. "Your wife is stunning."

"She is."

"So are you," he murmured, reaching around to grasp my neck. His thumb soothed in circles along my pulse with that same sense of affection he'd doted on Mads.

I fucking preened at his touch, all but purring my desire for him.

He crowded in close along her front, and she sighed as he pressed his mouth to mine. Another slow tasting of tongues and nipping of teeth stirred my dick. "Damn delicious too," he murmured before pulling away with a smirk I wanted to bite off his lips.

Sliding his hands down my back and slowly easing space between us to get his hands on my wife's hips, his focus flitted between the two of us. "I just had the best sex of my fucking existence, but since it's honesty or nothing, I gotta admit I'm feeling needy as hell."

I understood the sentiment and swallowed hard as Mads cradled his face in her hands. "All three of us have issues," she told him. "Wounds that are going to cause problems from time to time, but we're in this, Colton. Hudson wouldn't have given his body to you unless he planned to pursue a future. His doing so wasn't just because it's what I wanted, trust me."

Colton shifted his focus to my face.

Unable to form words, I nodded at the truth she'd spoken for both of us.

Wetness filled his eyes, causing my own to sting. "I've been looking for love my entire life, a place to truly belong, and I'm scared as fuck this is all going to get ripped away. I'm not fishing," he hastened to add, and a seemingly nervous laugh escaped him. He shifted to move back, but I reached out to clasp his hip, holding him steady, adoring how vulnerable he allowed himself to be.

I could learn a lot from Colton.

"Stay," I murmured, hoping he could read the craving stirring deep inside my soul through my eyes. He'd instilled a need that would never be fully sated, a fire no one but him would ever be able to dampen.

Colton swallowed hard but listened, allowing me to tug him closer, our gazes locked in understanding, as though he felt the same.

Our lips met again, warm and promising, with languid strokes that only made me burn for more.

So goddamn much my entire body hungered for him.

The second we broke apart, he dropped to his knees and hugged Mads tight, his cheek on her soft belly.

A tear slid down my cheek as she sighed and slid her fingers through his dark, wet locks.

Kissing my wife's neck, I hoped she recognized my thankfulness for her loyalty, her persistence in opening my eyes to all we could be.

45

MADELINE

I woke before both of my lovers, the barest hint of sunlight filtering through the blinds.

Colton rested in front of me, his warmth against my chest. He half-sprawled over Hudson who lay on his back, mouth open and breathing heavy with sleep. Their tangled fingers rested over my husband's heart.

Wetness filled my eyes as my throat swelled tight.

Never in a million years would I have guessed Hudson would open himself up again to a relationship outside the two of us. But there had been something in Colton from the very beginning...a drawing outside physical attraction that had refused to relent.

I wanted to spoil him rotten. Hold his head to my chest and scratch at his scalp until he rested against me. My heart yearned for him to feel accepted. Loved. I hoped his soul would find the belonging he'd never had as a child.

He'd missed out on adoption twice, and I expected insecurities of thinking he needed to be on his best behavior would trouble him from time to time.

But I would make it my mission to show him that acceptance and love *could* be unconditional. I was determined to trust and edify him until he recognized his worth in our lives...because he was there to stay.

Knowing without doubt I would wake with him again the next morning, I snuck out of bed, contentment in my heart and a smile on my lips.

Peaceful silence reigned over our home as I slipped on my robe and crept down the hallway. The sight of the almost emptied baby's room sent a pang through my heart. There would always be lingering sorrow I would never escape—and didn't want to—but I'd risen above debilitating depression.

Some days, I expected, would be worse than others, but hope for the future gave me something worth focusing on.

The sun barely peeked over the horizon, hints of it lighting the kitchen window.

I started the coffee and leaned against the sink.

How many times in those two weeks had I stood in that exact spot watching Colton build our back deck? How often had I taken him a snack or drink just so I could hear his voice and enjoy lighthearted conversation?

Even with the lack of arousal and lust back then, I'd felt stirrings inside my chest for him. During those days, it hadn't been his youthful body or hard cock I'd drooled for but a deeper draw as though the energy between us had always been meant to entwine together.

But it had been Hudson's insistence, his gentle prodding, that had opened me up to so much more with the young man who'd caught my attention.

A tear of thankfulness slid down my cheek, and I swiped it away with my palm, turning toward the coffee pot that finished its gurgling.

So much happiness spread through my chest, curving my lips into a smile.

I looked forward to our future again—even without children...

The thought trailed away as I pulled mugs down from the overhead cabinet. Colton had grown up without loving parents in a system that failed too many, he'd told me. The sharing of his heartaches as a child had hit me right in the feels, but I considered at that moment that there were hundreds—thousands of others just like him.

Looking for love.

Desperate for a home to call their own.

My throat went tight, and I closed my eyes, allowing tears to slip free. A quiet sob escaped me—and warm arms surrounded my waist, the familiar warmth and scent of my husband easing me against his chest.

"Shh," he murmured against my ear, but I knew he didn't mean to shush me. Clasping his hands atop my belly, I let the release happen, a cleansing cry rather than one that would lead me back into darkness.

Tears for our loss of both Maya Joy and the relationship we'd thought would last through thick and thin poured down my cheeks. I didn't mourn Peter's disappearance from our lives though. Hudson and I had found a soul ten times more worthy of our love and affection. Thankfulness sent a few more droplets from my eyes—for both my husband's willingness to try and Colton's easy forgiveness and acceptance.

Only a sweet ache remained in my chest once I finished.

Hudson kissed beneath my ear. "Okay, love?"

"Yes." I spoke the word with quiet assurance before one last shuddered sigh slipped through my body.

"What do you need?" he asked, and I knew in the

deepest parts of my soul Hudson would kick Colton from our house without question if that was what I told him to do. Regardless of how he'd given in and offered himself to the younger man, his love for me would dictate he make that kind of choice when I wouldn't ever be able to do so for him.

"Could you love him in the way you do me?" I asked quietly, my eyes still shut as I leaned against him.

He paused from answering but eventually exhaled heavily. "Yes."

I smiled, my heart growing lighter. "That's what I'm hoping for," I spoke honestly. "That's what I can feel on the horizon, Hud. I know it's possible if you would allow him an equal share of your heart."

"Are you willing to give up a portion?" He nuzzled my neck, his whiskers soft on my skin.

"Yes," I didn't hesitate to reply. Turning, I wrapped my arms around his broad shoulders and studied his sleepy, hazel eyes.

Unguarded, he peered right back. "What else do you want...I can see there's more."

I nibbled on the inside of my lip, still pondering over the newfound yearning in my heart.

"Mads," he whispered, tucking me in close against his body.

"I want to foster then maybe adopt." I let the truth whisper off my tongue. "The three of us could give lonely children the chance Colton never had."

A slow smile crinkled the skin around his eyes, softening his gaze with loving warmth. "Yeah?"

"Yes."

He kissed me, a soft press of lips. "Anything for you, love."

"Shit."

The muttered, tear-filled word pulled my attention over Hudson's shoulder.

Colton stood shirtless in the doorway, hands limp at his sides where his unbuttoned jeans clung to his trim hips. Wetness flooded his dark eyes, making them look like melting chocolate.

"You heard?" I asked quietly, my heart wanting to break all over again.

He swallowed hard and nodded.

"Come here, boy," Hudson said, his rumbling voice full of warmth. He angled slightly away from me and clasped Colton's waist as he moved closer.

We both looked at him, the tremble of his lower lip causing my eyes to well again.

"I knew there was something special about you the first day we met," Hudson said. "You brought a sense of excitement back into my life that scared the shit out of me. I'm sorry it took me so damn long to get my head out of my ass, but I'm going to try like hell to be a better man for both of you."

Colton's throat worked as he stared at my husband. "I promise to do the same," he whispered.

"I'm going to get pissy sometimes," Hudson warned.

"So will I." Colton's smile wobbled.

"I can be an insecure, gruff bastard."

"I've already seen that firsthand, and I'll be honest— I'm kind of fond of that part of you. Brings out the brat in me."

Hudson clasped the back of Colton's neck. "Are you willing to take a chance on my old ass?"

"Fucking *love* your old ass," Colton said with a chuckle, grabbing Hudson's backside. "Almost as much as your wife's." He palmed one of my cheeks and squeezed. "But yeah. I totally am. Never wanted anything more."

"Mmm," Hudson hummed his approval and drew him in, their lips pressing lightly in a chaste kiss.

I sighed and snuggled in closer, all the warm fuzzies flooding my soul. "Feel free to make out while I get us some coffee and breakfast." A quick smooch on each of their cheeks, and I started to pull away.

Both men yanked me back into their little bubble where hungry mouths and fingers worshiped me right there in the kitchen.

The coffee ended up burning in the pot.

EPILOGUE

COLTON - FIVE YEARS LATER

Hudson ordered me to bed with a sloppy, well-used hole in celebration of flipping my second house and padding our shared bank account. Even after all our time together, the man still loved me being a mess of cum and lube, slack and ready for him if he woke in need of having his cock warmed.

Pressure against my ass and the slow, steady thrust of his dick roused me in the middle of the night exactly as I'd expected. It was Hudson's way of showing dominance and boosting his insecurities about my always being there for him, no matter where or when.

I assured Hudson I would give him whatever the fuck he wanted—*whenever* the fuck regardless of my success in life, but I knew he still struggled to accept I would remain loyal. That I would never desire or allow another man inside what he owned.

Sometimes he got caught up in his emotions, and I would become the forceful one, eating out and fucking his ass until he calmed down and just gave in to letting me take over his mind and body for a short period of time.

Eyes firmly shut and smiling, I shifted my backside toward my man, staying relaxed and snuggly with Mads's softness all along my front as he sighed and wrapped his arms around me.

I fu*king loved being plugged up and cherished by both my lo*rs.

*thing compared to a Young/Colton sandwich.

*ot even the chicken salad with purple grapes Madeline pa*ed in my lunches. She spoiled me rotten, and I did the s*e for her whenever possible. Flowers, peanut butter *ps, neck kisses she adored, and spending Sunday after-*ons baking in our kitchen together. Hell, I'd even given in *o the whole yoga thing and had become addicted myself.

Hudson refused to join us, but his loss.

Rubbing my nose in Madeline's hair, I rested, fully content with how the two shared my heart in equal measure. Missing Link had helped me find the love I'd been looking for my entire damn life.

Smiling like a dork, I sought out sleep to once more take me into oblivion where no worries of the day, our schedules, or work demanded attention.

A sweet scent filled my nose, and I sniffed as wakefulness returned what seemed mere minutes later.

Cinnamon buns.

"Mmm," I groaned, stretching against Hudson's chest pressed to my back.

His dick had slipped from my ass during sleep but still rested sticky and half-hard against my thigh.

Saturday, I realized as I blinked my eyes open to find our alarm clock showing past seven when we both got up to head to work.

The house sat silent—rare even for a weekend.

I climbed out of bed without disturbing Hudson who'd

learned to sleep like the dead. Blaming his changed sleeping patterns on old age had gotten me a red ass the night before —and that sloppy hole he'd thoroughly taken advantage of.

Grinning at the memory, I cleaned up in the bathroom and slipped down the hallway and stairs, desperate to keep quiet to enjoy the peace for as long as possible.

Madeline was in the kitchen, no big surprise, the scent of cinnamon and coffee filling the room. I'd beaten Hudson to her lush backside that morning, the same as I'd been doing as of late, wrapping my arms around her delicious curves and soaking in her warmth.

"Morning," I murmured against her neck, still smiling like a goddamn dork as the sweet scent of honeysuckle filled my nose.

She turned, giving me her mouth, her hands were affectionate as always in mapping out my face, neck, and hair while I loved on her lips.

"Mmm," I hummed. "You taste like coffee."

Bumping against my groin, she pushed me away. "Give me a second to pull these rolls from the oven, and I'll pour you a cup."

"I can get my own, woman." I slapped her ass as she turned, loving the jiggle in her stretch pants.

She grabbed up the oven mitt and swatted it at me, but I sidestepped with a chuckle.

I almost dropped the mug as she bent to retrieve our breakfast.

"Goddamn, your body is like a back road, baby," I groaned. "Gorgeous curves and delicious bends I could spend all day exploring."

A soft shot of laughter from her warmed my chest.

"You *love* that I can't get enough of your soft skin and sweet taste," I insisted.

She set the tray atop the oven, slipped off the mitt, and pressed into me, backing me against the counter. "I love *you*," she corrected me, the warmth in her blue eyes sending tingles rushing through my chest.

"Mmm." I grabbed her backside, squeezing while grinding my morning wood into her soft belly. "Not nearly as much as I love you."

Smiling, she kissed my chin. The corner of my mouth. Tipped my head down to reach my nose. "I adore every inch of you, Colton."

"Same, Lin." I sighed and swiped my tongue over the seam of her lips.

It had taken Hudson eight long as fuck months to give in and repeat what I'd been telling him daily since Madeline and I had first exchanged those words a few weeks into our relationship.

It had been the same day Peter had been found guilty of possession with the intent to sell. He'd gone to prison for nine months, and according to what we'd heard through the grapevine, he'd stayed clean upon getting out and had moved across the country with Ryan Foley of all people.

None of us had cared what the hell he did as long as he kept his distance, and our lives had continued on after he'd left, the three of us looking forward as a committed throuple, planning for our future.

A shuffle of footsteps sounded upstairs in the hallway.

A door opened—a murmur of voices. So much for our peaceful moment.

But there would be more to steal. We always managed to find time regardless of circumstances.

Filling my lungs to bursting, I rested my forehead against Madeline's. "Are you ready for today?

"Are *you*?" she asked me, knowing how much the events ahead of us would twinge my heart with the sweetest pain.

"Yes."

The stairs creaked, and we both turned our gazes toward the kitchen opening.

Hudson soon filled the doorway, sleepy two-year-old twins perched on either of his strong arms. Devon clung to his rumpled T-shirt with her chubby hands, nothing short of a death grip.

Dax's dark eyes landed on Madeline, and the binkie popped from his mouth, falling to the floor as he reached for her. "Momma!"

I swallowed hard, my hold dropping from Madeline as she retrieved the little guy from his papa.

A loud thump lifted my focus overhead, a grin stretching my lips.

"Cimmimim wolls!" Feet thundered down the stairs. "I wants one!"

A terror of brown skin and riotous black curls bounded past Hudson's legs and tore into the kitchen.

I grabbed up the boy we had adopted the year before, blowing raspberries into his neck as he squirmed and wiggled to be let back down.

"Cimmimim wolls!" Izaak repeated, knowing I loved them just as much as he did and ought to be just as excited.

"Yeah, little dude, but you gotta chill your butt down," I told him, walking him over to the breakfast table. "If you sit here for two minutes—"

"One!"

"Two," I insisted, holding up my fingers against his index pointing at the ceiling, "then I'll let you have one of mine."

His dark eyes widened as he flopped into his chair. "Weally?"

"Really."

"I can be good," he stated, nodding like he wanted to pop his head off.

Ruffling his hair, I grinned. "You are a good boy, Izaak. The very best son we could ever wish for."

I turned to find Hudson and Madeline watching me, the love in their eyes piercing straight through my damn chest like a fiery bolt. My smile wobbled as I took Dax from Madeline's arms so she could get the shifting kid behind me his promised breakfast.

Once I had Dax settled into his highchair alongside Isaak and smooched his chubby cheeks, I turned toward my man who snuggled the most precious child on the planet.

"Hi, sweet girl." I bopped her on the nose as she attempted to smoosh into Hudson's chest and hide from me, the little tease. "Loves you," I whispered to her and gave her a kiss like I'd done to her brother.

"Morning, old man," I told Hudson while tucking some of Devon's wayward hair behind her ear.

Hudson narrowed his gaze at me but let me smack my lips against his. "Didn't get enough last night?"

"Oh, I had plenty." My ass still ached from him, but I loved to be sassy at him until he scowled. "I'll be feeling it all day," I whispered against the ear opposite Devon. "And thinking about when I can return the favor."

Hudson grunted. "Dream on."

"You love it." I nipped his earlobe. "Almost as much as you love me."

He grumbled something under his breath.

"What was that?" I asked, snaking a hand around his waist and shoving my hand down into the back of his sweats to palm his furry ass.

"I said you're needy as hell," he muttered.

I pressed my lips to his even though mine stretched in a grin. "So are you, man of mine."

Unable to help myself, I continued to play with his backside while turning my attention back to the relaxed lump of baby fat in his arms. I nudged my nose against Devon's while pretending to tug her white lamb from her clutch. "Did you sleeps good?"

She shook her head, her eyes still sleep-crusted and hazed.

"Did your brother wake you up?"

"Yeah," she whispered and snuggled her face back in Papa's strong chest.

She and Dax still shared a crib, clung to each other for dear life, and sometimes cried when separated. While in their eight months with us they had healed from the wounds their mother had inflicted on them before the state intervened, we expected it would be a while before they settled in fully.

Devon had taken to Hudson immediately, wrapping him around her little finger. Dax was a momma's boy, but the twins continued to keep their eyes on each other as much as possible.

"Mooooommmmmmaaaaa!" Izaak whined, and I tsked, shaking my head at the little man who'd stolen my heart.

"Shh," I shushed him, giving him my stern eyes he hated while his momma fixed his breakfast plate, including cut-up strawberries and bananas.

Little face scrunched, he sat on his hands. "Wants!" he whispered at me, his dark eyes flashing in a scowl, and I fought to keep from grinning.

Madeline didn't torture the poor kid any longer. She set a paper plate with two cinnamon rolls on it in front of him and kissed the top of his head as he dug in.

"You have to eat your berries and bananas too, young man."

"So I can gwow up big and stwong like papa and daddy!" he stated loudly around his food.

"Don't talk with your mouth full," Madeline chided gently as always.

Dax's binkie hit the floor again, and he reached for Izaak's breakfast. "Me!" he demanded, his voice raspy.

"Mine!" Izaak shouted, yanking his plate away from his brother's hand. "Momma gets yours in a mimute. Be pastents!"

I bit back my chuckle while Madeline dealt with the two brawlers who went at it almost daily but always ended up snuggling on a beanbag with Devon to watch cartoons.

Hudson released a heavy sigh, and I turned to find his eyes damp rather than annoyed by their boisterous bickering that filled the house more often than not.

I wound my arm around him again but left his backside alone. "Ready to officially add the two munchkins to our family today?"

He kissed the top of Devon's head, her downy wisps of blonde hair sticking to his whiskers. "Yeah," he whispered, his smile wobbling.

The moisture in his eyes thickened my throat. Hudson rarely shut down on us anymore. The walls blocking off his vulnerability no longer clung to his soul, and a new man had emerged, one who allowed all his feelings to show, one who didn't hold back his emotions.

"I honestly couldn't love you any more if I tried," I told him, offering the same reassurance I did every day.

"Same."

"Nuh uh," I said, shaking my head. "I want the words."

"Needy little—"

"Tell me you love me, old man," I interjected before he could call me a brat or his little cock slut in front of our children.

Fire lit in his eyes, the kind that sent shivers straight to my balls.

Fuck did I love my silver fox.

"Say it," I pushed with all the sass I had available in my tone.

"Love everything about you," he grumbled, his cheeks flushing.

"Damn right you do." I hip-checked him, slapped his ass, and made my way to the breakfast nook. "Now sit your fine backside down here and let wifey spoil us all rotten."

He did as told.

And Mads loved on us in her favorite way, filling my heart to overflowing.

THE END

ABOUT THE AUTHOR

USA Today bestselling author Lynn Burke is a CrossFit and coffee addict. Her three spawn and two fur babies dictate how often she can be found hunched over her Mac, typing as fast as her fickle muse cooks up hot stories.

You can find more about Lynn at her website: www. authorlynnburke.com

ALSO BY LYNN BURKE

Abel's Obsession

Divulging Secrets

Healing Storms

In Between

Reluctant Lumberjack

Resisting his Mate

Billion Dollar Love Anthology

Blood Born Series

Bonds of Worship Series

Dark Leopards MC

Darkest Desires Series

Devil's Outlaws MC

Elite Escort Series

Elite Escorts MM Series

Fallen Gliders MC

Forbidden Obsession Duet

Found by Fate Series

Midnight Sun Series

Missing Link Series

Risso Family Series

Sandy Ridge Series

Sinful Nature Series

Vicious Vipers MC